KEEPING FAITH

MILITARY ROMANCE — WITH A SCIENCE FICTION EDGE

ANN GIMPEL

Edited by
ANGELA KELLY
Illustrated by
FIONA JAYDE

CONTENTS

KEEPING FAITH

GENTECH REBELLION, BOOK FIVE

Military Romance
(with a science fiction edge)
By
Ann Gimpel

BOOK DESCRIPTION: KEEPING FAITH

Faith fled her compound one wintry night with four other genetically modified women. Glory, Honor, Charity, and Hope have all found men who adore them. Faith is happy for her sisters, but it's lonely on her own. A man piqued her interest, but she ran the probabilities, and the odds of him ever being interested in her are thin. Tough and forbidding, Reginald was a field surgeon in the Middle East. He eats and breathes medicine. Besides, he's married to the CIA. No wives in his past. Faith hacked into the personnel database to check.

Reginald Thomas agreed to run the CIA's infirmary after a bullet nailed him in Afghanistan. He's one of a handful of scientists who produced the original batches of genetically modified humans, and he's laid low since their rebellion. The catastrophe rankles, but he hasn't given up finding a fix for their genome problems.

A permanent bachelor for a host of feeble reasons, he's substituted immersion in medicine and science for a personal life. Easier that way. And a whole lot cleaner. The status quo might be sterile, but at least it's trouble free. When Faith catches his eye, he fights his attraction to her, but it's a losing battle. Loving her fulfills him, and he can't walk away. What will happen if she discovers he helped create those like her? In a radical departure from his normal forthright manner, he buries that fact deep. If she never finds out, it can't ever come back to bite him.

Series Backstory:

Sometime between the interminable wars in the Middle East and 9/11, the United States moved forward breeding a race of super humans. Clandestine labs formed, armed with eager scientists who'd always yearned to manipulate human DNA. At first the clones looked promising, growing to fighting size in as little as a dozen years, but V1 had design flaws that grew worse in V2.

Seven years ago, a rogue group turned on their creators, blew up the lab, and hit all the other breeding farms, freeing whomever they could find. In the intervening time, they've retreated to hidden compounds and created a society run by men. Women are kept on a tight leash because the men fear if they discover their innate power, they'll launch their own rebellion.

CHAPTER 1

Faith walked slowly across the CIA's extensive grounds. She'd just seen Hope and Charlie off at the terminal building next to the airstrip. They'd looked deliriously happy, and Faith was grateful Charlie's near miss with death hadn't left lasting problems. She stuffed her hands into her pockets, wishing she'd brought gloves. For once it wasn't raining, but it was almost dark, and the wind had a bite to it.

Milton Reins, head of the CIA, had been there to wish Hope and Charlie well too. He'd also been chockful of instructions about the Gulfstream business class jet until Charlie reminded his boss he was qualified to fly it.

Not quite ready to return to her apartment building and all the new women who'd been assigned housing there, Faith wandered aimlessly. Glory, Honor, Charity, and Hope—women who were like sisters to her—had hooked up with men they loved dearly. It seemed like an impossible fantasy come true.

A few months back, they'd lived at a compound in Washington State, sharing a dormitory with seven more genetically modified women just like them. Glory's bravery freed the five of them who'd been willing to trust her, and Faith blessed the CIA every single day for taking a chance on them as agents.

More women had joined their ranks during a raid they'd just completed in Maine. Twenty to be precise. It made her heart glad the women had been able to lay their reservations aside and take a chance on a new life. One where they'd be treated like human beings rather than slaves.

She really should hustle back to the apartment building and see if any of them wanted to go to dinner. Faith remembered her first days on the sprawling CIA campus. How lost and overwhelmed she'd felt. It had helped that Glory was already there. The least she could do was pass on the goodwill to the new gals.

"Faith. Hold up."

She glanced over her shoulder at the sound of Frank's voice, but kept walking. Frank was genetically modified too, but he'd been one of the Nameless Ones, men who'd made the women's lives holy hell in the compounds. He was also a genetic researcher. Her friend Charity had fallen in love with Tony, the scientist Frank defected with, but Faith didn't harbor fond feelings for any of the genetically modified men.

During the seven years the CIA had hunted those like her, they'd labeled them freaks. The tag stuck, and she still thought of men like Frank as freaks, but not necessarily her or the women.

How's that for hypocrisy? She smothered a snorting laugh.

"What's so funny?" Frank caught up with her.

Faith shrugged. "I was thinking about how the CIA calls us freaks, and I'm good when it means you. Less good when it means me."

"Doesn't matter what they call us," Frank countered. "They took us in. Gave us homes and work. They didn't have to. How'd Charlie look? I'd meant to check him over one last time before he left, but didn't get there in time."

"Like the old Charlie. None the worse for wear. Dr. Thomas was there. I'm pretty sure he had some of the same concerns you do, but Milton told him to go back to his infirmary."

Frank hooted laughter. "Bet that didn't go over very well."

"No. It didn't. The doc stayed until Charlie and Hope headed out onto the tarmac." Faith narrowed her eyes. "You've gotten to know him pretty well, huh?"

"Who?"

"The doctor."

"In a manner of speaking, yeah. After Tony and I pulled a rabbit out of a black hole and saved Charlie, the guy decided we weren't just a bunch of uninformed quacks pretending we knew something about physiology."

"You're mixing your metaphors."

"So?" Frank angled his unusual amber eyes with their vertical slit pupils her way. Like all the genetically modified men, he was tall and broad-shouldered with a rangy build. Unevenly cut jet-black hair hung to his shoulders.

"So, nothing. Just pointing it out. Um, did you want something? I really should get back to the apartment building. We have all those new women, and—"

"Yeah I did," he interrupted in true Nameless One fashion.

Faith shook off irritation. "Whatever it is, hurry up."

He tucked a hand beneath her elbow in a distressingly familiar gesture. "How about joining me in the cafeteria for dinner? Tony and I got done early tonight, and he's spending the evening with Charity."

Faith jerked away from his touch. "The new women are my first responsibility," she said stiffly, wishing Frank would take the hint and leave. If he were human, he might've, but subtlety and picking up on social cues weren't part of how any of them had been programmed.

"Bring 'em along." He grinned rakishly. "You may not like me, but one of them might."

Faith stopped walking and stared at him. "What the hell, Frank? Any woman in a storm?"

"Now who's mixing metaphors?" He looked down his nose at her.

Faith felt her face heat. "I'll be in the dining hall in half an hour or so. If you want to sit with us, that's fine—so long as none of the women object. They're much fresher from a compound than me, so they may well run screaming from the room if you get too close."

Frank closed a hand around one wrist, effectively trapping her. "Get real, Faith. I wasn't in your compound, but it wasn't as if we flogged the women. You make it sound as if we were the devil incarnate."

"To us, you were. You rationed everything from food to blankets to when we had to show up to have our eggs harvested." She angled her head to one side. "The men in my compound ate what they wanted. They weren't half-starved like us. I bet they had more than one blanket. And they had private rooms; they weren't stuffed twelve to a dorm like we were—"

"You can stop now." Frank held up his other hand. "I'm sorry. I felt bad I didn't do more at the time, and I still do, but you living in the past and hanging onto hostility and bitterness isn't wise."

"Why not?" she demanded. "What's the phrase? He who forgets history is doomed to repeat it."

"George Santayana said that, but you're living in a different world now. The odds are better than seventy percent the CIA will effectively quell the rebellion sometime in the next six months. V4 has proven unstable. God only knows how many freaks were made with that configuration, but they'll implode, which will further thin their ranks."

"Fascinating," she muttered, "but I need to get moving."

Frank released her wrist. "I'd like to get to know you better, Faith, but I won't be heavy-handed about it. Give it some thought, and let me know."

She took a step backward. "What about wanting to give the women a thrill by having dinner with them?"

"Eh, I just said that to see if you'd react. Be jealous or something." He actually looked mildly uncomfortable when he twisted his mouth into a frown. "You weren't, and I'm crushed, but I'll get over it."

Without waiting for a response from her, he spun and took off at a quick lope.

Faith ran hard the other way, heading for her apartment building. Her thoughts were a roiling mess. Charity may have managed to square hooking up with a nameless one, but Faith didn't have it in her to overlook their years of horrific treatment. The women may not have been beaten, but they'd endured every other type of abuse.

Except sexual.

Intimacy was forbidden in the compounds. The reason Glory had run away was because a Nameless One tried to rape her. She'd used her kinetics to kill him, been scared half to death, and gone out a window in the thick of winter with only a worn pair of tennis shoes and a threadbare sweater. It was hard enough in Washington, but by the time she'd hitchhiked halfway across the country to Minnesota, the cold had almost killed her.

Frank was a hunk of a man. All the Nameless Ones were, but Faith couldn't see herself letting her guard down long enough to allow him inside her hopes and dreams, let alone sleeping with him. The thought of physical intimacy with someone like him made her vaguely ill.

She reached her building and tipped her chin so the retinal scanner could trip the lock and let her in. She was capable of employing kinetics to spring any lock, but so long as she was here, she'd do things the CIA way. After she nodded to the security guard patrolling the lobby, she pulled open a stairwell door and headed for the third floor.

Faith employed telepathy as she hastened up the stairs to see which women might be interested in joining her for dinner in the cafeteria. By the time she got to her floor, seven of the new recruits waited for her, milling about in the hallway. Faith recognized three of them since they were part of a group assigned specifically to her for weapons and martial arts practice.

A thought struck Faith. "I never asked, and we mostly communicate via telepathy when we train, but did you ever swap out your identification numbers from the compounds for names?"

A woman from Faith's group squared her shoulders. Like all the genetically modified women, she had long, thick dark hair and clear green eyes. The women had sleekly muscled bodies, and were both tall and strong. "Some of us did," she replied.

Faith smiled grimly. "That was one of the concessions we insisted on in my compound. We got sick of numbers, so we named ourselves and refused to respond when Nameless Ones called us by our numbers. Tell you what. Before we're done eating tonight, at least the seven of you will have picked names."

"Sounds like a plan," another of the women said.

"Tell us about Hope and Charlie." Another pressed forward and clasped her hands together. "It seems like such a fairytale romance. Everything went well? They're off on a honeymoon?"

"Well, they're not exactly married, so honeymoon isn't the correct word," Faith replied. "But I watched their plane take off, and they did look happy."

A collective *ahhhhh* surged through the group, and seven pairs of green eyes shone with delight for one of their kind who'd found happiness.

Faith could relate, and it made her both sad and angry. Up until she'd fled the compound, the thought of falling in love was just a fantasy. Something that happened in movies she watched on the Internet, but nothing that would ever happen to her. Frank's invitation—and his obvious interest—nagged at the back of her mind.

No. I'd rather be dead than hook up with a Nameless One. Charity may have, but I'm not her.

"Dinner?" Faith urged to quell her churning thoughts and trotted back down the stairway. If they got there after eight, the steam tables would be closed. Snacks were always available, but they weren't as satisfying as a hot meal.

The women trailed after her, chatting among themselves. They sounded carefree, another emotion that had eluded them in the compounds where they'd had to watch their backs every single minute.

"What do you think about goddess warrior names?" One of the women joined Faith.

"It doesn't matter what I think," Faith offered. "A name is important. It symbolizes who you are. Humans don't get to pick their own names, but some of the research I've read indicates that people grow into their given names—for good or for ill."

"So I should pick a name where I have an affinity for the woman, right?"

"Sounds good to me," Faith replied. "In our compound, we picked simple names that had meaning for us. We figured if we selected anything too complicated, we'd never get the men to quit hollering out our numbers when they wanted something."

Another woman closed on Faith's other side. "Was it easy?" she asked.

"The transition?" Faith glanced her way.

"Yeah. How long did it take them to give up and use names?"

Faith buried a snort. "Some got on the bandwagon in six months. Took others a year. And they cut our rations and assigned us extra duties to force us to give up on having names. We held firm, though. It was our first victory, and we wrangled every last bit of pleasure we could out of it."

"The men don't have names." Someone spoke up.

"Yeah, they do. They just never used them around us. One guy slipped up. It was what gave us the impetus to demand names for ourselves." Faith slapped her palm on the reader plate outside the cafeteria and pushed the door open.

"Get your food," she instructed, "and we'll push some tables together. In fact, I'll do that while you're in line, so the table will be ready."

Amid repeated *thank yous*, Faith strode to the back of the large room. All the tables seated four, so she pushed three together. That done, she stopped by the drink table for a cup of coffee and left it in front of her place before crossing to the steam tables lined up at the far end. The cafeteria had zero ambience, but it served good food under the harsh glare of banks of fluorescent panels.

By the time she slid into her seat, the other women were already eating.

One set her fork down and smiled self-consciously. "This—" she waved a hand around the table at the overflowing plates "—feels like more of a miracle than anything else. We never, never had enough food."

Faith remembered all too well. "At least that part of our lives is over—I hope," she murmured and began to eat.

Other women from the Maine compound filtered in, and Faith pushed more tables in line with theirs.

"What happens with practice tomorrow?" one of the women who'd been on Hope's team asked.

"Well, out of the five of you assigned to Hope, two will come with me, and three with Charity for the week Hope is gone."

Faith did a quick nose count. Three of the women from Hope's group were there. "You two—" she pointed "—will be with me and my five. And you—" she pointed again "—will join Charity."

"Which one is she?" the woman asked.

The woman sitting next to her leaned close. "The one who hooked up with a Nameless One."

"Ohhh." A knowing look creased the first woman's face. "I know who she is."

Faith licked dry lips. She should keep quiet, but a need to

speak up for her friend won out. "Charity is amazing. You're lucky to have her for an instructor. She's one of the V3s with an unstable genome, but she got past it by being one strong bitch of a woman."

"But a Nameless One..." The woman who'd asked the question looked at her plate.

"Charity had a hell of a hard time swallowing that," Faith said. "But Tony saved her when her genome hit a downward spiral, and he adores her."

"I suppose it's possible," a woman on Faith's team muttered, "but it kind of makes my skin crawl."

Murmured assent rose from several women.

"Names." Faith changed the subject. "You all need to pick names —unless you already have them." She stabbed her fork into china and realized her plate was empty. The abrupt motion told her how difficult the conversation about Tony and Charity was for her to hear, let alone be part of.

It brought Frank's earlier invitation front and center again too.

She pushed to her feet. "I'm going to call it a night. You can remain here as long as you want. Work on those names. No one will kick you out of the cafeteria. For those of you on my team, we'll meet at zero eight hundred sharp in the underground arena. Unless we receive other orders between now and then. If that happens, I'll alert you myself."

Faith loped toward a door and snapped her coat off a hook, sliding into it as she walked out the door. She kept her head down, mostly so she wouldn't have to think about anything, and plowed right into Dr. Thomas.

Faith halted abruptly. "I— I'm sorry," she muttered. "Wasn't watching where I was going."

"It's all right, Faith." The doctor smiled pleasantly. His dark hair, which had been shorn close to his head when she'd first met him, was growing longer. He had green eyes, but a darker shade than hers. Tall and thin, he'd been a field surgeon in the Middle East. He was the one who'd pitched nine kinds of fits about Frank and Tony treating Charlie, but to his credit, he'd backpedaled fast.

Hard to argue with success, and the doctor hadn't tried.

He was still gazing at her. It made her uncomfortable, so she studied him to give herself something to do. She was used to collecting data with her computer-esque brain. He'd tossed a fur-lined coat over scrubs and was probably intent on dinner.

"So long as I ran into you—rather literally it turns out—I've been meaning to ask you something." He quirked an inquisitive brow her way.

Faith thinned her mouth into an aggravated line. What was it about men and asking her things tonight? "I'm waiting." She ditched her discomfort and latched her gaze onto his before she remembered humans didn't appreciate that level of directness.

"You have some good skills. I've seen you patch the women up when they get hurt in the arena. Did you do any work in the labs in your compound?"

"Not the labs, but I did do some medical support work, why?" Before he could answer, she hurried on. "I really enjoy field work, uh, sir. Not sure I'd want to be stuck in someplace like the infirmary all day. Not that it isn't nice and all—" Faith realized she was blithering and cut off her flow of words. She'd take whatever tasks the CIA assigned. To do anything else would be the height of ingratitude.

"Stop by the infirmary tomorrow," he said. "Say around noon. That shouldn't interrupt your morning training schedule. I've been extremely impressed with Frank and Tony's knowledge base, and I have an idea I'd like to float past you."

"I'm not a Nameless One," she mumbled.

"Oh yes, that is what you women call them, isn't it." He smiled again. "See you tomorrow, Faith. I'm looking forward to our chat."

Reginald Thomas touched his palm to the scanner and disappeared inside, leaving Faith staring after him.

She forced her gaze away from watching him through the glass door and turned toward her apartment building. Efforts to keep her mind blank failed. Where Frank's invitation had creeped her out, the doctor's fascinated her. Was he interested in her as something other than some kind of guinea pig? A hybrid type of medical personnel who could think outside of standardized training?

Her heart gave a funny little flutter, and her statement about preferring fieldwork hit the skids. She'd give up weapons practice, telepathy skills enhancement, and martial arts workshops in a hot minute if it meant she got to spend her days next to Dr. Thomas.

"Oh, put a lid on it," Faith muttered and walked into her building.

"What was that, miss?" the security guard asked.

"Nothing. Just talking to myself. Good evening, Greg."

"And a good evening to you as well, Miss Faith."

She took the stairs three at a time and ran down the hall to her apartment, letting herself in. Faith paced in circles for a long five minutes before engaging her kinetics. She'd be in big trouble if she were caught, but she was determined to hack into the CIA's personnel database and find out everything she could about Reginald Thomas.

I'll stop the minute I find a wife, she promised herself, but wondered if she'd be disciplined enough to quit there.

hree hours earlier

Reginald Thomas—Reg to those who knew him well—watched Faith surreptitiously as she and Hope hugged in the airport's terminal building. While he'd known about the genetically altered CIA additions, he'd kept a very low profile after the first five women showed up.

For the best of reasons.

He'd been deeply involved in creating that race of super-humans. After two tours in the Middle East as a field surgeon, he'd seen the writing on the wall, and the message didn't bode well for the United States. The countries they fought were ruthless and had no compunctions about using their soldiers as cannon fodder. For every man killed, two more sprang up to take his place, many not more than young teenagers.

He'd opted for some hard lab time after that second tour and floated his brainchild past the scientific community. Their level of enthusiasm surprised him. So did the reality of established breeding farms flying beneath the radar.

The upshot was he'd spent the next few years fine-tuning his model and working on creating alterations when V1 turned out to have significant flaws. Things appeared to be running smoothly, so he'd signed on for one more overseas tour and returned to Iraq and Afghanistan. Lab work was fine, but he missed the adrenaline punch of kneeling in the mud engaged in hand-to-hand combat with death.

He'd won against the Grim Reaper enough times to keep coming back for more. Like as not, he'd still be crouched in a flapping canvas field tent tending wounded, but a bullet had shattered his femur and sent him back to the States. Milton had chased him down in a VA hospital, filled him in on the CIA's quiet little war against the freaks he'd created, and offered him a job.

Reg had struggled hard with the proposal. His leg was healing, and the Air Force would clear him for active duty again. In the end, his decision hinged on two things. Guilt and responsibility. The freaks may not have been his original idea, but he was one of three primary researchers who'd fielded the V2 configuration. No way of getting around the fact that the damage they were doing—and the lives lost as the CIA fought them—were his fault.

Also, he liked Milton. He'd served with him and Roy Kincaid and Charlie McClaren at different times in the Middle East. To be surrounded by men he respected was important. Still, it hadn't been an easy transition. The CIA infirmary was his baby, but it lacked the grittiness of dodging bullets, grenades, and landmines...

When you cut to the heart of things, he was a live-life-on-the-edge junkie just like every other career military man.

Faith and Hope were still chatting animatedly, their green eyes aglow with pleasure. It was clear the women were close—and that Faith was delighted her friend had found a man to love.

His attempts to maintain separation from the freaks had come to a crashing halt when Charlie ended up in the infirmary—surrounded by freaks determined to save his life. Reg's attempts to shoo them out of his nice, neat clinic failed, but that was a good thing because he'd learned a lot about how his creations turned out.

Not my creations. They manipulated the pattern I started with and made it ever so much better.

Still watching the women, because he couldn't tear his gaze away, Reg cringed internally. He'd left before his V2 genome fully played itself out. It took a few months to unravel, but it had been an unmitigated disaster. And the pivotal event spawning the rebellion. He'd been in Afghanistan when he'd caught wind of the bad news. Not much he could do about it from ten thousand miles away, so he'd gone back to fishing for shrapnel in the patient he'd been working on.

He'd done enough doctoring, much of it could be relegated to autopilot, so he'd spent a whole lot of time feeling shitty and replaying the gene sequences to figure out where he'd gone wrong.

"Hey, Doc!" Charlie strode to his side. "I'm cleared from your end, right?"

"Yup. Just stopping by to see you off." He extended a hand, and Charlie clasped it.

"Thanks for not chasing Frank and Tony out."

Reg bit back a snort. "I have a funny habit of listening to people when I've run up against a dead end." He let go of Charlie's hand. "I'm pleased and fascinated their intervention worked, but I do want to see you every two weeks so I can take serum samples and see what, if anything, is changing in your physiology."

"You got it!" Charlie grinned and walked to Hope and Faith. "Ready to go?" he asked Hope."

When she trained her green eyes on him, they brimmed with enthusiasm and joy. "You betcha. Sooner we're airborne, the sooner I can take over the flight computer. I've always wanted to fly one of those things." She pointed out the bank of windows.

Charlie hooked an arm beneath hers. "That can be arranged." He lowered his voice to a stage whisper. "Just don't tell Uncle Miltie."

Hope stared right at him and inquired, "Uncle Who?"

Charlie rolled his eyes. "Come on, sweetheart, before Uncle Who changes his mind."

"Take good care of that plane," Milton cautioned for the umpteenth time with a deadpan expression.

Charlie cast a serious side-eye at his boss, and both men broke out laughing. They were still chortling when Charlie and Hope walked through the door and out onto the tarmac. Duffels hung off their shoulders, along with an assortment of firepower.

After a final wistful glance at her friend, Faith turned to leave. Her emotions were easy enough to read. She was happy for her friend, but she wanted the same thing: a man of her own to love. Out of the four women she'd arrived at Langley with, she was the only one still by herself.

"Hold up for a minute, Faith." Milton's tone was stern.

"It's past six, sir." She twisted to face him. "Was there more work you wanted me to do tonight?" Her expression was open, unguarded. And her words had been sincere without a hint of sullenness.

Reg had to hand it to her. Most normal humans would've been piling arguments atop arguments that they'd done plenty for one day and could they please be excused to their quarters. Not Faith.

"One more thing," Milton's harsh demeanor softened.

"Name it." She stood straighter, waiting.

"See if any of our new female recruits want to go to dinner with you. I'm sure things here still feel uncomfortable, and having a seasoned pro show them the ropes will get them into the swing of life at Langley. Make them useful agents that much sooner."

Faith smiled, and the classic planes of her face shifted into something profanely beautiful. Reg stared at green eyes, slanted cheekbones, a high forehead, and a defined chin with a dimple dead center. Her teeth were very straight and very white.

"I'd planned to do that anyway, sir. Thanks for being so kind to Hope and Charlie."

The corners of Milton's mouth twitched. "Don't spread it around. Kind isn't how I want anyone to see me. Gets in the way of my badass reputation."

"Your secret is safe with me." She turned toward the door and let herself outside.

Milton turned to Reg and quirked a brow. "Feel like a cup of coffee?"

"Do you suppose it's too early to put a splash of whiskey in it?"

Milton made a grunting noise. "Wasn't aware booze had a time limit on it. Come on." He pushed the door open and motioned Reg through. The whine of jet engines revving said the Gulfstream was on the move.

"Were you wanting to come back to the infirmary?" Reg asked.

"It's closer than my house, so sure. You still bunking in Charlie's building?"

"Yeah." Reg shrugged, suddenly uncomfortable. "I spend most of my time in the infirmary. My bed there actually sees a whole lot more of me than the one in my apartment."

Milton made a noncommittal sound and broke into a lope once they got outside. Light was fading fast, and the temperature was dropping. Reg ran alongside him, enjoying the feel of pushing his body to work at something physical.

"Good that your leg healed so well," Milton observed. "Shattered femurs can go either way."

"Got lucky on that one." Reg paused a beat, decided what the hell, and asked, "Were you ever going to tell me you got Cortexiphan?"

Milton cast a pointed, sidelong look his way. "No."

Reg sucked in a breath, not sure where to go with that. On the one hand, everyone under his care—which included all of the CIA's personnel stationed on this base—were supposed to reveal every aspect of their medical histories and treatment. On the other, he reported to Milton, which made things sticky.

"If I'd had any intention of letting anyone know about Frank and Tony's Herculean efforts to save my life, that scenario would've played out in the infirmary. I didn't want them to get into trouble, or be kicked out of the CIA, if they guessed wrong and I died."

"Oh, you mean like I threatened to do when the dynamic duo did pretty much the same thing with Charlie?" Reg tried to keep a sour, disapproving note out of his voice.

"They did a whole lot more to save Charlie's bacon than to save mine."

They reached the infirmary, and Reg tilted his head to let the scanner read his retina. Once the latch clicked, he pushed the door open with his hip and led the way up three flights to his office on the clinic's top floor.

Milton followed him into his domain and let out a long, low whistle. "Cyclone get loose in here?"

Reg looked at the piles of books, papers, and two printers spewing still more paper. "Been doing some research," he admitted. "I prefer reading things on paper than on the screen, and this way, I can file things where they're easy to find again."

Milton pushed a stack of paper off a chair and dropped into it, folding his hands in his lap. "Research on what?" His voice was bland.

Reg dragged the room's only other chair around, clearing its seat so he could sit too. "On the freaks, what else. Did you want anything in your coffee? I'll get us a couple cups before I settle in."

"Sure. A shot of booze would go down well."

Reg moved to a coffeemaker plugged in on the far side of the room and sloshed the pot's contents. It didn't look too thick and sludgy to drink, so he divided what was left into two white, ceramic mugs. "Pick your poison." He dragged bottles of scotch, bourbon, and Irish whiskey from a cabinet.

"Whiskey, please."

"Excellent choice. It's what I drink, but I keep the others for impromptu guests."

"Like me?" Milton smiled.

"Exactly like you." Reg handed him a cup, sat across from Milton with his own, and waited. He knew the CIA head of operations well enough to understand he wanted something.

"Yeah, I do want something. Actually a few somethings," Milton latched his direct, dark gaze onto Reg.

He narrowed his eyes. "Did the ability to read minds come along with the injections, or the Cortexiphan?"

"It was there before, but it got a whole lot stronger with the addition of Cortexiphan," Milton said. "First off, I want you to stop blaming yourself."

"Huh? I had nothing to do with your decision to add Cortexiphan after your injection series headed south."

"Not that. You're still feeling responsible for the freaks' genome malfunction."

Breath hissed from between Reg's clenched teeth. "It's because I am responsible. I designed V2. Not singlehandedly, but I was the senior researcher in that lab, and I fucked things up. No way to sugarcoat it."

Milton cocked his head to one side. "We all make mistakes—"

Reg made a chopping motion with the hand not holding his mug and belted back the coffee-whiskey mixture. "This was a whole lot more than a mistake. I know exactly what I did wrong. The V3 fix the freaks came up with ameliorated some of the problems, but not all of them. I actually believe I've developed a better—"

"Which would explain why you sleep here," Milton broke in. "Damn it, Reg, the genetically altered don't need anything further from you. They're satisfied with V3. The ones still in compounds have discovered V4 is far worse than the V2 you came up with, but they're not our problem."

"When I fuck something up, I like to fix it." Reg cringed at how the words sounded. Like a whiny twenty-year-old seeking justice in an arbitrary world.

"Yeah, we all do, but sometimes your best bet is to pack up your toys and move on. Is all this—" Milton waved an arm expansively to encompass the messy office "—research on building a better genome?"

Reg felt his face heat. "Not all, but maybe ninety percent."

Milton leaned toward him. "I'm going to be out of line here, so be warned. In all the years I've known you, you've never had much of a personal life. Why not?"

Milton's question caught him by surprise. He was in the process of swallowing, and he choked on the hot liquid. "That's more than out of line," he sputtered, wiping coffee off his chin with the back of one hand.

"That would be me. No boundaries. Are you going to answer me? Or should I just cull through your mind?"

Reg surged to his feet and placed his mug atop a stack of books on one corner of his desk. His hands balled into fists before he realized what he was doing and shook his head. "Yeah, like I'm going to keep you out of my private places by punching you."

"Not the best idea," Milton agreed, and took another swallow of coffee.

"You have access to my personnel records," Reg said stiffly and unclenched his hands.

Milton blew out a frustrated breath. "This isn't the Middle East, and you haven't been captured. It's not a name, rank, and serial number event. I've known you a long time, and I care about you. You've never married. What? Do you like men? I won't judge."

Reg's shoulders sagged and he dropped back into his chair. "No. Not men." He reached for his cup, and then changed his mind. "I grew up on Chicago's lower east side. We were beyond poor. Never enough food. No heat. Often as not, the water and gas were turned off. The cockroaches and mice in our two rooms fared better than the people did. I worked from the time I could walk, and Mom and Dad just kept having more kids. There were ten by the time I left home."

Milton made come along motions with one hand. "Keep going."

"Not that much to tell. I got mixed up with gangs when I was thirteen. I'd have sunk into oblivion and graduated into the adult penal system, but one of my teachers in juvenile hall kicked sense into me. God only knows what he saw in a smart-mouthed kid who was hell-bent on destruction, but he hung in there with me. Eventually, I moved in with him and his wife. They didn't have any kids of their own, and they adopted me. I finished high school with good enough grades to get scholarships, and the rest is in my personnel records."

"Indeed it is," Milton said. "Harvard Medical with highest honors and a residency in Internal Medicine. From there, you joined the Air Force and headed for the Middle East."

"Actually, I joined up before medical school. The Air Force underwrote part of my training, and I owed them four years of service."

"But you liked the military and chose to stay."

It hadn't been a question, so Reg didn't answer it. He took another drink from his mug.

"Why not so much as a girlfriend?" Milton persisted.

"I had my share. In med school, a gal and I grew close during our last year, but she was also close to a few other docs in training. It was like a game for her, keeping us from finding out about each other."

"What happened when you did find out?" Milton furled salt and pepper brows.

Reg shrugged. "Predictable. We ended up shouting at each other. She said some things that hurt. So did I. Whole thing set me off my game for days. So much so, I made a mistake in clinic. If one of the residents hadn't noticed, I'd have killed a patient. It wasn't a particularly complicated case, but you can kill anyone if you give them the wrong drug, or the wrong dose of the right one."

"So you decided love and medicine weren't good bedfellows."

"You might say that. My patients have always been my first priority."

"You made them that because you got scared." Milton got to his feet. "Thanks for trusting me. I'll never say a word, but I want you to hear me out."

"Do I have a choice?" Reg beat back half a smile.

"No. I came from humble beginnings too. Not as bad as yours, but bad enough. Being perfect was my hedge against falling back into the slime pit I came from. Perfect in my job, that is. I took another tack when it came to women and blew through marriages. Until I decided I was done. Honor changed all that for me, and I'm damn glad she came along."

"What exactly are you saying?"

Milton set his mug down, walked to the door, and spun to face him. "Just this. It's a lonely life. You're past forty. Unless you want to be sixty and still dragging test tubes and research papers to bed with you, take a good, hard look at your priorities. I wish someone had given me a swift kick in the backside, but they didn't."

"Why do I feel like I've stumbled into a bad episode of *Dr. Phil?*"

"Not *Dr. Phil.* When Roy tried to sit me down—after I pretty much blew it with Honor—I told him I didn't do chick flicks. Regardless, stop blaming yourself for V2. If it hadn't been for you, the genetically altered might have vanished after V1 didn't pan out. They're quite a gift. So what if your research model wasn't perfect? Whose is?"

Before Reg could formulate an answer, Milton was gone. Most of what he'd said had been eerily accurate, and being dissected with such skill was damned unsettling. Reg reached for his mug and drained it. The alcohol buzzed pleasantly, soothing some of the rough edges from Milton's advice session.

He cares about me. He didn't have to bother, but he did.

The revelation was disconcerting. Reg did hold people at arm's length, hiding behind his M.D. to keep a comfortable distance. Milton had smashed through his defenses like a hot knife cutting through butter.

Question was, what would he do about it?

Reg gazed about his office and really looked at how sterile it was. Outside of his ego wall, nothing graced the walls. Not so much as a photograph of places he'd been.

"Yeah, right," he muttered. "Not the vacation type. I've been to war zones. They're not exactly photographic material. Dead bodies and landmine holes. Broken buildings and rubble."

Out of nowhere, Faith's face flashed through his mind. She'd caught his eye while Charlie was in the infirmary, and she'd come to visit him and Hope. Since she arrived about the same time every day, it had been easy to be close by. He'd wanted to get to know her better then, and he still did. But how? His enforced solitude had spanned twenty years. Dating felt awkward and uncomfortable.

An idea bloomed. As he turned it over, looking for holes, it appealed to him. He could offer her research work in the infirmary. It would be a good fit for her computer-like brain. That way, she'd be close enough for them to chat. Maybe they could have coffee—or a meal.

At the thought of food, his stomach growled. He hadn't eaten since breakfast—another bad habit—and he got to his feet. If he was going to have dinner in the cafeteria, he needed to hurry.

His plan to get to know Faith was far from perfect, but maybe it would be a start. He strode out the door, hearing it latch shut behind him. His cock, a badly neglected appendage, sent sharp sensations shooting through him, and he pulled his lab coat closed to cover his erection. It wasn't that he never indulged, but the last time had been months ago. Thinking about Faith kindled his libido, and he welcomed the heat spilling through him.

Beneath everything, he was still a man.

"Night, Doc," rang from several clinic staff as he passed them on his way to the front door. He wished them a good evening in return, nabbed a coat off a hook, and walked into the night.

Even though it had been awkward and embarrassing while it was happening, Milton did him a huge favor by reaching out. Next time he saw him, he'd find a way to say thanks. His inner critic—the one that avoided anything smacking of the personal—winced.

He told it to man up and shut up.

CHAPTER 3

Faith leveraged her enhanced genetics, pushing them for more speed as she ran across campus to make her agreed upon meeting with Dr. Thomas on time. Practice had gone particularly well this morning and had continued longer than expected. So long, she hadn't gotten lunch, but she could eat later. She'd tossed and turned the previous night until she'd put her mind in sleep mode. It wasn't the same as actually sleeping, but at least it shut off her thoughts.

What did the doctor want with her? She'd met him during Charlie's crisis, mostly because he'd always been somewhere near Charlie's room when she showed up. Was his constant presence because he was taking extra special care of Charlie after his near-death experience?

That had to be it. Most clinic patients weren't all that ill. Medical emergencies were farmed out to level one trauma centers in nearby McLean, Virginia or another metropolitan area. While the infirmary did have isolation rooms, in case personnel were exposed to something best quarantined at Langley, insofar as she could tell those rooms had been empty during Charlie's stay. Except for the one he was in. Not that he had anything contagious, but he'd been quite a handful after a Cortexiphan infusion nearly killed him.

She stopped in front of the infirmary. It was quarter past twelve, and she hoped she wasn't too late. He'd said *around noon*, which could mean a lot of different things.

I have to get over apologizing until I discover if one is needed, she lectured herself, wishing she had some of Charity's abrasiveness.

A palm plate and a retinal scanner graced the doorjamb, but neither unlatched the lock when she tried them. She'd tripped the locks with kinetics when she came to visit Charlie, but didn't want to get off on the wrong foot today. Stepping closer, she pushed the buzzer.

"State your business," a tinny female voice said.

"I was supposed to be here at noon," Faith replied.

"For what?" the voice prodded.

Oh yeah, that would be important, huh? Faith's face warmed with embarrassment.

"I have an appointment with Dr. Thomas."

"Just a moment."

The crackling, hissing speaker quieted. Rather than it coming back online, the door made a buzzing sound as the lock disengaged.

Faith shouldered her way inside and stood in the familiar foyer, waiting. She had no idea where Dr. Thomas would be meeting her. The clinic held a utilitarian aspect. No cushy furniture here. No dog-eared magazines. The pungent smell of antiseptic burned her nostrils, and a row of card table chairs lined one wall. Perhaps because it was the noon hour, the reception area was devoid of people.

She clasped her hands behind her back, still scanning the no-frills waiting room and sent her kinetics zinging wide to figure out if anyone was here besides whoever had buzzed her in. Several people worked behind walls on both sides of the room she stood in. Others were on the upper two floors. She located Dr. Thomas easily enough, grateful when his energy moved toward her. She'd begun to wonder if he'd forgotten about his invitation from the previous evening.

It was a possibility, given how busy he was.

His unique emanations grew closer. He had to be in the stairwell she'd always taken to get to Charlie's room on the second floor. Sure enough, the door opened, and he strode through. His teal smock and white lab coat were splattered with blood, its distinct metallic scent sharp in her sensitive nostrils.

"Faith." His deep, rich voice did funny things to her stomach. "Sorry I'm late and didn't have time to grab a clean coat. Got caught up in a last minute surgery."

"It's fine. I was late too." She squeezed her clasped hands tighter together, waiting to see why she'd been summoned.

"Follow me back upstairs," he said. "We're meeting in my office." Without waiting for her assent, he turned and opened the stairwell door, holding it for her. Once she was through, he moved past her and hurried up the stairs. "Hope you don't mind," he called over a shoulder, "but I ordered lunch for us. Only chance I'll get to eat today, and I figured the same might be true for you."

Faith emerged on the third floor, a part of the infirmary building she'd never seen beyond the building's schematics that lived in her database brain. The doctor turned hard right and went to the end of the hall. Just like the outside door, his office had dual scanners.

"Why both palm and retinal security here?" she asked.

"Everyone who works here has palm access," he said. "The retinal scanner mounted by this door only admits me, and I can disable the hand plate if I want to keep everyone else out." He held the door for her, waiting. "Rank has a few privileges. Not many, mind you."

Faith walked into a spotless office. So spotless it didn't appear anyone ever worked here. Books, file folders, and file boxes lined shelves built into one wall. A computer terminal with dual monitors and two printers stood on an enormous desk that took up a third of the floor space. Degrees decked another wall, interspersed with certificates from the military and the CIA. What looked like a miniature lab sat against the back wall complete with a microscope, test tube rack, and clipboards.

"Your office is so…organized." Faith bit hard on her lower lip. How he kept his workspace was none of her concern.

"Not always. Actually, I just cleaned it late last night. Yesterday, even clerical was complaining about having to wend their way through stacks of books, journals, and stray papers."

Not sure what an appropriate response would be, she asked, "Where do you want me to sit?"

"Right there." He pointed at one of two chairs turned to face each another. A small, round table sat off to one side. "Our lunch should arrive presently. I hope ham and Swiss on wheat is acceptable."

"Sure. I eat almost anything. They starved us in the compounds. Teaches you not to be picky." Faith felt like she was babbling, so she sat down fast and folded her hands in her lap.

"Thanks for arranging your schedule to accommodate mine on such short notice." He took the seat across from her. "What I'd like to talk with you about is spending at least half your work hours here." He held up a hand. "Hear me out, please, before you ask questions."

Faith nodded, and he continued. "Frank and Tony brought up some very interesting points after they saved Charlie's life—a feat neither my skill nor my training could accomplish. I'd like to figure out a way to create a safer, easier injection series for our agents. I'd also like to modify the Cortexiphan so it could be used to augment the benefits from those injections. Minus the harsh side effect profile"

"That's all fine and well," Faith cut in when he stopped to take a breath, remembering too late he'd said to hold her questions. "Never mind," she said. "Sorry. I was supposed to wait."

"No. It's all right. What were you going to say?"

She took a deep breath. It might be cutting off her nose to spite her face, but she had to be honest. "I'm not a geneticist like Frank or

Tony. Those are worthwhile projects, but don't you think you'd be better served with one of them working here?"

"They're already knee-deep in both those projects. Generally in science, a two-pronged approach delivers the most robust results. We'll take what comes from their lab, compare and contrast it with what emerges from this lab, and create the safest, most effective products possible."

Faith licked her lips. Being this close to Dr. Thomas did strange things to her insides. They felt light and fluttery. A knock on the door almost sent her hurtling out of her seat.

"Come in," Dr. Thomas called.

The door opened, and a smiling orderly—or maybe he was a nurse—delivered two brown paper sacks, dropping them on the table next to her chair. "Here you go."

"Thanks, John. What do I owe you?" The doctor stood and dug a wallet out of the back pocket of his scrubs.

"Ten bucks."

Dr. Thomas extracted a bill, and the other man took it and left. "Feel free to begin," he told Faith. "I'm going to wash up and get out of these blood-stained scrubs." He hustled through the door that hadn't fully closed.

Faith stared after him, wanting him to come back, but then she got hold of herself and grabbed one of the lunch bags. Better to eat than to moon over the impossible. She hadn't found much during last night's hacking session in the personnel database, but that didn't mean the doctor was single. He might have a love interest he wasn't married to.

Unwrapping her sandwich, she began to eat. She'd promised herself to stop if she unearthed a wife while hacking, but there hadn't been one. About all she'd found were his illustrious school transcripts and degrees, his military deployments and decorations, and records from him being wounded and transferred to a VA hospital before he went to work for the CIA two years ago. If he had a family, and he damn near had to, there'd been no mention of it.

The door latch clicked before Dr. Thomas swept back into the room wearing a clean lab coat and scrub top. "Thank God for laundry, huh?" He made a grab for the other lunch bag, extracted his sandwich, and took a couple bites, chewing and swallowing. "One of the worst parts of field deployments is getting back into the same stinky, putrid clothes every single day. The nose adapts, but the spirit doesn't."

Faith smiled. He had an easy way about him that put her at her ease. "This is a good sandwich. Thank you for thinking of me."

"You're welcome." He pulled a can of soda from his bag and popped the tab, taking a long drink.

"Back to your job offer," she said. "I don't have anything by way of scientific training. I'm not sure what I could do to be helpful. In truth, I'd be dead weight until someone trained me—and I downloaded relevant data into my brain."

He sent a speculative glance skittering her way. "You just nailed it with your download comment. You'd learn very fast because of how your mind is configured. Much faster than a normal human beginning at ground zero."

"Why not use one of the other Nameless Ones?" she persisted. "We just got a bunch of guys who defected. Maybe one of them has lab experience."

"Faith." He set his soda on the table. "Would you like to spend about four hours a day working for me? Before you answer, it's a simple question and has nothing to do with the qualifications you believe you lack."

She swallowed around a suddenly dry throat and pulled her own can of soda out of her bag. "Uh, not sure, sir. What would happen to the women assigned to me?"

"I'd cover that ground with Milton. He's the original solution guy. I've seen him pull off amazing feats with a paperclip and a hand grenade. That's not the question, though."

Faith studied her lap as she ran probabilities. Could she work here and rein in her attraction for the man seated across from her?

What if something slipped out and embarrassed the holy hell out of her? More to the point, did she want to learn the particular skillset he was offering?

The answer to the last question was a resounding yes, but the odds attached to the first two queries ran in the fifty-fifty range.

"Faith?"

She felt his shrewd green eyes studying her and mumbled, "I'm considering all the ramifications."

"Would you care to share your thought processes—so I can understand how they work?"

"No," she blurted and clapped a hand over her mouth. "Sorry, that came out wrong."

His expression shifted, eyes gleaming with curiosity. "If I had the injection series and the Cortexiphan, I'd be able to gather the answers from your mind. Since I haven't done either of those things, you need to talk with me."

Thank fucking God you can't read my thoughts.

She rode herd on her autonomic nervous system before she turned bright red. "Well, I am interested in learning more about the science that drives Frank and Tony's research. It's grounded in who I am and how my genome works. Who wouldn't want to know more about those things?"

He angled his head to one side. "Is that a yes? Or a maybe?"

She tried not to smile, but felt the edges of her mouth curve into one despite her best efforts. "It's a maybe-yes. Enough of a yes that you can talk with Milton and see if he's even willing to spring me from my other duties."

Dr. Thomas nodded solemnly. "I will. I appreciate you being open to trying something new. I believe we have a lot we can learn from each other."

"Pfft." She waved a dismissive hand. "You have plenty to teach me, but I'm just a woman from a compound. They liked us stupid— and went to great lengths to keep us that way."

"No." His voice was sharp. "You were smarter than the men, and they knew it. It's why they were so hard on you."

"Yeah, I understand all that, but it doesn't make any of it easier or more palatable. Life in the compounds was hell for us women."

He polished off the rest of his sandwich in a few quick bites, and she did the same. "Someday, I hope you'll tell me about those compounds."

"Why would you want to know?"

"Chalk it up to the scientist in me. Firsthand accounts are always more interesting than reading about things." He looked at a bag of chips, made a face, and laid them aside.

"Don't like potato chips?" she asked.

"Not particularly, but they're good for extra calories, so I always order them."

"And then don't eat them." Her eyes widened. "Aw geez. I'm sorry. You might be my boss, and that was way too casual, not to mention inappropriate." Faith shook her head. "I'm still getting used to all the social rules normal humans have. It's not easy."

"No apology needed. Would you like to see where we'll be working? I have a state-of-the-art lab one floor down. Got specialized funding from CDC during the last Ebola outbreak in Sub-Saharan Africa. They weren't sure how many additional labs they might need that were iso-standard. Mine was, so I got the money and created the lab of my dreams." He paused for a beat. "I'm ready for those Ebola samples, but at least so far, no one's ever sent me any."

Faith crumpled the paper that had held her sandwich and tossed it into a nearby waste can. "Sure. I'd love to see your lab. Now that you mention it, Frank and Tony were drooling over it after they synthesized that stuff they injected into Charlie. They're still talking about all the bells and whistles you have that they want. Last time they requested some item—and justified the request by saying you had it—Milton told them to stuff it."

Dr. Thomas laughed. "I can just see him doing that." He stood and dropped the remains of his lunch in the trash too. "Shall we?"

"Sure, sir. I know roughly where we're going, but I'll follow you."

"Drop the sir," he said. "My name is Reg."

She stopped dead. "I can't call you by your first name. It's not right."

"You can and you will. Everyone else who works for me does."

"They do not." She stood straight. "I've heard them call you doctor and Doc Thomas."

"And I correct them when I'm thinking about it." He led the way out of his office, and she trotted after him.

Was she making a mistake? Her brain whirled feverishly with questions and probabilities as she went down the stairs and another long hallway to yet one more dually protected door. One thing was certain, Frank and Tony would be green with envy once they found out that she—a mere woman—had daily access to a lab they'd lay down their lives for.

"Ha!" she mumbled under her breath.

"Ha, what?" Dr. Thomas—Reg, she mentally corrected herself—asked without turning around.

"Nothing. You weren't supposed to hear that."

"I may not have your enhanced genetics—" he pulled the door open for her "—but I have very sharp ears."

"I'll keep it in mind." Faith gazed around the lab. While she didn't recognize most of its contents, every wall and alcove was bursting with equipment. She walked to one of the long walls and began reading labels, checking off the name of each item with the database in her mind. "It's going to take me days to figure out what each of these things is."

"But you know how to find those answers, right?" He'd closed the door, but he still stood next to it watching her.

"Oh sure." She walked to another item and touched it. "All I have to do is look up the name for this in my head, and I can find out what it is and what it's used for. When I need more information, I link to the CIA's mainframe. It's the same process as when you institute a search, except I'm doing it with my mind rather than a keyboard."

"Excellent and precisely what I was hoping for. It's almost one. Where do you need to be this afternoon?"

"That holodeck thing in the underground arena. We'll be doing some simulated MMA scenarios."

"You should get moving, or you'll be late. Let me run interference with Milton, and I'll get back to you with his answer."

She should leave. She'd clearly been dismissed, but she couldn't stop one word from escaping. "When?"

Rather than being annoying, her lack of control over her mouth seemed to amuse him. "As soon as I have an answer. Now get moving. You'll have lots of time to catalog what's in my lab next time you're here."

"How do you know there'll be a next time?" Faith tossed her hands skyward. "Don't mind me. I'm sorry. I'm not usually like this. I may not have been here long, but the CIA has taught me about protocol and manners and—"

"Go." He made shooing motions with one hand. "I'll be in touch."

Faith spun, tugged the door open, and fled down the hallway, taking the stairs three at a time in her hurry to escape. She'd behaved abysmally, been forward, treated the doctor like a friend not a boss.

Yeah, the list is long.

The minute she was outside, she broke into a run, pushing hard. She'd made a fool out of herself. The next thing she'd hear from Dr. Thomas was that Milton said no. Hell, he'd probably never even talk with Milton. She'd proven herself way too high maintenance today. He was looking for a lab assistant, not someone to provide a running commentary on everything from soup to nuts.

Faith was so engaged in kicking herself, she ran right past the underground arena entrance and had to double back.

I have to get over myself right now.

Wiping her mind clean so none of the freak women would be able to read it, she waited for the elevator to drop her two hundred feet to their shielded practice arena. The end of today couldn't come fast enough. She wanted to hide in her apartment, crawl into her bed, and pull the covers over her head.

Only reason he looks so good to me is because all my friends found someone special.

Fancy words. If I believed them—and I don't—I could forget about Reg and move on.

CHAPTER 4

*R*eg tweaked a couple of experiments percolating in the lab before making his way back to his office. He needed to check on the leg ulcer he'd lanced, cleaned, and stitched just before Faith showed up, but that could wait. Too bad the agent hadn't presented for treatment sooner. The wound had been purulent, spewing bloody fluid when he opened it.

It had been hard chasing Faith out of the lab. She'd clearly wanted to stay, and he'd wanted her there. Her quick mind and forthright manner appealed to him. This was one woman who wouldn't play games—or engage in subterfuge. Her reaction to his offer pleased him. She hadn't shot him down out of the box, which had to be a good sign.

Not necessarily.

She said maybe to a job offer, one that will shed light on how she's made. It's a long way from there to going out with me.

Reg slowed his pace. Was that what he wanted? Why clutter up his nice, neat, sterile life with a woman after all these years? He grimaced because he'd just answered his own question. His life was sterile, just like his instruments. If he didn't make some changes soon, he'd grow so set in his ways, no woman would ever want him.

Hell, he was almost at that point now.

He pushed the door shut behind him and grabbed the telephone, intent on raising Milton. Surely, getting him to agree with allowing Faith to spend time in the lab would be a slam-dunk. Or would it?

Guess I'm about to find out.

Reg tapped the phone's display.

Milton had his own ideas about the genetically modified women. He'd gone out on a limb with the brass, building a case to allow the women to remain and become agents. That particular battle spawned a proprietary interest, and Milton kept a close eye on everything the women did at the CIA.

"Yeah? What is it?" Milton barked, sounding even more put out that usual.

Probably wasn't the best time to blurt out a request for any departure from protocol, so Reg switched tactics fast. "I'm headed to the gun range. Haven't done my required monthly practice session—"

"And you still hate guns and were hoping for company," Milton interrupted.

"Something like that." Reg loosened his grip on the receiver before he broke the plastic. "Are you going to save me from myself? Or do I have to drill those targets alone?"

"What is it that bothers you so much about keeping your skills sharp?" Milton asked, his voice edging from pissed to weary. "If it was some surgical procedure, bet you'd read up on it damn fast. Maybe even hunt down a lab animal or two to practice on."

"True enough, but I put bodies back together. Practicing to destroy them never sat well. On an intellectual level, I recognize—"

"Can it. Be there in thirty. I could use a break." Milton disconnected, leaving Reg staring at the phone in his hand.

So far, so good.

He went to the small closet at the rear of his office and shucked his scrub top and lab coat, exchanging them for a dark sweatshirt blazoned with the CIA's logo. He glanced down at the paper covers on his tennis shoes—left over from this morning's surgery—and swapped out the low-slung footwear for a stout pair of boots. So long as he was changing shoes, he also traded out his scrub trousers for sweatpants.

He left his office at a run, stopped to check the wound he'd dressed earlier, upped the IV antibiotic, and hustled outside to one of the pool cars. No way could he make the gun range in the few minutes he had left. Milton was punctual, and he expected the same from his subordinates.

It took breaking Langley's thirty-five mile-per-hour speed limit, but he arrived at the range right after Milton, who was just emerging from his own car. Reg parked and jumped out, running to join the other man.

"Meant to jog over here," Milton said.

Reg snorted. "Yeah, me too, but I had to check on a surgical patient from this morning and—"

"You ran out of time. Never enough, is there?" Milton headed into the building and stopped in the munitions room to gather firearms and ammo. The agent working there checked them in.

Reg collected his own set of guns and ammunition. "That's the third time you've cut me off today."

Milton turned his steely, dark gaze on Reg. "Your point?"

"Nothing, but sometimes it's instructive to allow people to finish their sentences."

"Noted."

Milton trotted into the cavernous firing range and placed specialized protection over his ears. The headsets muffled gun noise, but allowed normal conversation to filter through.

Reg settled his own headset in place and slapped a clip in his automatic rifle. Raising it to a shoulder, he drilled a distant target. Guns weren't his favorite toy, but he'd become proficient firing them. The Air Force had seen to that. They'd also made certain he was certified as both a fixed wing and helicopter pilot—mostly so he could fly himself out of dicey situations in the event his pilot and copilot were killed. Doctors were always in short supply, and the military did everything it could to ensure they wouldn't lose any.

Standing next to him, Milton burned through several clips in three different weapons. Reg followed suit. The stench of expended ammunition filled the air. Acetone from cordite, the musky, sulfuric stench of gunpowder, and the acrid bite of propellant. When he ran out of clips, he set the last gun he'd fired—a .45 semiautomatic pistol—aside, and turned toward Milton, who was also out of ammo.

No more excuses. He had to broach Faith with Milton, or this trip to the firing range would turn into a waste of time.

Not totally. I did need this month's practice session.

Milton dragged off his headset and turned to Reg. "What did you really want?"

"That transparent, am I?" Reg furled his brows into question marks.

"You didn't answer me."

Three agents shouldered into the range, taking up spots down the firing line.

Milton tapped Reg's upper arm. "Let's get out of here before I have to put my headset on again. I'll follow you back to your office."

"Sure." Reg filed out after Milton and dropped the guns off at central munitions. They checked him off for this month's mandatory practice. By the time he walked outside, Milton and his car were gone.

As he drove back to the infirmary—at a more sedate pace that wouldn't alert campus security—he turned over a number of approaches to float past Milton.

And discarded every single one of them.

Milton was sharp. He'd see through almost anything Reg came up with. Even though he'd chided his boss about cutting people off midsentence, the hard truth was Milton hated wasting time. He listened until he didn't need to hear anything further, and then he chucked his opinion into the mix. Reg had worked with him in the field in the Middle East, and Milton's management style hadn't changed.

He slid his car into a parking space next to the infirmary and walked inside and up the stairs. Milton was already in his office.

"How'd you get inside?" Reg sputtered. "I had the palm reader locked out."

Milton sent a pointed glance his way. "Kinetics. What the fuck happened? Cleaning bug bite you?" He waved his arms, gesturing at the newly pristine office.

Reg stepped through the door and kicked it shut behind him. "Nah. Not so much, but I got to thinking about what you said, and I cleared and filed all the genome research. It's still here, arranged in files and binders—in case I want to take another peek."

"Mmph." Milton crossed his arms over his chest. "What's up? You didn't ask me over here to admire your office."

"I didn't ask you over here at all. You invited yourself."

Milton screwed his face into a frown. "You're sparring with me. You want something, and it wasn't just company at the gun range."

"Are you using your kinetics?"

"Not yet, but if you drag your heels much more, I might. Am I wrong about you wanting something?"

Here it was. Truth time. Even if Milton pitched a fit and said no, there was no reason he couldn't pursue Faith, but the proximity of having her in the lab would make things so much easier.

"Would you be willing to free up Faith from her other duties for four hours a day?"

Milton's frown deepened. "Why? So she can do what?"

"I spoke with her about working here in my lab."

Milton trudged across the office and pulled open the cabinet where Reg kept the liquor. Selecting the whiskey, he uncorked it and poured a couple fingers into a mug. After he'd put the bottle back, he drained the mug's contents.

"Let me be sure I have this straight," Milton growled. "You spoke with her about a change in her duty assignment without first checking with me?"

"Yup." Reg nodded. "That's right."

"What would the Air Force have thought about that breach of protocol?"

He shrugged. "Probably not much, but docs have a whole lot of latitude. Most of us can do ever so much better in the private sector, and—"

"Spare me." Milton made a hacking motion with one hand, reached for the liquor cabinet door, but then changed his mind and set his cup aside. "Why do you want her here? Why not Frank or Tony? I assume you're looking for a research associate."

Reg beat back a smile, but he wasn't fast enough.

"What's so funny?" Milton demanded.

"Faith asked exactly the same question."

"Are you going to answer it? What'd you tell her? We've got a dynamic balance here between the original five women and the new recruits. If I'm going to alter it, I need a damn good reason."

"Frank and Tony are working on a version of the injection series that will be easier to tolerate."

"Yeah, I know that." Milton flapped a dismissive hand. "They're also working on developing Cortexiphan that doesn't have such a shitty side effect profile. So what?"

"I'm working on those same things in this lab. Once we've all come up with answers, we'll pool them and synthesize better chemicals."

"I'm still not understanding why you need Faith for that. Why not see if one of the other freak men has a science background."

"Since when do I not get to pick who works with me?" Reg bristled. In the military, the best defense was often a strong offense.

Milton rolled his eyes. "God preserve me from medical personnel. You guys get the special snowflake treatment from the second you enter medical school, and you never get over it."

"How about this?" Reg edged toward the coffee pot and poured himself a cup. It was too early for booze—at least in his book. The coffee was bitter, but he slugged back half a cup, waiting for the caffeine to hit him.

"How about what?" Milton's voice held an exasperated tone that meant he was close to walking out the door. Patience had never been his long suit. Neither was subtlety. Even in the field, he'd been a "let's go in and blow the fuck out of them" type.

"Let me have her four hours a day for the next quarter. Then you can reinstitute her normal duties."

"Does that mean you'll be done fine-tuning the injections and Cortexiphan by then?"

Not very fucking likely. Unless Frank and Tony are miracle-workers.

Reg produced a sunny smile. "Maybe. I'll be close enough I might not need an assistant at that point."

"What aren't you telling me?" Milton stepped closer, a calculating expression on his face. "How about Honor? What if I reassign her to this project? Would that meet your needs?"

"No. I want Faith. Last thing I need is your wife reporting back to you every single day. Science isn't linear, and there will be lots of days when it looks as if we're losing ground."

"She's not my wife. Not yet, anyway."

"Same difference." Reg kept his gaze leveled at Milton.

"Want to know what I think?" Milton walked around Reg and headed for the closed door.

"Just like the other day, you'll tell me regardless."

Milton reached the door and turned a hatchet-faced look Reg's way. "You took our little heart-to-heart the other day seriously. Faith appeals to you, but it's been so long since you've spent time with women, you want her to be here. On your turf. That way, it's a comfort zone for you, and you can explore your attraction to her at your leisure. Am I close?"

Reg felt his face heat. Damn Milton, anyway. "Yeah. Close."

Milton's stern countenance shattered, replaced by a warm smile. "Excellent news. Those women are amazing, but know this—" he fisted one hand and drove it into his other palm "—if I catch wind of you mistreating her or making her unhappy, you'll catch hell from me. And I will find out. Those five gals are close. They have no secrets from one another."

"Does that mean you approve of the reassignment?" Reg forced a neutrality he was far from feeling as he double-checked Milton's words. Getting Faith here was only a first step, but a very important one.

"It does, but—"

A flurry of footsteps in the corridor was followed by a frantic knock on the door. Milton was closest, so he pulled it open.

"Doctor. Thank God. I tried to buzz you, but your pager's off." A harried looking blonde nurse in dark blue scrubs rocked from foot to foot.

"What's happened, Mary?" Reg crossed the room in a few long strides and pulled a lab coat out of the closet, slipping it over his sweats. He'd learned long ago to cover what he could with clothes that withstood bleach. He also glanced at his pager. It was, indeed, off. He hadn't wanted any interruptions during his meeting with Faith and had neglected to click it back on.

"Accident at the gun range, sir. It's bad. Medics are bring them in now." She spun on her heel and ran down the corridor with Reg right behind her.

"How many?" Reg called after her.

"Three."

"I'm coming," Milton announced. "I want to know what happened. Our range is absolutely safe. If there's been carnage, I want to know why."

Reg didn't argue. When they arrived at the door to his small emergency room, he glanced back at Milton. "You can come in, but you'll need a mask and gloves."

"Fine. Where are they?"

He tapped a closet and pulled it open, handing things out. "The gloves are sterile, once you get them on, don't touch anything or they won't be anymore." Hitting the automatic door opener with his hip, he strode into the room he'd converted into an emergency triage area. The door to the outside stood open, and medics hustled in wheeling a gurney. Leaving the man strapped to it with Reg, they ran back outside presumably for the others.

Reg bent over the first man, assessing damage. It appeared bullets had grazed his chest, but he'd had the presence of mind to wear a vest, which probably saved his life. A lump at the base of his skull suggested blunt trauma.

"I'm here," Mary announced. "Let me know what you need."

"Get an IV line cooking."

"On it, sir," she snapped.

The man was unconscious, probably because of the whack he'd taken at the back of his head. Reg propped one eye open, intent on evaluating neurological damage. The unmistakable amber pupil of a freak stared sightlessly back at him.

A harsh intake of breath from Milton told him he'd seen the same thing.

"Mary," Milton asked, "are all the victims genetically altered?"

"Not sure, sir." She inserted a cannula smoothly into an arm she'd exposed after cutting through the man's clothing. "Doctor. What do you want in the IV?"

Good question.

Reg had been familiar with freak physiology, but V3 changed a lot of parameters.

"Could you raise Frank or Tony?" Reg glanced at Milton.

Rather than answering, Milton tapped keys on his wrist computer and barked orders. When he was done, he clasped his hands behind his back.

Good. Meant he'd remembered Reg's instructions. The wrist computer meant Milton's gloves were no longer sterile, but so long as he kept his hands off anything in the room, they'd be fine.

Since the first man wasn't in immediate danger of checking out, Reg moved to the next two. Both were freaks, but one of them was dead. A bullet through the heart had taken care of him. Why hadn't this guy worn a vest like the first one? The last man was in worse shape than the first, but would pull through, judging from his vitals. No vest on him, either.

"In here," Milton shouted just before Frank and Tony burst into the already overcrowded space, pulling on masks and gloves.

"What the fuck?" Frank asked, bending over the first man.

"Aw, crap! This one's dead." Shock and dismay ricocheted through Tony's voice, and he went toe to toe with Milton. "How did this happen?"

"I don't know, but I'm going to find out. Can you save the other two?" Milton demanded.

"Yeah, they'll live," Frank said.

"I'll let you know what I find out." Milton turned to leave.

"Like you did when my chopper was sabotaged?" Frank's question cut like a whip.

Milton didn't answer, just hurried out the door, stripping off his gloves as he went.

"Fuck!" Frank punched the air with a fist.

"We don't have time for that." Reg bent over the first man. "We have an IV set up. What should we put in it?"

"What would you use in a normal human?" Frank countered, still looking furious.

"Ringers and an antibiotic."

"Works here too," Frank said. "Stay away from the quinolones. They don't go well with our physiology."

"Good to know," Reg muttered.

"This guy's lost a lot of blood and we have to get a bullet out of him," Tony said. "It's lodged in his shoulder."

"I'll take care of it." Reg moved next to Tony. The victim was unconscious, which would make probing for and removing the bullet straightforward.

He rustled up several sealed, sterile instrument packets, put on fresh gloves, and went to work.

"Someone's out to get us," Tony said.

"Ya think?" Sarcasm rolled off Frank's response.

"They put the guy responsible for the last mess with your chopper in lockdown," Tony pointed out.

"Shut up," Frank hissed. "We're not supposed to know about that."

"I'll never tell," Reg said. "Neither will Mary here."

"This is horrible," the nurse said, checking vitals. "Who would target freaks, er the genetically modified? It's not as if you haven't had a rough enough go of things."

"The ones who still label us freaks, in the worst, pejorative sense of that word," Tony replied.

The man he and Tony had just pulled a bullet out of moaned, the sound cracked and tortured. He began to writhe on the narrow table he was strapped to.

"It's all right." Tony splayed a gloved hand across the man's chest. "You're going to be okay. If you can, direct your kinetics to go to work on that hole in your shoulder."

The man's amber eyes fluttered open. "Why bring us to Langley?" he asked in a deep, throaty voice. "If you only wanted to kill us, you could've done that back at our compound in Maine."

Reg bent over him. "Whoever did this will be brought to justice. Court-martialed."

The freak rolled his eyes. "Yeah, right." He tried to twist his head.

Frank must have intuited what he wanted. "Stay still. One of you didn't make it."

"I know. I saw Chris take a direct hit. We gave Aaron a raft of shit when he put on a bulletproof vest. Turns out he was the smart one. He's fine, right?"

"Yeah, sort of fine," Aaron called from his gurney. "Got a hell of a headache, but I've instituted a healing sequence."

Reg scanned the telemetry monitors, gratified by what he saw.

"Shall I move them to beds upstairs?" the nurse asked.

"Yeah. I want to keep them at least overnight," Reg replied.

"Monitor their vitals and report in if anything looks amiss. I'll check on them before I turn in for the night."

"Is your pager back on?" Mary looked up from swabbing the bullet wound with Betadine.

"Yes. Sorry about that. I hardly ever turn it off."

"Can we talk with you?" Frank skewered Reg with his amber gaze.

"Sure." He followed Frank and Tony outside.

Tony led the way to a grove of trees shielding the infirmary from the next building over and leaned against a stout trunk. "So far, everyone else is okay, but we may not be able to remain here."

"That's a discussion you need to have with Milton," Reg protested. "My slender power base begins and ends with the infirmary."

"He has competing priorities," Tony said flatly.

Reg narrowed his eyes, thinking before he said, "Milton will protect the integrity of the CIA, but not if it means shielding a murderer from justice."

"It's not *a murderer*," Frank said.

Reg's muscles tightened. "If you know something, tell me."

"After my chopper was shot down, Tony and I began doing some digging. There's not much that's sacrosanct around here—"

"Yes, I understand you can hack into any computerized system," Reg cut in.

"What we found," Tony said, "was an organized cadre who don't believe we belong here. They have plans to take us out one by one, making it appear accidental."

"Do you have names?" Reg asked.

"Oh yeah," Tony replied.

"How come you haven't told Milton, or have you?"

"We weren't totally done with our investigation," Frank replied tersely, "but that may not matter now."

"Get those names to Milton, stat. That's an order. Beyond that, there's no way today could ever look accidental." Reg clamped his jaws into a tight line.

"Of course there is," Frank said. "Those men got sloppy and shot each other. They'll deny it, but there won't be any witnesses to corroborate one version or the other."

"Of course there are. Two of those men are very much alive—" Reg began when Frank's meaning sank in. "Are you suggesting I need guards in the infirmary?"

"Not a bad idea, but I'm not expecting an attack while they're in your shop," Tony replied. "Those men will need to disappear, though, and damned fast. Before they can testify about who attacked them."

"They're conscious. I'll have Milton send legal up to take depositions today."

"It's a start," Tony said, "but they still need to vanish."

"Or else we could engage in a little counter-terrorism with the group we discovered," Frank interjected. "If we scatter a few bodies around, maybe they'll give up."

"Not how we handle things, "Reg said. "I'll alert Milton right now."

A thought blindsided him. "Charity and the women. They're not in danger, are they?"

"You're kidding, right? That group has plans, and they won't rest until we're no longer cluttering up their turf. Women aren't exempt." Tony sounded bitter, his words terse. "Charity is fine, though. Thanks for thinking about her."

Reg sprinted for his car. Langley's campus had just turned into a war zone. He'd lived in enough of them, he recognized how they felt. Spy versus spy, raised to the tenth degree. One thing was certain, nothing would happen to Faith.

He fired the engine and headed toward Milton's building. Exactly how he'd protect Faith wasn't clear yet, but he'd figure something out. She didn't have to return his interest for him to shield her from injury. She and the other women had suffered plenty in the compounds. He'd make good, goddamned sure she wasn't in harm's way here.

His tires squealed as he braked hard. He might get a citation, but he left the car at an angle in the *No Parking* zone that fronted Milton's building. As he ran for the side door, realization dawned that Faith's kinetics were far better protection than anything he could provide.

Doesn't matter. I'll still do everything I can to keep her safe.

CHAPTER 5

The afternoon was almost shot. Faith knelt on the mat, teaching one of her charges a karate hold, when Honor's mind voice blasted her with shielded telepathy. *"They're killing us. Do you know everyone in the arena?"*

"Hang on," Faith told the woman she was working with and let go of her.

"What do you mean?" she asked Honor. *"Who's killing us?"*

"The agents who don't want us here. Same ones who sabotaged Charlie and Frank's last mission. Is anyone down there with you that you don't know?"

"Not sure. I have to check. It's a big room."

"Use extreme caution. If anything doesn't feel right, use your kinetics to stun."

"What's wrong?" the woman she'd been paired with asked. "I know you're talking with someone, but you're shielding the words."

"Not sure yet," Faith hedged. No reason to get the new recruit panicked about an amorphous threat. Not yet anyway. "Someone may want to harm us—" she began.

"Nameless Ones, right?" the woman cut in, followed by, "Can we kill them?"

"Not Nameless Ones. Not this time." Faith blew out a tense breath. "Look. I really don't know anything. Not yet. Stay close and keep your guard up. If anyone looks cross-eyed at us, flatten them with kinetics."

"We're in danger? In the middle of the CIA?" The woman switched to telepathy, and her green eyes developed a pinched, worried look. Faith recognized that look from her years in the compounds.

"I don't know, but I rethought you remaining with me. Go back and tell everyone they get a five minute break." Faith gripped her arm. "Do not say anything about any of this."

"Got it." The woman nodded sharply and pulled out of Faith's grasp. "If you need help, we'll be there fast."

"Thanks."

"Well?" Honor was back.

"Don't know yet. I'll be back in touch when I do. Jesus, Honor, it's been like ninety seconds. I'm on it."

Faith walked a few feet from the mats and sent her kinetics outward, checking who was in the arena. She located her seven charges easily, but she hadn't been concerned about them. Charity and her eight had staked out the far side of the large gym. Half a dozen men, none of them freaks, wrestled with each other in the corner near the holographic projector.

"Six men are here that I don't know," Faith told Honor. *"None of them are freaks. Did you alert Charity, or just me?"*

"Just you." Tension radiated through Honor's mind voice. *"Charity can be a loose cannon."*

"Return to your practice. Now." Milton's voice blasted her. He hadn't mastered any of the subtleties of telepathic speech. *"Appear normal. You'll have company soon."*

"Good or bad?" Faith asked, feeling a familiar tightening in her gut, but Milton was done talking. The same apprehension that had dogged her every time a Nameless One approached in the compounds was back in spades. They only showed up when they wanted something, and it was usually extra work details.

The other women in her group were on their feet moving toward her with quizzical expressions on their faces.

"Are we done for the day?" one asked.

Faith shook her head, and the woman she'd been sparring with frowned and said. "Of course not. I told you gals this was only a break."

"Better watch it," one of the other women shot back. "You're starting to sound bossy, just like the Nameless Ones."

"Enough of that. We have another hour to go here." Faith herded her charges back to the mats. "Let's get cracking." She kept her words lighthearted. "If you do really well, we'll spend tomorrow outside."

The woman she'd been sparring with was quick on the uptake. She must've sensed Faith's inner turmoil, but she grinned and said, "Outside would be a plus for tomorrow, but I'm hungry right now. Sooner we're done, sooner I can have dinner."

"Heh! Not as hungry as we were in the compound," another woman spoke up.

Faith demonstrated two different chokeholds. "Pair up," she instructed. "Pick different partners this time."

"Why can't we use kinetics?" a woman asked.

"Yeah," another chimed it. "They're quicker, cleaner, and a whole lot less work."

"It's not that you can't use your kinetics," Faith replied. "Look at mixed martial arts as another tool in your quiver. Same as weapons practice." She clapped her hands together. "No more talk."

The next quarter hour dripped past. Who was Milton sending? Were the men, still yukking it up as they threw one another around on the far side of the arena, some kind of threat? Milton had apparently discovered a new link to the sabotage Charlie, Hope, and Frank faced on their last mission to Maine...

Faith shut off her overactive brain. She had a boatload of questions, but no answers at all. Not even about her earlier meeting with Dr. Thomas. No matter how hard she tried, she couldn't bring herself to think of him as Reg. Had he spoken with Milton, and would she be cleared to work in the lab?

She'd told the doctor she preferred field work, but the lure of finding out more about how she'd been constructed was damn near irresistible.

Who am I kidding? I want to spend more time with him. Maybe if I'm there, he'll see me as something more than an employee...

Don't get your hopes up, a second inner voice cautioned.

Because her attention was elsewhere, the woman she'd paired with defeated her hold easily. Faith laughed. "Want to try that again?"

Her partner shook her head. "Nope. I'm good with stopping when I'm ahead. My turn to be the aggressor."

"Fair enough." Faith stretched her arms over her head to work out the kinks and was in the process of trading spots when the doors at the far end of the arena flew open, clunking against their stops.

Frank, Tony, Milton, Roy, Honor, Glory, and Reg burst into the room, heading for the tight group of men near the holodeck.

"What's that all about?" a woman from Faith's team pointed at the men who weren't laughing anymore.

Milton angled his head and said something to Honor. She tapped Glory's shoulder, and the two women switched direction. From the other side of the room, Charity sprang to her feet and ran toward Faith with her team strung out behind her.

"What the hell is going on?" she demanded, reaching them about the same time as Honor and Glory.

Honor tossed her head back. "Wait till we're all here," she said.

Shouting ensued from where Milton and the others faced off against the men. It was tempting to listen in, but if she did, Faith wouldn't hear whatever Honor had to say.

Honor gestured them into a tight circle and switched to telepathy. *"Not going to sugarcoat this,"* she began. *"After Frank got back from his last mission—the one that was sabotaged—he suspected a rat. He and Tony dug into all the computers here and unearthed an organized group that wants us either dead or gone from Langley."*

Faith fought a deeply sinking feeling. She'd finally, finally felt safe, but it was illusion. Maybe *safe* wasn't in the cards—for any of them, ever.

"Faith!" Honor snapped her fingers beneath Faith's nose. "I'm not done."

"I'm still listening," Faith responded dully.

"Frank and Tony unearthed names. Milton is rounding everyone up. They'll be interrogated and court-martialed. That should be the end of it."

"This time," Faith replied in mind speech.

"Hatred is a funny thing," Glory said, not bothering with telepathy. "People are afraid of what's different. They'll go to great lengths to distance themselves from *different*, because they perceive it as a threat."

"Another name for that is bigotry," one of the new women cut in.

"Yeah," someone else said. "Like when they shoved Indians onto reservations or enslaved Africans or forced Jews into gas chambers."

"Just scared, small-minded men protecting their turf," the woman who'd labeled different as bigotry added.

Milton ran over to them, light on his feet and agile. Lines of stress carved deep into his forehead. "It's handled," he said brusquely.

Honor glanced at the open double doors. Three of the half dozen men who'd been practicing wore handcuffs and were being led outside. The other three followed.

"A few more details," she prodded Milton.

"Should be clear enough," he growled. "This was a recruiting effort. Three of them were part of the group and they were soliciting the other three to join."

"They're not cuffed." Charity stuck her face in front of Milton's. "Why are you so sure they're innocent?"

"They'll be questioned." Milton returned Charity's stare. "For now, that's all you need to know."

"Did you get the rest of them?" Honor's voice cracked with strain.

"Yes. These were the last ones." Milton's expression softened fractionally. "See you later." He spun and ran full tilt after the men who'd disappeared through the doors.

"What happened? I want details." Charity stalked in front of Honor.

"Why single me out?" Honor trained her clear green eyes on Charity.

"Because you're here and Tony isn't. I knew he and Frank were researching something really hush-hush. He kept saying he'd tell me —as soon as he was certain."

"I want to know too," Faith said.

"We all do." One of the new recruits pushed closer to Honor.

"There was an attack at the gun range today," Honor replied in tones that could have etched glass. "They killed one of the men—"

Faith chewed on her lower lip. "A Nameless One?" At Honor's nod, she went on. "I'm not fond of them, but I don't particularly want CIA agents murdering any of us. Do we know why?"

Honor shrugged. "We're different, and they're afraid of us. Because they're afraid, they don't want us anywhere near their nice, clean little lives." She sucked in a noisy breath. "Frank and Tony unearthed plans to kill enough of us, the rest would get scared and leave on our own."

"How many were involved in this scheme?" Glory asked. "Jesus, I feel guilty. And responsible. I'm the reason all of us are here."

"No." Honor rounded on her. "Nameless Ones are why we're here, and don't you ever forget that. They hounded us, targeted us, almost raped you."

"Yeah, not much of a choice, but still." Glory squeezed her eyes shut. "I'm getting sidetracked. How many?"

"From the digging the men did, they found nine."

"How do we know that's all of them?" Charity demanded. Fury

blazed from the depths of her eyes, and the air around her crackled from her kinetics.

"We don't," Honor said shortly. "After today's attack, Dr. Thomas ordered Frank and Tony to give Milton everything they'd uncovered."

"What were Frank and Tony doing in the infirmary?" Faith asked.

"I presume the doctor requested their help with his not-quite-human patients." Charity's tone was laced with sarcasm.

"Look here." Honor speared all of them with her direct gaze. "Not all normal humans are bad. Just like not all Nameless Ones are bad. When we start thinking like that, we're no better than the cadre who decided we didn't have a right to draw breath."

Charity looked at her feet. "Thanks. I needed that."

"We all did," Faith said. "Does anyone feel like dinner?"

"Not particularly," Glory replied, "but we should show up in the cafeteria same as usual. If we hide in our quarters—or leave campus for takeout—it will send a message we're running scared."

"Particularly since we're not certain Frank and Tony's intel was complete, I agree totally," Honor said. "I usually eat in with Milton, but I'm coming with you."

Faith nodded slowly. "No matter how guilty this group of nine was, they're agents. I haven't been here long, but they all seem to stick together, and we're going to get a ton of flak over this."

"Yup." Honor clacked her teeth together. "Milton already warned me about the same thing. You can't stuff change down people's throats."

"Tony threw down a gauntlet and said we're here to stay—no matter what," Charity said defiantly.

"Obviously." Glory's tone was grim. "I'm not letting anyone run us out of the CIA."

Faith kept her mouth shut. Roy was an attorney. He could easily find work elsewhere, and Milton could have retired years ago. If they left, Glory and Honor would go with them.

"Let's get that dinner over with," Faith muttered. "Meet all of you at six thirty in the cafeteria. It wasn't much fun when the Nameless Ones turned us into underlings who were one step up from slaves—"

"—but at least they weren't out to kill us," one of the women finished Faith's sentence.

Honor spread her hands in front of her. "Milton believes the problem is under control."

"I hope he's right," Faith said and sprinted for the door. "See you in an hour," she called over one shoulder.

The elevator was waiting, but for once she took the stairs. Twenty floors was a lot, but she needed to burn off her outrage—and her fear. Was she destined to be on the run forever? It hadn't worked out very well for Glory, and she'd only been on her own for a couple weeks before Roy stumbled onto her.

The top of the long stairwell caught her by surprise. She could've climbed double what she had and longed for more. Faith slapped her palm over the reader plate and let herself out into fading daylight.

"There you are." Dr. Thomas straightened from where he'd been leaning against a post. "I was watching the elevator, but the other women said you opted for the stairs." He eyed her. "I'm impressed. You're not even breathing hard."

Faith met his direct gaze. "Not trying to be rude, but I have to hurry. I'm meeting the other women for dinner, and I'd like to clean up first."

A subtle alteration in his expression suggested she'd said the wrong thing. His words clinched it. "Any chance you could get out of that obligation? I was hoping you'd have dinner with me. Milton approved reassigning you to my lab, and we could discuss your new job."

Faith raked her hands through her hair. It had mostly escaped from its clips and rubber bands. She wanted to have dinner with Dr.

Thomas, but she owed it to the women to be in the dining room as a show of solidarity.

"It's not that I don't want to eat with you and find out what my new job duties and responsibilities will be," she began, her tone formal as she debated what to say next.

"Then it's settled." He smiled encouragingly. "Would you like to eat off campus? I know a lot of quiet little restaurants in McLean where we could go. What do you like to eat?"

Faith shook her head. What she needed to say hadn't gotten through.

Because I danced around it.

"I can't. It's been a hard day. The wounded from the gun range ended up in your infirmary, so you know what happened."

"I do, and I'm appalled. Milton's on top of it, though." Kindness and concern streamed from him in waves that she picked up with her kinetics.

Faith spread her hands in front of her, flexing the fingers as she organized her thoughts. Thank God the doctor wasn't pushing her, and she added compassion to the other traits she admired in him.

"The women have always stuck together. Ever since the rebellion that is," she said. "We had to. If we didn't, our plight in the compounds would have been worse than it was." She cast a sidelong glance his way, but he was just watching her.

She straightened her spine. "It's important for us to put in an appearance at the cafeteria together. Especially tonight. We have to show the ones who view us as subhuman that we're just as good as they are. That we're not going to slink off to our quarters and hide just because they've targeted us for destruction."

Approval danced in the centers of his green eyes. Like hers, but not. "Good for you." He angled his head to one side. "Would you mind if I joined you in the cafeteria? We could still eat together, and maybe my presence at your table would help. Just in case Frank and Tony missed a few of the agitators when they culled through all the PCs here."

Faith swallowed hard. "You don't have to do that—" she began.

"I want to," he cut in. "Wouldn't have offered if I didn't." He set his jaw in a harsh line. "You don't know much about me, but I grew up poor. Really poor. So destitute, your life at the compound was a picnic compared with what I faced every day. I know what it's like to be on the receiving end of prejudice and disgust. Of people thinking they were better than me because they had cleaner clothes and didn't go home to a slum."

Faith opened her mouth, but he waved her to silence.

"What's taken root here at the CIA is pure evil, driven by weak men who need someone to look down on. When they prey on those they view as less than them, it validates their insecurities, makes them feel like men, when they're nothing but pale imitations of what it means to be one."

"Pretty words." Faith latched her gaze onto his. "But they were here first. We're the interlopers."

Dr. Thomas shook his head. "Nope. Last I checked, this is America. You have just as much right to be here as anyone else. Have faith in Milton. He'll clean up this mess. He faced worse in the Middle East where corruption was rampant. So bad, you didn't know whom you could trust."

Faith inhaled raggedly. "I'll try."

"It's all anyone can ask. Now about dinner. May I join you and the women?"

"I'd like that, and I know they would too. Everyone's been swooning over Hope and Charlie. In their secret hearts, they're hoping to find someone for themselves."

Her face grew warm, but she stopped shy of slapping a hand over her mouth. "Sorry. That was way too personal."

Dr. Thomas took a step closer, his eyes glittering with sharp interest. "How about you? Are you hoping for a Charlie of your own?"

Heat swooshed over the top of her head, oblivious to her efforts to exert control over her autonomic nervous system. "Don't know," she mumbled. "Haven't thought much about it. Um, we're meeting at six thirty. See you there." Without waiting for him to answer, she took off, running at Mach 10 before he could offer her a ride.

If she couldn't do a better job keeping a lid on what came out her mouth, she'd be better off not talking at all. What the fuck was she thinking, going on about Hope and Charlie? She could apologize over dinner, but the more she thought about it, the less appeal an apology held. Maybe if she never mentioned it again, neither would he, and they could start fresh discussing what she'd be doing in the spotless lab she'd visited earlier that day.

Feels like a million years ago.

Yeah, but it wasn't.

She reached her building and raced inside. If she hurried, she'd have time to wash and dry her hair and dress in something besides her shapeless sweats.

CHAPTER 6

*R*eg watched the graceful flow of Faith's body as she ran for her quarters. The way she moved was pure poetry, and he felt his body responding. What would she feel like crushed against him, mouth on his? Would her body look as amazing as he suspected with high, tight curves and long, lean lines?

He shook his head hard to clear tumbling images of a naked Faith, lips swollen with passion, nipples puckered, and labia slick with her arousal, but the imagery was so seductive, it refused to leave.

Not the time for that. Maybe later, but not now.

To redirect blood away from his swollen cock, he broke into a jog, heading back toward the infirmary. He wanted to trade his bloodstained clothes for something clean before he subjected everyone in the dining room to his presence. Blood didn't bother most agents, but the freaks' senses were much sharper than normal humans' were, and he didn't want to ruin anyone's supper.

Years of strict discipline took over and he forced himself to focus. The plot Frank and Tony had unearthed was deeply troubling. Nothing quite like a cadre of trained agents to come up with ways to sow distrust and dissention. That they'd been in the arena expressly to add to their ranks was damned disturbing. That they'd chosen to be there at the same time the women were on the posted schedule worried him even more.

The reason Frank and Tony had held silence was because they'd only worked their way through around seventy percent of the thousands of computers at Langley, and they'd cautioned Milton they hadn't checked more than a quarter of the agents' cell phones.

Which meant the group determined to rid themselves of proximity to the genetically altered might run far deeper than the nine men they'd apprehended so far. They'd be interrogated, but agents were trained not to crack under pressure, so the odds of them spilling names wasn't all that great. Reg wondered if Milton would even gather enough to expel everyone in the group from the CIA. It depended exactly what data Frank and Tony had collected.

A sharp lawyer would argue the information had been obtained illegally, and the men's cases could be tied up in the courts for years. During that time, they'd be on administrative leave. And still on the CIA payroll, which was an egregious waste of resources.

Not my problem.

He reached the infirmary and let himself in past a phalanx of agents guarding the building's primary entrance. He nodded at one of the men he knew. "Is anyone stationed outside the ER door?"

"Yes, sir." The agent nodded crisply. "By the fire escape too. No one will get in here that we don't know about."

"Excellent." Reg hurried up to the second floor and checked on his patients, including both freaks and the man he'd operated on that morning. Everyone was doing fine.

"Hey!" Aaron called before Reg had cleared the room.

He turned back. "Yes? You're healing nicely. Nothing to worry about."

Aaron scrunched his amber eyes in annoyance. "I know how I'm doing. I instituted a healing sequence earlier. We need to leave, Ben and me."

"I'll clear you for discharge tomorrow morning if nothing's changed." Reg smiled pleasantly.

"You didn't hear me, Doc. We're not safe here."

"Of course you are. Agents are posted all around this building. I can add a sedative to your IV if you'd like."

"No!" Aaron thundered. "Last thing I need is to be knocked out. Agents are who attacked us. We already gave statements. Ben and I will be safer in our apartment building, surrounded by others like us. We'll post our own sentries and sleep in shifts."

"That's scarcely necessary—" Reg began.

"What if I think it is? Look. I understand this is your clinic, but I'm not in any danger of dying or doing anything to repudiate your medical care. Release us. Please. Tonight."

"I'd need to clear it with Milton," Reg hedged. He didn't want the injured men to leave before twenty-four hours had elapsed to rule out a host of complications that might arise.

"Our physiology is different," Aaron hissed. "That twenty-four hour rule is for normal humans, not us."

"You were in my head."

"Of course. Easier to counter arguments if I know what they are ahead of time." Aaron grinned, but with zero warmth.

"I'll get you an answer presently." Reg turned and left, taking the stairs to his office one floor up. The invasion of his thoughts was disquieting. What was more so was that he wanted to be able to do the same thing. For the first time, he considered the ramifications of taking the injections series and following it with Cortexiphan. He could volunteer to be one of Frank and Tony's guinea pigs once all of them had come up with a safer configuration of the chemical cocktails.

Inside his office, he picked up the landline. It was scrambled, so it felt safer than his wrist computer or cellphone.

Milton answered on the first ring. "Did something else happen?" His words were gruff.

"No." Reg cut to the chase. No reason to waste energy on

pleasantries like asking how Milton's last hour had gone. "The freaks here want me to release them."

"Are they medically stable?"

"At the moment, but I always like to watch patients for twenty-four hours to make certain—"

"Spare me your medical CYA," Milton cut in. "Unless you think they're in danger of dying, let 'em go. I'll send Frank over to round them up. He's been nattering about exactly the same thing. For all I know, they've been in telepathic communication."

"About that..." Reg's voice trailed off.

"About what, doctor? I'm swamped here."

"Nothing. I'll get Aaron and Ben unhooked from their IVs and machinery. They'll be good to go in about a quarter hour."

After a non-verbal grunt that could have meant anything, Milton disconnected, and Reg ran back downstairs. "You're leaving," he told Aaron. "Frank will be here soon. Meantime, I'll get that IV out of you."

"Thanks." The harsh look in Aaron's eyes softened. "I appreciate you taking care of us. I know you wanted to give us the best medical oversight possible."

Reg didn't know quite what to say. Apologizing for the attack that had landed Aaron and Ben here was too little and too late. "We'll get to the bottom of this," he promised and winced at how lame his words sounded.

"Maybe we'll leave in the meantime. We've been talking about it, but the group is undecided."

"Did you include the women in that discussion?" Reg drew his brows together. He did not want Faith leaving. And he was certain neither Roy nor Milton would approve of their women living anywhere but with them. Charlie too, but he and Hope wouldn't be back for a week. Events unfolded fast in war zones, so maybe the current spate of problems would've settled before then.

An uncomfortable look flitted across Aaron's sculpted featured.

"Erm. No. Probably a big omission on our part. I'll alert the other men."

"To what?" Frank stuck his head in the doorway with Ben standing next to him. "I unhooked him." He tossed a glance Ben's way. "They'll need something to wear."

Energy crackled across the small space. Reg had seen enough of it when Tony and Hope were pulling Charlie back from the gates of Mordor to understand they were talking telepathically.

"None of that," he snapped.

"None of what?" Frank inquired blandly.

"I want to hear what you're hatching up."

"Just planning on getting together with the rest of the men once Ben and Aaron are ready to leave," Frank replied.

"I'd asked about the women," Reg persisted.

"No decision's been made yet about them." Frank spoke stiffly.

Reg finished with Aaron and turned to face Frank. "You can't make decisions for the women. Not anymore. They make their own choices. Plus, all of you signed contracts with the CIA. You can't just walk out on them."

"We can if you're trying to kill us." Frank met Reg's unrelenting stare head on.

"It's only a small subset intent on your destruction," Reg clarified. "I'm certain all the agents milling around here will be reassigned to guard your quarters."

Frank spread his hands in front of him. "I respect you, Doc, but you'll excuse me if I'm suspicious of the CIA's protection. I understand a splinter group was behind today's attack—and the earlier sabotage of the chopper Charlie and I were in. I also know Tony and I weren't finished checking the extent of the scheme to bring us down. Until we know more, it's in our best interest to remain vigilant."

"I get that. I do. But when you work with us—rather than pitting yourselves against the world like you've done for the last seven years—you provide a far stronger base to fight back from"

"Say more," Ben spoke up.

"You can't go it alone," Reg replied. "You've been on the run for seven years with inadequate food and supplies. Eventually, you'd have all died out because instabilities in your genome would have caught up with you. This way—"

"I fixed the genome problems," Frank cut in.

"To some extent," Reg said, "but it's not perfect."

"Better than what the scientists stuck us with," Aaron said. "Besides, what would you know about that?"

Reg shrugged. He'd said too much and was quick to clear his mind of anything that might give away his earlier role at the breeding farms. "I did some research into the problem when I got back from Afghanistan."

"I want to know what you came up with," Frank said, "but not just now. Where can we find clothes for Aaron and Ben?"

"Closet next to the ER downstairs has an assortment of sweatpants, shirts, and jackets." Reg glanced around Aaron's room. "Your shoes are right there." He pointed. "Ben's should be in his room."

"Yup. I got them," Ben said.

"We're on our way out of here," Frank said and turned to go.

Aaron sat on the edge of his bed for a moment before standing.

Reg watched him closely. "You feeling dizzy?"

"A little, but it's passing." He walked to his shoes and scooped them up. "I'll put them on downstairs after I'm dressed."

"Good plan." Reg left the room and hollered after Frank who was disappearing through a stairwell door. "Hold up, soldier."

Frank turned. "I assume you mean me."

"Yeah. Sorry. Old habits die hard." Reg hurried to where Frank stood half in and half out the door. "Listen up. What's coming next is an order."

"That so?" Frank furled his dark brows.

"Yes. Any plans you make tonight are to be shared with Roy,

Milton, or both. In other words, do not leave the CIA campus without their express permission. Do I make myself clear?"

"Abundantly," Aaron said from behind them.

"What happens if we ignore that?" Frank asked, his tone bland as yesterday's egg whites.

"You'll be back on the run. The CIA isn't a revolving door. Either you're here and on board with us. Or not."

"I'll make certain the men know," Frank said.

"One more thing," Reg said.

"Yeah?" Aaron sounded surly, but he probably had a hell of a headache from the blow he'd taken to the back of his head.

"Leave the women out of your plans. They've settled in nicely here."

Something sharp jabbed the side of his head. Kinetics. "Stop that!" He leveled his gaze at all three men. "Just because you can cull thoughts doesn't mean you should, and whoever did that was clumsy as hell."

"Sorry," Ben muttered. "It was me. Guess I'm off my feed from the attack. Why do you care so much about our women?"

Heat began in Reg's chest, moving upward. He opted for covering his real feelings with faux anger. "I outrank you. This is my clinic, and you will not question me. You don't trust us. The women don't trust you, and I don't want them put in an uncomfortable position. Their lives have been hard enough."

"Got it," Ben said sullenly. Pushing around Frank, he bolted down the stairs.

Frank sent an odd, calculating look Reg's way before turning to join the other man. Aaron padded down the stairs after them.

Reg trudged into the stairwell, moving up, rather than down. He still needed to change clothes. The stench of dried blood clung to him, mingled with antiseptic and the peculiar plastic smells of monitors and medical equipment.

Should he call Milton and share his concerns the freaks would bolt? Aaron and Ben had been intransigent about leaving, so much so he suspected they'd have pulled their own IVs and been gone before morning no matter what he thought about it.

He made an effort to sort through why what happened to them was so important to him. It ran far deeper than his Hippocratic Oath responsibilities. He didn't have to dig far before he ran into a sense of responsibility mucked up with failure. If he hadn't left for the Middle East, had been stateside when things went south with V2, he might've made a difference. By the time he returned the dye was cast, and it was too late to do much but watch from the sidelines.

Not that he was the only competent scientist assigned to the project, but the others, fearing for their lives, fled at the first hint of rebellion. Maybe because of all the time he'd spent with bullets flying over his head, he'd have stayed the course, no matter the personal consequences.

Yeah. The rest of them probably had families. Reasons not to put their lives at risk.

He reached his office and looked at the phone, still considering whether to call Milton. He'd sounded so grumpy and out of sorts, leaving things well enough alone might be the wisest course of action.

As if it sensed his indecision and stepped in to solve the problem for him, the phone blatted the annoying klaxon burst that meant Milton was calling. Reg crossed the room and snapped up the receiver.

"I was just going to call you—" he began.

"Saved you the trouble." Milton was in prime form, forging through other people's sentences.

Reg didn't bother to say anything else. He just waited to see what his boss had on his mind.

"Aren't you going to say anything?" Milton demanded.

Reg rolled his eyes. "Why? You'll cut me off before I'm done. What did you need? I'm late for dinner."

"Dinner might not happen. There's been an incident—"

The sound of running footsteps pounded toward him right before someone beat a fist against his door. "Hold on, Milton, someone's here." Reg moved to the far side of the room and pulled the door open.

Faith and Charity burst into his office.

"You have to come," Faith cried.

"Five men with hoods attacked us on our way to the dining room," Charity snarled.

"Why are you here?" Reg asked. "Why not find Roy or Milton or Tony?"

"Milton's building is locked," Charity hissed. "Our kinetics couldn't blast the lock. I can't find Tony. Something's up. I—"

"Which women are there?" Milton demanded.

"Faith and Charity. Let me put you on speaker." Reg pushed the button and held the phone between them, saying, "It's Milton."

"Why the hell is your building locked?" Charity demanded.

"Was anyone hurt?" Milton demanded. "I heard the part about the attack."

"Yeah." Faith drew her lips back from her teeth in a snarl. "The men are dead. All five of them. We ran for your office, but couldn't get in. Charlie's gone. Jesus! We're in the infirmary because it was the only place I could think of to go."

Another set of footsteps pelted toward them. Charity screeched, "Tony," and ran down the hall.

"Thank God you're all right," Tony's distinctive bass boomed from outside Reg's door.

"First off," Milton's voice was steel, "I did not purposefully lock anyone out of my building. Roy and I have been here for hours interrogating the nine men from earlier. Frank was here until he headed your way. Tony left as soon as word of the attack reached us."

He and Charity walked into Reg's office. Fury rolled off Tony in thick waves that even Reg could feel. "That Milton?" He gestured at the phone. At Reg's nod, Tony moved closer and said, "Someone jammed the locks in your building between when Frank left and when I did. They obviously wanted to keep you and Roy in there—"

"How'd you get out?" Milton interrupted.

"Blew my way through a door. What are you going to do to keep my people safe?"

"Good question, son." Milton sounded tired. "I just sent a cleanup crew to pick up the dead. It will be instructive to see who they are. It might help Roy and me get more intel out of our captives, who've been amazingly close-mouthed. So close-mouthed, I'd bet money they knew about the attack the women stymied and were running out the clock." He made a disgusted, clucking noise. "I'll raise maintenance to work on the busted door—and the locks."

"What about our safety?" Tony repeated his question. "I can keep Charity safe, but there are twenty other women—"

"Faith and Charity. Did you know any of the men who attacked you?" Milton asked, ignoring Tony's demand.

"No," Charity said. "And I pulled their fucking face coverings off once they were dead."

"Was it just the two of you?" Milton asked.

"No. Ten of the new women were with us," Faith replied. "Honor was there too. In truth, there was no contest at all. Once we saw their knives—and heard them say they were going to kill us for being freak bitches—we sent kinetics to stop their hearts. It was over in minutes."

"Where are the other women?" Milton asked.

"I sent them back to their quarters," Faith replied. "Not Honor, but the rest of them."

"With strict orders to dismantle the elevator mechanism and seal off the third floor with kinetics," Charity added in a growl.

"I'm truly grateful you can protect yourselves—" Milton began. "Hold up. Honor just got here. Charity said you were there tonight—"

"Yes," Honor cut in. "I was there. I helped kill those fuckers. We have to fix this. We'll never—"

"You think I don't know that?"

"Don't yell at me," Honor shot back.

"Milton." Reg broke in before the argument could escalate. "Next steps? Faith, Charity, and Tony are still in my office."

"I'm calling an emergency meeting in the big conference room in ten minutes. Everyone's attendance is mandatory," Milton growled.

"What's that going to accomplish?" Tony asked, his words lined with bitterness, as if he'd given up.

"Your job," Milton inserted as if Tony hadn't said anything, "will be to use your kinetics. Delve into everyone's minds. Even those you think you know. If you sense anything that even hints at someone being part of this conspiracy, I want to know right after the meeting."

"You want all of us involved, right?" Charity cut in.

"Right," Milton said. "Every single freak. Split up the room and check everyone's motives. Twice. I'm going to cut this thing off at the knees, and that starts now."

The line developed the hollow buzzing that meant Milton had disconnected. Reg looked at the grim-faced group. "You heard him. Ten minutes. We need to get moving. Use telepathy to let the rest of you know we need your particular talents tonight."

"Nice to have permission," Tony muttered. Linking an arm through Charity's, he hauled her through the door.

Reg glanced at the bloody lab coat he still hadn't changed out of and slipped it off his shoulders. His sweat top could do with a pass through the laundry too, but at least the blood didn't show on black material.

"I'll wait for you just outside so you can change," Faith said and moved into the corridor.

"Thanks," he called after her.

Reg didn't chide her for being in his mind, just grabbed fresh clothes and threw them on before joining her. "I have to check on a patient, and then I can go," he told Faith. "You don't have to wait for me."

"I want to. You must have missed dinner. I know I did. Is there a stash of chips or something here that we could bring with us?"

He liked the sound of *we* when it rolled off her tongue. "Sure. Meet you downstairs. There's a small kitchen next to the ER. Help yourself to whatever you want and get double rations. I'm not picky. Whatever you choose will be fine."

She nodded sharply. "See you by the front door." Turning, she hustled down the hall toward the stairs.

Reg followed her, stopping on the second floor to make sure the man he'd worked on this morning was still stable.

A dark-haired nurse was taking vitals, and she smiled at him. "Evening, Doc. Our guy's doing great."

Reg lifted the blanket and noted a fresh dressing. "You just changed this."

The nurse nodded. "I did, and the wound was clean. No evidence of infection."

"I won't disturb it." Reg shook the man's hand. "Have a quiet night. You can return to your quarters tomorrow."

"I'm sorry I let my leg go for so long." The man rubbed his whiskered chin ruefully. "Kept thinking it would get better, but it never did."

"No worries, soldier. That's why I'm here."

Reg left the room. Despite the horror unfolding on Langley's campus, he was eager to join Faith. She could've left without him, but she hadn't. It had to be a good sign.

Maybe it just meant she didn't want to brave the campus by herself.

If he were in her shoes, he'd go armed to the teeth. Since he was passing the clinic's gun safe, he spun the combination and plucked a .38 semiautomatic off a shelf along with some clips and a shoulder holster. He didn't have kinetics to deploy, but he'd be damned if anything happened to Faith because he couldn't defend her.

Who am I kidding? Tonight proved she can defend herself, but that doesn't mean I can't help.

CHAPTER 7

Faith rustled through the kitchen's refrigerator, selecting two varieties of cheese sticks. Next she hit the cupboards and added an assortment of crackers in small, plastic packages to the sack she'd grabbed off a hook. Two apples and two bananas followed along with napkins.

She was surprised she wasn't more rattled from the attack, except it had been laughable. Neither she nor the other women had ever been in serious danger. It would take a whole lot more armed men to be any kind of threat. Now that they understood they had to practice vigilance, anyone even getting as close as the five men had would be unlikely.

A thought slapped her hard. They were far more competent fighters than even the most highly trained humans. It was what they'd been designed for, but their ability had never truly been put to the test before they blew up the breeding farms and fled.

Too bad they didn't program us to be good at farming. Would've made those seven years a whole lot easier.

A wry laugh escaped.

"What's so funny? I could use a joke about now." Reg walked into the kitchen buckling a shoulder holster into place and sliding a pistol into it.

She offered him a shy smile. "Nothing, really." She extended her full carry sack. "Did you want to munch on something while we walk over there?"

"We should drive. Those ten minutes are up, and it's at least a fifteen minute walk." He reached into the bag and extracted a bag of crackers. "Good choice. Totally devoid of nutrition, but they taste great."

"Would you like me to get something else?" Faith chewed her lower lip. Pleasing Dr. Thomas was high on her list.

"Not at all. These are great. That wasn't a criticism. Let's go." He snagged a set of keys off the board near the front door and glanced at the number of the pool car so he could find it easily.

Faith followed him outside. He waited until she drew even with him and took the food bag. "Thanks," she said.

"Car's over there." He jerked his head at a row of identical black SUVs lined up on the far side of the street. "How you holding up?"

"Fine. You'd asked what was funny earlier. I was thinking about how I'm made. We were developed to be warriors, not farmers. If we'd had a few more practical skills built into our processing units, compound life would've been easier."

"No one expected you guys to bolt." Reg walked around the car and opened the door for her. He settled behind the wheel, still munching crackers, and flicked the ignition, positioning the food bag on the console between them.

"Do you blame us?" She dug down to the cheese and unwrapped a stick, chewing quickly.

"No. Not after what happened with V2." He pulled away from the curb, driving faster than Langley's speed limit, but the road was empty of other traffic.

"How would you know much about that? You were in the Middle East then."

Reg looked sidelong at her. "And you know that how?"

Faith felt her face heat. Even in the dimly lit car, she was certain she turned color. "I might've peeked."

"I gathered that, but did you take the information from my mind or from the CIA's personnel records?"

"Little of both," she muttered, wondering how to change the conversational topic without being obvious about it.

"Why did you care enough to bother?"

The question was pointed, direct. Something a freak might've asked. "Since it was looking like I'd be working for you, I wanted as much information as possible." Faith sucked in a ragged breath. Not exactly the whole truth, but close enough.

"Did you check up on Charlie when you were assigned to his squadron?"

"Didn't have to. Charity already had."

Reg started to laugh. He was still laughing when he pulled the car into a spot a block from Milton's building and got out.

Before he could come around and open her door, Faith jumped out, still clutching the bag of food. "Glad I can be a source of amusement," she said stiffly. He was laughing at her, and she wanted him to stop.

"Not amusement," he clarified. "Awe, amazement, admiration. You women are really something. My hat's off to you."

"Really?" she stammered. Her face grew warm all over again, and she redirected blood away from her overactive capillary beds.

"Really." He closed a hand around her lower arm and pivoted until he faced her. "We're already late. Two more minutes won't matter much."

Faith squared her shoulders, waiting. Was he going to tell her he'd rethought having her work in his lab because of the unrest at Langley? Maybe his compliment had been salve to grease the bad news that was coming.

"You look like you're waiting for an axe to fall." He caught her gaze with his. "If anything I say makes you uncomfortable, ever, please tell me."

"I will." Faith stopped shy of telling him to get on with whatever he had to say.

"I was really looking forward to sharing dinner with you and the other women tonight. In the cafeteria, not sitting in straight back chairs around a conference table with Milton issuing orders. Maybe tomorrow after work, we can catch supper somewhere. I'd like it if you'd let me take you off campus to something a little more private than the cafeteria. A place we could get to know one another better."

Her eyes widened, and when her face grew hot, she didn't bother squelching it. "Y-you—" she spluttered. "Did you just ask me on a date?" Her voice was high and squeaky, and she felt like an idiot.

Dr. Thomas smiled. "I guess I did. Will you accept?"

"Yes. I'd like that." Her heart did galloping flip-flops in her chest. She cautioned her overly reactive body that it was nothing. He was being kind. Still, she couldn't help hoping this would be the beginning of her very own love story.

Whoa. Whoa. Whoa. Talk about getting ahead of myself.

"Excellent. I promise I don't bite, and I'll behave. Now that we have that settled, we should go inside. I get some latitude for tardiness because of my patient obligations, but especially tonight, I don't want to push Milton too far." He took the food bag and tucked it under one arm. "Feel like a jog?"

She loped next to him as they ran toward the meeting room. Tonight was critical. Between her and the other freaks, they'd be able to identify dissenting thought patterns. Once they'd reported names to Milton and Roy at the end of the night, they might be able to put an end to this particular problem.

"Have you heard anything about further attacks?" she asked.

"Not since what happened to you."

"Not what I meant. I was referring to outbreaks like the one that leveled the CIA installation in Los Angeles."

Reg slapped his palm against a reader and held the building's door open for her. "No. But I'm often not in that loop. Milton doesn't usually bother me unless he needs something medical."

She ran down a hall and up a set of stairs with Reg right behind her, the feel of his energy solid and reassuring. He had a quiet strength and competence that appealed to her. Not flamboyant like Milton and Roy and Charlie, but just as capable.

The double doors leading into the big conference room stood open, and she ducked through. The large conference table was absent, and chairs had been set up theater-style in tight rows.

"Nice you could join us tonight." Sarcasm sheeted from Milton's greeting.

Reg waved cheerily and headed for the first empty row of seats, which was about two-thirds of the way back.

"Drinks and sandwiches are on the table," Milton went on. "Get food before you sit."

Reg bent toward her, speaking low. "Do you want something to drink?"

"I'll get us coffees," she offered. "Unless you'd prefer something else."

"Coke, please." He winked. "Another of those empty calorie indulgences. Need something equally devoid of nutritional value to match up with our snacks."

He made his way to the end of a row while Faith strode to a table laden with food. She got a can of Coke, a cup of coffee, and piled two roast beef sandwiches atop napkins on a plate.

Your assignment is the six rows immediately in front of you. Frank's mind voice intruded into her pleasant musings about Dr. Thomas. She loved listening to the doctor talk. He had an easy way and a deep, sensual voice. Particularly when she compared it with Frank's that had all the allure of a buzz saw—even in its telepathic form.

"Got it," she replied. *"Both sides of the aisle, right?"*

"Exactly. Why were you late?" Frank asked.

Oh-oh.

Faith considered not answering, but Frank could be relentless. *"I don't report to you. I was helping in the infirmary."*

"You wouldn't by any chance be the reason the doctor is so concerned about the women?"

Faith made her way back to where Dr. Thomas was waiting. She felt Frank's scrutiny and knew he was waiting for her to respond. Reg took the sandwich plate from her, and she settled next to him.

"Well?" Frank prodded.

"I have no idea what Dr. Thomas is concerned about or why," she retorted. *"Leave me be and scan your part of the room."*

"What was that about?" Reg asked softly. "I can feel the kinetic energy that means you're talking, but that's as far as it goes."

Faith shook her head and broke off a corner of sandwich, stuffing it into her mouth. She really was hungry. "Nothing. Just my assignment."

He looked like he wanted to ask more. Instead, he started on the other sandwich.

Milton ran lightly to the double doors and shut them. "I've posted sentries," he informed the group. "No one leaves this room without my express permission." He returned to the front and stood facing the group.

"Seems a bit Draconian, sir," someone mumbled.

"No comments unless I request them," Milton snapped. "Everyone is here except for a few medical personnel manning the infirmary, and a bare bones IT crew monitoring incoming intel."

He clicked a few buttons on a computer terminal. "Medical and IT. You listening?"

After a chorus of *yes sir*, Milton scanned the group with his dark eyes. "We have a problem. Everyone likely knows something about it, but I'm going to fill in the blanks. We accepted genetically modified humans at the CIA because I was convinced they'd make exceptional agents. They haven't disappointed me."

He stopped to slug down something in a mug, probably coffee. "What has disappointed and disheartened me have been those of you—" he paused for effect "—who decided in your bigoted little hearts that you didn't want anyone but the purely human here. Who knows? Maybe the freaks' ability to converse telepathically got to you. Maybe their superior physical prowess made you feel threatened.

"Regardless of your reasons, this mutiny stops now. The genetically modified are not only here to stay, I'm hoping to add to their ranks as more and more compounds fold. This is America, folks. That means we accept everyone no matter what color their skin is or what their genetic configuration happens to be."

"It's not safe to have them here." A man near the front shot to his feet.

"Why not?" Milton countered.

The man jerked his chin toward Glory, who happened to be sitting not far from him. "Those women killed five of us tonight."

Honor bolted to her feet and rounded on him. "They attacked us first. What would you have had us do? Lie back while they shredded us with their knives?"

"Don't you people have something like stun in your arsenal?" the man demanded. "Did you have to kill them?"

"Yes, we can disable," Glory answered. "But we were set upon. They told us they planned to kill us. In my book, that's justification for us to strike first."

"That's your story," the man countered. "None of your victims are alive to tell theirs."

"Enough!" Milton thundered. "Sit down or I'll have you escorted to a cell."

"Someone has to speak for us," the man protested as he folded back into his chair.

Milton spread his arms wide. "Look around you. We have blacks and Asians in this room. Mexicans, Europeans."

"Do not forget mother Russia," an accented voice shouted from near where Faith sat.

"Yup." Milton snorted. "Even Russians. Some of you are straight.

Some are gay. Some have been married forever, and others have been divorced so many times, you've lost count. Some of you have children. Some not. Every college degree is represented, from English to engineering to medicine. We have diversity, people. The freaks are just one more aspect of that. They're here to stay. Get used to it."

He dropped his arms to his sides. "I will not tolerate any further episodes of antagonism against the genetically modified. I will court-martial, suspend from active duty, and take any other steps I feel are critical to achieving integration. We created an entire group of human beings, and then handed them the raw end of the stick when they rebelled because of our fuck ups. I'm not going to make that worse by standing by and doing nothing, while a few small-minded agents decide to be vigilantes."

Milton fell silent and blew out a weary-sounding breath. "Questions?"

A rustling susurrus moved around the room. Faith glanced at Dr. Thomas sitting beside her. Leaning close, she whispered. "He really meant that. I'm astonished he'd take up for us against those like him."

"Milton's like that," Dr. Thomas whispered back. "He'll go to the mat for what he believes. It's one of the reasons he commands absolute respect from his men. A lot of officers send their troops to do the shit work. Not Milton. He's always there in the thick of things, taking the same risks he ordered others to."

"Is this meeting over?" a woman asked from near the front of the room.

"Not quite yet," Milton replied and said something to Roy.

He moved through the room stopping for a moment beside each freak. When he paused next to Faith, she shook her head. *"No names from me,"* she sent telepathically. Roy could hear her because he'd had the injection series. He made his way to the front of the room and looked at Milton. She felt the kinetics from their awkward attempts at telepathy, but it didn't matter how clumsy they were. The humans in the room would never hear what Roy said.

Milton rattled off four names. "You will remain. Everyone else is free to go."

Faith pressed her lips together. Four wasn't a bad number. It was manageable. Even added to the nine apprehended earlier and the five who'd attacked them, it totaled eighteen. Balanced against the overall number of CIA employees, it was a small percentage.

"Grateful it's not more," Dr. Thomas murmured. "You ready to leave?"

"Not sure. Let me check with Honor.

"Are we dismissed?" she asked the other woman.

"Yes. Milton wants everyone out of here, including me."

Faith rose and gathered the paper plate and drink can, intent on throwing everything away.

"I'll get those." Reg pried them out of her hands and carried them to a waste can at the back of the room. "Hang on, and I'll give you a ride back to your quarters."

"What do you want to do with our snack bag?" she asked.

He shrugged. "I'll toss it in the car."

She joined him in the throng pressing through the doors. Faith tried to read expressions, but gave it up for a lost cause. She didn't understand normal human emotions that well, so she deployed kinetics and almost wished she hadn't. A mélange of anger, sorrow, compassion, and studied neutrality flowed from the folk leaving the room.

Too bad the doc couldn't communicate telepathically, but she didn't want to ask the questions bumping against one another in her head out loud. Once they were outside and had drawn away from others, she murmured, "It's harder working for the CIA than a more normal business, right?"

He turned, and his green eyes glittered in the reflection from a street light. "What are you asking? Whether agents and support staff here have difficult lives because of the work environment?"

She closed her teeth over her lower lip. "Something like that."

"Any kind of military work is challenging. Being an agent is damned hard. It's why so many of them remain single. The hours and the stress are real marriage killers. Why?"

Faith hesitated. Should she tell him she'd made a point of scanning the crowd as they exited?

They reached the SUV, and Dr. Thomas pulled a back door open to toss the food bag inside. He turned to look at her. "Feel like a longer run? I could accompany you back to your building and then come back for the car."

Faith nodded. "I'd love to go for a run. It's not that cold tonight, and there's a killer moon up there."

"Killer moon, eh?" The corners of his eyes crinkled with delight. "Didn't take you long to pick up our idiomatic expressions."

"I watched a lot of television in the compound. Internet too. It's why I know anything at all about you guys." She eyed the .38 cradled in his shoulder holster. "Planning to bring the gun?"

"You betcha. I don't have your kinetic ability."

They set off at a moderate pace. She could probably run faster than him, but that would defeat the whole purpose of spending a little more time together.

"You never did answer me," he prodded.

"About what?"

"Why you asked about job stress and the CIA."

Maybe because she was moving, her tongue was looser. This time, it wasn't a struggle to reply. "I was trying to read people leaving that meeting. When I couldn't tell much from their faces, I used kinetics."

"And?"

He sounded fascinated, so she went on. "Their emotions were all over the map. Sad. Angry. Empathetic. Most of the people projected a mix of all three."

"Makes sense." He blew out a breath, and it plumed in the night air. "I saw the same dynamic over and over again in the Middle East.

We were there to help a group of human beings who couldn't help themselves. They were enslaved, starved, slaughtered, at the mercy of ruthless regimes. Some soldiers made it through by immersing themselves in hatred. Others chose compassion. They fared better."

"Wonder what makes the difference?" she mused.

"Lots of things. How you were raised. How confident you are in your own skin. The ones who are angry and critical usually had shit childhoods."

"You're not that way," she spoke up and then could've kicked herself. She'd do better steering this conversation away from personal territory.

"That's right," he said. "I did tell you I grew up in pretty crappy circumstances." He made a shrugging motion but kept running. "Who knows why I ended up in medical school and the guy next door is doing life in prison? I did have an edge, though."

Despite her vow to stay away from the personal, Faith couldn't resist asking, "What was that?"

"A teacher saw something in me. Potential, maybe. He and his wife adopted me when I was throwing my life down the toilet with both hands. The first few months with them were pretty rocky, but they stuck by me, and eventually I pulled my head out of my rear end and stopped acting like a cocky little jerk."

"Thanks for trusting me enough to tell me that." They were nearing her building, but she didn't want the time with the doctor to end. Could she ask if he wanted to run some more without him thinking she was nuts? Maybe he was tired. He'd had a long day.

"What's going through that head of yours?"

"How do you know anything is?" she countered.

"You get this thoughtful look, and you draw your eyebrows together." He stopped in a grove of trees not far from the side entrance to her building and draped an arm around her shoulders.

Faith leaned into him. She thought maybe she shouldn't, but he felt warm and solid and reassuring.

He wrapped his other arm around her so he was facing her, and he cupped the side of her face with one calloused hand. "You're so beautiful. Do you know that?"

She shook her head. "No, but I'm glad you think so."

He traced the line of her mouth with his thumb. "And you have a wonderfully expressive mouth. What would you do if I kissed you?"

"I don't know. It's never happened before." Her breath hitched, and sensual heat spread outward from her belly. She wrapped her arms around him, holding him close and breathing in the scents of bayberry, forests, and antiseptic.

Slowly, ever so slowly, he covered her mouth with his in the gentlest of kisses, still cradling her head with one hand. She kissed him back, savoring the feel of his mouth beneath her lips. Her nipples peaked, tingling with wanting things she had no name for. She'd explored her own body thoroughly, but no one else had ever touched her.

What would that feel like?

He tightened the arm around her back, moving it lower until it circled her waist. The press of his penis, long, hot, and swollen, prodded her belly. Her breath quickened along with his, and he licked the seam between her lips. When she opened her mouth to his exploration, he slid his tongue inside.

She sucked on it, loving the sensations cascading through her. Time slowed as he deepened their kiss, alternating his tongue with small, teasing kisses. Faith felt her body melt against his as desire spooled in the dark, secret place between her legs. Her hips developed a mind of their own, and she rocked against him.

He moved his mouth away from hers, and she tried pulling his head back toward her. Kissing was amazing, wonderful. She hadn't had enough of it or the man in her arms.

Banked flames lit the backs of his eyes. "It's enough for now, Faith. But you feel wonderful. I'll look forward to seeing you tomorrow."

"We could kiss more." She looked away from his direct gaze. "Sorry if that wasn't the right thing to say."

"It's more right than you know." His voice had a husky catch to it. "We could, but then I'd scoop you up and bring you home with me. We'll have time, sweetheart. I want to get to know more about you before we make love. Come on." He let go of her and laced his fingers with hers. "I'm going to see you safely inside."

Before we make love. He said before we make love.

Her insides turned to mush. The man she wanted felt the same. She walked by his side to the well-lit entrance. "I guess I'm going to have to get over thinking of you as Dr. Thomas," she murmured.

"That would be nice." He made a sound between a laugh and a snort. "I'd love to hear you say my name."

She turned her face up, gazing at him. "Reg. Does it stand for something?"

"Reginald, but that's way too stuffy and formal. Reg is fine. Goodnight. Try not to worry about fallout from tonight's meeting. These things take a bit of time, but they always die down."

Faith smiled. "See you soon…Reg."

"That wasn't so hard." He kissed her lightly one more time before turning and loping off into the night.

Faith let herself into her building and started for the stairs. She still couldn't quite believe what had happened, but she wasn't going to ruin it by picking it apart, either.

After the attack, she'd dreaded what tomorrow at Langley would bring. Between Milton's speech and her run across campus with Reg, hope fanned bright. Maybe she and the women had found a permanent home after all.

Please. Please let it be true.

She floated into her apartment, reliving every exquisite moment of Reg's kisses. The feel of his mouth on hers and the scents uniquely his followed her into the shower and then into her bed.

She wanted to talk with Honor or Glory or Charity, but tomorrow would be soon enough. Tucked under the covers, she shut her eyes and ran her hands over her body pretending Reg was the one touching her. She pinched her nipples and slid a hand between her legs, rubbing her sensitive nub in hard, little circles. In her fantasy, his mouth covered a breast, suckling her, and the hand working her clit was his. The imagery shot her into a climax so shattering it stole her breath and left her wrung out but hungry for more.

CHAPTER 8

*R*eg pushed himself to run faster, but his erection didn't subside. Faith's wonderful scent eddied around him, and he could still feel her body pressed against his. She had a woodsy smell, like an evergreen forest after a downpour in tropical climes, and she'd felt like a goddess in his arms, all firm muscles but with curves in the right places.

He dragged himself out of his mental imagery long enough to assess where he was on Langley's campus. His infirmary was only a block away, but he really should retrieve the pool car—in case someone else needed it.

His cock throbbed mercilessly, making at least one decision for him. He switched directions, headed for the wooded perimeter of Langley. Once he passed the last building, he lost himself in shadows and drew to a halt. Visions of Faith danced behind his closed eyes, and he cupped a hand around himself. He hardly ever let himself get lost in sexual fantasies. Since he'd spent so much of his life by himself, there wasn't much point, but Faith—a buck-naked Faith—tantalized him.

Would she look the same as she did in his mind? If not, the reality would be even better than his imaginings. He stroked himself through his trousers, not sure what the hell he was doing. Was he just going to drag his cock out and masturbate right here beneath the canopy of leafless elms?

He smothered a laugh. That was the purview of adolescent boys, who had perpetual erections. For someone like him—a forty-something man—being so aroused he was desperate to come was ridiculous.

Wasn't it?

His cock didn't think so. It jerked in his hand, and he recognized a familiar tightening in his balls that meant orgasm would happen with very little effort. He untied the waistband of his scrubs, spreading his legs so his pants wouldn't end up on the ground, and closed his hand around his shaft. The shock of skin-to-skin contact drove everything from his mind but Faith. Her scent. The press of her breasts against him. The hitch to her breathing as she thrust her hips against his painfully erect cock. Her mouth glued to his in a kiss that had developed a life of its own.

Reg stroked himself faster, harder. He was pushing inside the heat of Faith's body, feeling her muscles tighten around him. It was as far as he got. Semen pulsed from him, splattering the mostly frozen ground. His heart thudded against his ribs, and he inhaled in a series of gasping pants as his climax wound down.

Still breathing hard, he wiped his hand on a nearby tree trunk and tied his pants back into place. He'd come in record time, and he shook his head ruefully. He'd have to pay attention to regaining control over his arousal. Coming in a couple minutes wouldn't satiate any woman, and pleasing Faith had moved to the top of his list.

She was a virgin. Tonight had been her very first kiss. Reg started back toward where he'd left the SUV. He passed the infirmary on the way, but skipped stopping in; he'd be back there soon enough. His thoughts returned to Faith. He'd have to make damned sure not to hurt her. She was human, yet not, in many elemental ways. If he kicked this door open—dated her, made love to her—it would be a lifelong commitment. She'd never understand a casual liaison, and it might harm her.

Never mind that failing at another attempt to be intimate would annihilate him, driving him even deeper into emotional isolation.

He slowed his pace. Could he lay aside a lifetime of avoiding a personal life? It wasn't just Faith dropping her barriers. He'd have to let his go as well, and his had been in place a hell of a lot longer than hers.

He thought about Zoe, the med student who'd cheated on him nine ways from Tuesday. In his secret places, he'd been certain she saw through his carefully crafted veneer to the insecurities he glossed over with a glib tongue. Because she viewed him as naïve and damaged, she'd cheated on him.

Except that wasn't true. What he hadn't been able to tease out as a twenty-two year old was crystal clear today.

She'd been sleeping with at least five other medical students. Cheating on all of them. Surely she didn't see all those men as damaged. For the first time, he understood that her insecurity drove her to sleep around. When she was naked with a man cooing over how flawless she was, she felt whole, but the feeling never lasted. And so she targeted one man after another seeking to fill the empty places in her own psyche.

Other realizations crowded on the heels of the first. Because of the wasteland of his childhood, her double-dealing had hit him hard. He hadn't chalked it up to her flaws, but had blamed his own instead. It was why he'd built a wall around his heart, one that grew thicker and thornier with the passing years.

Like as not, it was one of the determining factors that had driven him back to the Middle East time and time again. Not her infidelity *per se,* but his lack of interpersonal connections holding him stateside. His adoptive parents were both dead, and he had no idea where his birth parents or many siblings were.

Reg reached the SUV, dragged keys out of a jacket pocket, and got inside. Firing the ignition, he drove back to the infirmary, still lost in thought. He needed to understand himself and what made him tick before he could offer Faith much of anything beyond a sexual fling.

Being alone had been easy. He'd filled in his emotional vacuum with medicine.

Being part of a couple would require a skillset he'd never developed.

He backed into the same spot he'd gotten the car from and pushed his door open. Before he exited, he retrieved the food bag from the back seat, and then locked the car. The cloth bag still carried Faith's scent, and a bone-deep yearning filled him. Medicine could be a jealous mistress, and he'd done a damn thorough job of filling every waking moment with either practicing it or improving his skills.

Look at me. I'm headed into the infirmary to check on things. It's the middle of the night. I should go home, but I'll probably end up sleeping here.

Again.

Truth left a bitter taste in his mouth as he walked into the building and headed for his office. If anyone needed him, they'd have paged him if it were urgent, or left him a note for everything else.

He trudged up the stairs through a clinic that was silent but for the faint hum of medical machinery. When you cut to the bone, he had two choices. Business as usual—forever. Or taking a chance on the messiness, vulnerability, and joy two humans could find with each other.

What was it about Faith? Why was he even considering a change in a status quo that had worked for him?

Reg let himself into his office, shaking his head. Faith was attractive, but he'd crossed paths with beautiful women before. Some of them had made their interest in him clear, but he'd always ignored them.

"So what is it about her?" he asked the empty room and dropped into his chair. A cursory examination of his desktops—real and virtual—convinced him no one needed him.

Faith was lovely, but she was also capable and courageous. She trusted the strength in her enhanced body and wasn't afraid to use it. She had a forthright way of approaching the world. No flirting. No subterfuge. In many ways, it was like dealing with some men. The ones who were honest and aboveboard.

Should he tell her about his role in creating those like her?

"Humph. If I'm considering that, it must mean I've decided to lay my perpetual bachelorhood aside."

The sound of his voice surprised him. Maybe it would be better if he didn't fess up to his scientific wanderings right away. If he told her at the front end, it might scare her off, and then all his soul-searching would be for naught.

The more he thought about it, the better he liked the idea. By the time he told her, they'd have some water under the bridge and have come to trust each other. He would have to come clean before they made love, though. Definitely before they started living together. Surely, Faith would be enough impetus to drag him home from the clinic at night...

I am getting way, way ahead of myself here.

"No kidding," he muttered and glanced at his wrist computer. It was closing on midnight, and he needed to get some sleep. He pushed to his feet, heading out the door to a patient room at the far end of the hall that he'd converted into a bedroom, when his pager went off.

"Goddammit." He reached for the electronic device clipped to his jacket and tilted it to read the numeric message scrolling across its display. Reg's eyes widened, and he tapped the number into his wrist computer.

"Get over here," Milton growled. "Now."

"What happened?" Reg asked, but Milton was gone. Exasperation burned a path through him, and he raised Milton again. Before the other man could yell at him, Reg dove in. "I need to know what to bring. What kind of medical emergency do you have? And where are you?"

"My building. Interrogation rooms in the basement."

"That's the where," Reg prodded. "What's gone wrong that you need me?"

"One of the men may have swallowed his cyanide capsule."

Breath hissed through Reg's clenched teeth. "That's not easy to fix. Anything else I need to know?"

"Just get over here. Bring those emergency kits of yours, and do not call me back."

Reg stared at his wrist computer. "Yes, sir. Got it, sir," he muttered and ran down to the small emergency room. Once there, he grabbed several pre-packaged kits and ran out the door to the same car. Its keys were still in his pocket, which made things easier.

If he'd had a siren, he'd have activated it. As it was, he drove the heavy, rolling vehicle as fast as he dared, pulling into the *No Parking* zone right in front of Milton's building. Reg gathered his gear and bolted for the door. He'd never been to the interrogation chambers, but he took the stairs to the basement. He'd figure things out once he got there.

Turned out he didn't have to. A grim-faced Roy with a drawn look around his blue eyes waited at the bottom of the stairs. He didn't say a word, just took off at Mach 10 down a long, linoleum-lined hallway lit by fluorescents recessed into the ceiling.

Reg yelled after him. "Hey! I couldn't run that fast even if I weren't carrying all this shit."

Roy wheeled and raced back to him, holding out his hands for two of the four bags stuffed with medical accoutrements. "Sorry," he mumbled. "Milton's in a foul mood."

Reg rolled his eyes and fell into step next to Roy. "It's not as if he tried to find me and couldn't. I was right on top of the pager when it went off."

"It's not you." Roy lowered his voice. "It's the situation. Milton likes to be in control of things, and this scheme to rid Langley of freaks has more tentacles than a hydra."

"There are more agents involved?"

"Not so much here," Roy hedged.

Understanding slammed home. Agents from the various law enforcement branches and the military frequently knew one another. Roy's inference was that the plot extended beyond the CIA.

"Exactly," Roy said.

"Shit! You were in my head."

"Yeah. Sorry. It's become second nature. You should consider the injections."

"When would I have time to go through the hell you did?"

"Good incentive for you to make some improvements." Roy shot a rakish grin his way and looked a whole lot more like himself. "In here." He pushed a door open.

Reg strode inside. Frank and Tony were leaning over a prone man strapped to a cot. Milton stood off to one side, his expression reminiscent of an angry thundercloud.

"Where do you want your gear?" Roy asked.

Reg jerked his chin toward a long table. "Over there." He dropped his bags next to the other two and hurried to the unconscious agent with a stethoscope and blood pressure cuff in hand.

"What did the two of you do?" he asked Frank.

The geneticist glanced up with his odd, amber eyes. "Slowed the progression of the cyanide with some opposing chemicals."

"Move over." Reg bent over the man checking vitals. Nothing looked particularly promising, so he repeated his measurements with the same results.

"Well?" Milton moved closer.

"He's not doing great," Reg replied. "We could call for ambulance transport. There are a few things a hospital could do."

"No. He stays here," Milton said gruffly.

Reg rounded on him. "Why? What don't I know?"

"A whole lot," Roy cut in. "It all links into what you were thinking while we ran down the hall."

"Can't worry about that now," Reg said and focused his next words on Milton. "Why didn't you call me sooner?"

"What?" Frank stared at him. "You still have problems with us treating someone before you've assessed them?"

"Not what I meant at all—" Reg began.

"Enough," Milton roared. "I called you as soon as I knew what happened. Frank and Tony were already here. They were pressuring him—" he pointed at the man strapped to the gurney "—with kinetics, and he flicked his fake cap out of the way and swallowed his poison pill so fast none of us could get to him."

"Tried a charcoal lavage," Tony cut in, "but the guy wasn't the least bit cooperative swallowing it."

"How long ago did this happen?" Reg asked.

"Fifteen minutes," Milton replied.

"What else did you give him?" Reg asked Frank.

"Nothing."

Reg thinned his lips into a harsh line. "The good news is cyanide has antidotes. The bad news is they should already be on board. More bad news is I don't have any of them in my clinic, which is why I vote to transfer him to a hospital stat."

"What chemicals?" Tony asked.

"Hydroxocobalamin or a combination of amyl nitrate, sodium nitrate, and sodium thiosulfate."

"Got those last three in our lab," Tony said. "Amyl nitrate is an inhalant, right?"

Reg nodded. "Hurry."

Tony left at a dead run, his legs pumping so fast they were a blur.

Reg bent to unstrap the man from where he lay flat on his back. "Need to prop him up."

"I was considering Cortexiphan—" Frank began.

"Last resort if the chemical cocktail fails," Reg said, remembering how Charlie had almost died from Cortexiphan—

and he'd had the injection series to make him more like the freaks.

Reg worked over the comatose man, checking vitals every few minutes. "We have time before Tony gets back. How about if someone fills me in?"

"Not much to tell," Frank ground out. "The whole gig was laid out in this fucker's mind."

"What whole gig?" Reg continued to work on his patient, getting an IV line in place and readying himself for the chemicals Tony was bringing.

"Apparently, there are a few of these anti-freak vigilantes in the Army and the Air Force. Also in the FBI," Milton cut in.

"I'd identified all but the FBI players," Frank said, "when our victim cut my kinetic invasion short with his swan dive."

"What about the other three men you identified tonight?" Reg asked. "Or the earlier nine already in lockdown. Would they have the information?"

"Maybe," Milton said. "Not the other three from tonight, though. They were brand new recruits and knew nothing."

"Not quite true," Frank said. "They knew they hated us."

Beneath the anger and bravado, Reg sensed a sad, slow tension. Frank was strung tighter than frayed wire. What would happen if the threads separated?

Tony rushed back into the room carting a small sack that he passed to Reg. He reached inside and handed the amyl nitrate pearls back to Tony. "Break these under his nose one at a time. Give him about five minutes per pearl before you start the next one."

"How many ampoules?" Tony asked.

"Let's start with three."

Reg mixed the sodium nitrate and thiosulfate crystals with a pH neutral solution in a sterile test-tube from one of his bags. Once he was satisfied the reagents had dissolved, he transferred the mixture to a syringe and fed it into the IV line he'd set up.

"Well?" Milton hovered inches from the cot.

Reg exhaled sharply. "This is a human body. It will take time to see if this clears the cyanide."

"How much time?" Milton persisted.

"Hours." Frank bit off the word.

Reg silently blessed the freak. "Go home," he told Milton. "Get some sleep. If this man stabilizes, we'll move him to the infirmary."

"Not a good idea," Milton said. "He'll try to escape."

"Maybe not when he realizes how narrow his reprieve from death was." Reg straightened and tossed the empty syringe aside, plugging the IV line. He stared Milton down. "It's much easier for me to care for him in the infirmary where I have what I need."

"What can we do?" Tony asked.

"Nothing at the moment," Reg replied. "Which ampoule is that?"

"Last one." Tony broke it open and held it under the man's nose. "His color is better, and his heartbeat has stabilized. I've been linked to him with kinetics."

"We'll remain here in case you need us." Frank dragged a chair around and sat.

"I'm grateful you had the chemicals." Reg checked vitals again. Damn if Tony wasn't right about Agent No Name moving incrementally back toward the land of the living. "By the way, who is this guy?"

"John Moskowitz," Milton said. "Relatively new to the CIA. Recent grad from SUNY. Linguistics major. Fluent in Asian and Middle Eastern languages. It's why we hired him."

Reg clenched his jaws into a tight line. "You guys can erase some recent memories, can't you?"

Tony looked up from where he held the ampoule beneath John's nose. Frank's head snapped around, and Reg ended up looking into four very startled amber eyes.

"How could you possibly know that?" Tony asked.

"We never told anyone about that ability," Frank added, sounding as close to rattled as Reg had ever heard him.

Before Reg could weave a politically correct, plausible reason,

Roy spoke up. "He knows because he was one of the scientists who created you guys in the first place. Shit! I hunted for them almost as diligently as I hunted for you. It took me years to ferret that little fact about Dr. Thomas out from beneath lots of conflicting data. Most of their names were buried deep."

Milton didn't say a word. He grabbed Roy's upper arm and hauled him out into the hallway, presumably to a place where Frank and Tony wouldn't be able to hear what came next, even with their augmented senses.

"Damn!" Frank breathed the word. "It's true."

"Yeah. I just checked for myself." Tony kept his intense gaze focused on Reg. "Why'd you do such a shit job?" Bitterness underscored the question.

Reg bit back a host of excuses. Science was fickle. It took a whole lot of approximations before you hit the jackpot. He'd done the best he could… Instead, he looked first at one man, then the other.

"I am most humbly sorry. The breeding farms had been in full operation for years before I came along. I had very little to do with V1. I thought V2 fixed most of the V1 problems, but I wasn't here when your people decompensated. By the time I returned from Afghanistan, you'd staged a rebellion and moved beyond my reach."

"Might have been a good thing—for us," Frank muttered darkly.

"Not for me." Reg squared his shoulders. "If you ever choose to visit my office, I have reams of scientific experimentation with supporting data, and I believe I might be able to fix your instability permanently. Milton told me to drop it, that your V3 configuration was something you were happy with, so I put everything away."

"Thanks for not feeding us a line of shit." Tony spoke slowly. "I want to see everything in that research pile you referred to."

"Me too," Frank said. "When the topic came up before, I thought it was mostly anecdotal material. I had no idea you'd had hands-on experience. Would it be all right if we holed up in your office as soon as we're done here tonight?"

"More than fine. You don't need it, but you have my permission to defeat the locks with kinetics. In return, could I ask one favor?" Reg moved his gaze from Frank to Tony and back again.

"Possibly," Frank replied and narrowed his eyes to slits.

"Keep my secret."

Tony nodded. "We can do that. No percentage to telling anyone. Besides—" he exchanged a pointed look with Frank "—that way if your research pans out, we can claim full credit."

"There is that." Frank snorted. "Although, we've unearthed damn near every single paper and experiment that might help."

"I wouldn't be so sure you've seen the articles and papers in my collection. They go back ten years, and much of it was encoded to make it hack-proof. None of it ever hit the scientific journals for the best of reasons. We were flying under the radar, and hiding our project from public scrutiny was at the top of everyone's list."

"Who was everyone?" Tony asked.

Reg shook his head. "Nope. Not going there. Roy and his gang hunted for us for years. We covered our tracks well, and I'm leaving them buried."

"Fair enough," Frank said. "The important thing is gaining access to your research materials."

Reg exhaled briskly and turned back to his patient. The man was definitely stronger. "This is looking promising. I believe he's going to pull through."

"Want us to help you move him to the infirmary?" Frank asked. "It would be convenient since we can head up to your office after we get him situated."

"Please. I'll add him to the night nurse's patient roster."

"We'll stay in the building, even if we finish trolling through your library," Tony said. "It will guarantee this man doesn't go anywhere."

"And it will let you get some sleep." Frank's harsh, gravelly voice gentled. "You look trashed."

"Goes with the territory. Compensating for sleep deprivation is one of the courses in medical school." Reg tamped back a wry grin.

"That gurney will fit in the back of my SUV if you collapse its legs. I'll go get the rear gate open."

"We'll be right behind you with John," Frank said.

Reg placed everything he'd used back in his bags and hefted all four, two over each shoulder, as he walked out the door. "We're out of here, men."

The blitz of kinetics that meant Frank and Tony were talking telepathically tickled his back and made him even more determined to do whatever it took to make himself more like the freaks he'd helped engineer.

Next project, he promised himself. *Just as soon as we get the current problem under control.*

Another thought pummeled him. Milton had known about his relationship to the breeding farms. He'd also known Roy was hunting for the scientists to help with his ongoing war against the freaks. If Reg had ever wondered about Milton being his own man, tonight clinched it. He'd withheld information from Roy to keep the scientists, most of whom had escaped freak retribution by the barest margin, hidden from everyone's view.

Anything Roy knew was fair game for one of the genetically modified to pluck from his mind, and Milton had made his decision accordingly.

One more thing to thank him for...one of these days.

CHAPTER 9

Faith jolted awake to the incessant jangle of her cell phone. It startled her. No one called when they could use telepathy.

All that means is it's not a freak.

She shook her head to clear sleep from her mind and snatched the phone off her bedside table. "'Lo?"

"Faith. Thank God you're all right." Hope's voice blasted into her ear. "Charlie just fielded a call from Milton, and—"

"Whoa. Slow down," Faith cut in, amused she'd been wrong about the phone call not being from someone with her abilities. "I'm fine. Where are you?"

"Still in Montana. We were supposed to stay here for the rest of the week, remember?"

"Of course." Faith opened her eyes to a room that was still dark and checked her internal clock. "Jesus, Hope. It's zero five hundred."

"I was worried about you."

Faith rolled to a sit, the phone tucked between her chin and shoulder. "You called me so you wouldn't disturb Honor or Glory or Charity, huh?"

"Well, when you put it that way, I knew you'd be alone, and at least I wouldn't have awakened anyone else."

"Sounds like Milton's awake if he just called Charlie."

"So shoot me. I was worried about you. You're the only one by yourself, and Milton was focused on some dude who swallowed poison. I didn't get the whole story."

"What? Who poisoned themselves? I don't know anything about that. Must've happened after I went to bed." Faith exhaled briskly. "As long as I'm up, I'm going to get dressed and see what I can find out. Are you cutting your honeymoon short?"

"It's not a honeymoon. We're not married."

The corners of Faith's mouth twitched since she'd made the same distinction when one of the new women called Hope's trip a honeymoon. "At least tell me you're having a good time."

"Oh yeah. We were, anyway, until Milton called. I don't know if we're coming back early. Pretty sure Milton ordered Charlie to stay here for another couple of days, but you know Charlie."

"Not nearly as well as you do, but he does seem like the type who puts the CIA before everything. Or he did until he met you."

"No comment. I'm relieved you're okay. I did catch the part about the five guys you killed last night. Good for you." Satisfaction simmered through the phone lines. Faith did smile then as she remembered Hope breaking a man's nose for a far lesser offense than threatening to kill her.

"Can't take full credit. I had lots of help. Those other women would've done you proud if you'd been here."

Hope made a low, growling noise. "Wish I had been there. Every single one of those fuckers who looks at us as less than worthy should hang."

Faith's practical streak took over. "You can't be everywhere, hon. What you're doing is important too."

"And pretty darned wonderful." Hope's strident tone softened.

Thoughts bumped up against one another in Faith's head. For

Hope to truly have a life with Charlie, normal humans would have to accept freaks. And that was a long way from happening.

"Pretty quiet," Hope observed. "What aren't you saying?"

"Last night didn't do us any favors. It gave the ones who see us as a threat ammunition for their arguments to banish us from government installations like this one." She stopped to suck in a breath and blow it out. "It's like it was in the compounds. We hated the Nameless Ones. They had control over us, but it didn't stop us from hating them."

"Not the same. Normal humans don't have control over us. Or us over them. I do agree, though, that as long as they don't trust us, we'll never get to the far side of this to a place we can integrate with them."

"Yeah, we can't intimidate them into accepting us. Makes sense."

"It's actually damned smart," Charlie's deep voice buzzed in the background.

"Tell him hi from me," Faith said. "I'm going to get moving and find out what went down last night."

"Talk with you later," Hope replied. "Give everyone our best."

"Will do." Faith tapped the *End Call* button and laid her phone aside.

She dressed fast, layering up against the early morning chill. When she was ready to trot over to the cafeteria for breakfast and coffee, she reached out to Honor. *"You up, sweetie?"*

"You're kidding, right?" The other woman answered immediately.

"Feel like meeting me for breakfast?"

"Can't. I'm at the infirmary. How about you meet me here?"

A totally irrational fear clenched Faith's gut into a tight knot. *"Reg, er Dr. Thomas. He's all right, isn't he?"*

"Yeah. Why wouldn't he be? He may have saved the day last night, but he was never in any danger."

"What the hell happened?" Faith demanded, feeling like mice were chewing through her skin with tiny, razor-sharp teeth.

"Get over here, and I'll fill you in." Honor severed their mind link.

Faith shut her mouth with a *clack* once she realized it was gaping open and left her apartment at a dead run. Forget the cafeteria. She could grab coffee or snacks in the infirmary.

The darkened sky spit sleet as she ran across sodden grass and icy pavement. Faith pulled her hood up and ran faster. It hadn't even been midnight when Reg left her side. A whole lot could've happened in the last six hours. She considered reaching out to Frank or Tony telepathically, but her comfort zone with Nameless Ones still had gaping holes in it. One thing to talk with them when they ended up in the same meeting or training situation. Quite another to seek them out.

She'd bet her ass they knew what happened last night since they had their paws in damn near everything, but she could wait to find out from Honor.

Frank's sarcastic query of *"You wouldn't by any chance be the reason the doctor is so concerned about the women?"* rattled in the back of her mind. The man was sharp. She had to give him points for making that connection, but she hoped he wouldn't bring it up again.

Not very fucking likely. Once he gets his teeth into something, he keeps picking at it until either it's broken or he gets what he wants. All the Nameless Ones operate like that.

She ground her teeth together. Nothing she could do about Frank. Yeah, he'd propositioned her. And yeah, he'd probably be pissed if her relationship with Reg turned into what she hoped it would.

She turned hard left, selecting a wooded lane that led to the infirmary. What if remaining at the CIA weren't an option? Surely, she and the other women would have to face some kind of court proceeding for last night's carnage. Since normal humans lacked her ability to tell if someone was telling the truth with kinetics, they'd have to rely on words. All the courtroom-based television shows she'd watched formed a kaleidoscope in the mind. None of the information was reassuring.

Stop. I don't know a thing. No reason to waste energy on what-ifs. Besides, Roy and Milton and Charlie have kinetic ability.

Faith skidded to a halt at the infirmary's front door. Night was giving way to a pallid, gray dawn. She slapped her palm on the reader, hoping someone had given her access since she'd be working here.

The latch snicked open, and she barreled inside, deploying energy to determine where everyone was. Second floor. Her feet were moving almost before the information registered, and she took the stairs three and four at a time, galloping up them.

Reg, Milton, Honor, Frank, and Tony were smushed into a patient room. A youngish man lay strapped to the bed. Brown hair had been cut close to his skull, and waves of resentment rolled off him. "Goddammit!" He writhed against his bonds. "Another one. You people killed my father. Get out of here."

Faith stopped in the doorway. "How is that even possible?"

"His father was one of the scientists at the breeding farms," Milton said. "A little detail John conveniently left off his documentation when he applied for a position with us."

"What kind of intelligence agency can't unearth a simple fact like that?" John sneered, narrowing his brown eyes to slits.

"The same one that buried their identification in the first place," Milton shot back. "Do you want to salvage any type of future here, son?"

John shook his head. "No. Not if it means working with *them.*" He jerked his chin at Frank and Tony.

"They saved your life." Reg moved right in front of John and crossed his arms over his smocked chest. "Even though they knew how much you hated them, they still bailed your sorry ass out with charcoal. And Tony was the one who offered up the chemicals I injected that pulled your butt out of the fire."

"Fine. They're heroes, and I'm an ungrateful bastard."

"I finally put two and two together," Reg went on, ignoring John's comment. "I knew your father. He was one hell of a scientist.

He believed in what he was doing, and he'd be devastated by your reaction to the genetically modified humans he helped create. He died a hero—"

"Died being the operative term." John twisted his features into a grimace. "You have no idea what his loss did to our family. I have younger brothers. They grew up fatherless. Big M.D. like you. You have no idea what impact something like that—"

"Want to bet?" Reg skinned his lips back, baring his teeth. "Your family doesn't hold the market on pain, soldier. It's outrageous for you to assume you're the only person to experience loss."

Milton made a weary, chopping motion with one hand. "Enough. Lectures aren't helpful. Is he well enough to transfer to a cell?"

Anger rolled off Reg, mixed with grief and resignation. "Yeah. He's stable."

"What are you going to do to me?" John demanded, but he didn't sound as arrogant as he had a few moments before.

"What do you think happens to agents who turn against other agents with no provocation?" Milton countered.

"How about if I save you the trouble and resign?"

"You could do that," Milton said, "but you'll still be held to answer for willful disobedience under the Uniform Code of Military Justice. You can run, but you can't hide."

Reg turned on his heel and walked swiftly from the room. Faith followed him. "What happened?" she asked.

"Interrogation gone bad," Reg muttered and held the stairwell door open for her. "Frank or Tony pushed with their kinetics, and John swallowed his cyanide capsule."

"There's an antidote for that?" Faith was surprised. She'd always assumed it was a death sentence.

"Yeah. If you catch it in time."

"Did you get any sleep?"

"Enough. Frank and Tony sat with John after we got him back

here. Don't worry about me. I've had worse nights. What are you doing up so early? It's barely zero six hundred."

"Hope called. She heard about last night and was worried about me." Something Milton had said fit with her earlier fear about a hearing. "That Uniform Code. Will the women and I stand trial for last night?"

They'd reached Reg's office and he pushed it open, waiting for her to go through. "Not so much a trial as a hearing. You have nothing to worry about."

Faith crossed to the coffee pot, then feared she'd been presumptuous. "May I have a cup?"

"Of course. I should have offered."

She poured steaming liquid into a mug and wrapped her chilled fingers around it. "There aren't any witnesses from last night—" she began not quite sure how to frame her question.

"Maybe not, but we have machinery that functions a lot like your brains. It can determine truth from lies by your body's reactions to both questions and answers. You'll be questioned separately. To the extent your answers match up, that will also add credence to your stories."

Faith squared her shoulders and drank some of the scalding liquid, welcoming its bitterness and heat. "I've watched a lot of TV. All the police procedurals discount lie detectors."

He pushed the door shut with a foot and walked to her, prying the coffee out of her hands. Once he'd set it on his desk, he wrapped his arms around her. "It will be all right. All you have to do is tell the truth. Everything else will take care of itself. I'm not going to let anyone hurt you."

She slumped against him as weariness and hopelessness battled for ascendency. "You don't have to stand by me in case—" She swallowed around a lump in her throat. "In case things don't go well."

He tightened his hold on her. "My choice. Not yours. I know

we'd planned on dinner, but how about breakfast? I could use a break from this place."

Frantic pounding sounded on the door. Faith scanned with kinetics and recognized Honor's energy. She pulled out of Reg's embrace and crossed the room to pull the door open.

"I told you I'd fill you in—" Honor pursed her lips into a thin line "—but when I looked for you, you'd left. I tracked your energy here."

"I filled her in," Reg said. "Wasn't all that much to tell."

Milton materialized behind Honor. "I'm taking you home."

Honor turned to face Milton. "Only if you come too. I got some sleep last night. You didn't get any."

Faith watched love and concern flow from one to the other, and an unpleasant thought intruded. Maybe because she and Reg had just been talking about hearings and trials, her next words left the safety of her throat before she could stop them.

"A hearing is pointless."

Milton shifted his dark gaze her way. "Not my take. John will sit through a court-martial. So will the rest of the batch we have in the brig. Every last one will do jail time and lose access to any military or government benefits they've accrued."

"So long as you brought up the prisoners," Reg said. "How about giving Frank and Tony free rein to see if they can scrub the parts of their memories that're wrapped up in the plot we foiled."

"Excellent idea." Milton's nostrils flared. "I'll take care of it before we leave. If we did that to everyone involved, it would almost ensure an end to this particular problem."

Faith held up her hands. "We got sidetracked. I didn't mean the insurgents when I said a hearing would be pointless. I was referring to a hearing for those of us who killed the men last night. Honor was there. She's your woman. No one will believe the hearing process was fair if it finds us innocent." She paused fractionally, and then added, "Because of you."

"Yes, they will." Milton's dark eyes turned to steel. "I've built my reputation on objectivity and evenhandedness. This charade will end soon, or I'll see heads roll." He gripped Honor's arm and guided her out of the office.

Faith watched them leave. Milton obviously believed what he'd said, but Faith wasn't so sure.

"How about that breakfast?" Reg asked, cutting into her bleak thoughts.

Faith nodded. "Not very hungry, but okay."

He shut the door for a second time and walked to her side, weaving his arms around her. "You're not in a compound anymore. I have confidence in military justice. It's actually far better than the civilian courts."

"But I—"

He placed two fingers over her mouth. "Hush. I know a little breakfast place in town. Let's get away from here for a while."

Faith tried to gin up a smile, but it felt fake, so she gave up.

Reg cradled the back of her head in one hand, holding her close. "What did Hope have to say? Are she and Charlie enjoying Milton's horse ranch?"

Faith understood he was diverting her from her worries, and his concern touched her. She felt awkward about thanking him, so she settled for saying, "They're appreciating time with each other. We can leave."

"Good plan. Let's implement it before anything else happens." He smiled at her, and it changed his face from stark and austere to striking, highlighting his high cheekbones and square, stubble-covered jaw.

"Hang on. I should let Roy know I'm leaving. What time will we be back?"

"Before nine. Much as I'd love to spirit you off somewhere for a week and get to know you, I can't leave this clinic unless I secure a backup doc."

"Is that hard to do?"

"No. There are temporary services, but I need to call and schedule them. Sometimes they have someone right away, but usually it takes a day or two." He let go of her and pointed at the door. "Sooner we leave…"

Faith threw her kinetics open, hunting for Glory. At this hour, she almost had to be with Roy. *"Hey there."*

"Hey yourself," Glory's mind voice sounded sleepy.

"Ask Roy if it's okay if I start my class at nine today instead of eight. I can run it an hour later to make up the lost time."

"You could ask me yourself." Roy's voice echoed in her mind.

"I could, but it felt less intrusive to wake Glory. About my request?"

"Last night was intense," he responded. *"My plan was to give everyone R&R until noon."*

"Thank you." Faith started to close off her mind link, but Glory wasn't done.

"What exactly will you be doing between now and nine?" the other woman asked, her inflection unmistakable. The five of them knew each other far too well. For Faith to ask for any time off from a work project had to mean something significant was up, and Glory wanted to know what it was.

"Tell you later." Faith cut their connection fast. She strode to her abandoned coffee and drained half of it.

"Ready," she told Reg.

He held the door for her and followed her down the stairs. They didn't say much leaving the building, but the silence felt comfortable, not strained. He headed for the same vehicle they'd taken the previous night, unlocked it, and stood by while she got inside.

"I'm not used to being treated like a girl," she commented after he'd slid behind the wheel and started the car.

"Is that what I'm doing?"

Faith tried not to be obvious about it, but she couldn't stop looking at him. "Yes. All the door opening and stuff."

He glanced sidelong at her. "You can open doors for me and bring me flowers. Or junk food and candy. I won't take it amiss."

Rolling the window down, he flashed an ID badge at the gate guard, who waved them through.

"I'll keep it in mind. You know, this is the first time I've left the CIA campus—other than to go on missions—since I arrived. It feels like I'm cheating or playing hooky or something."

"Know what you mean." He looked sheepish. "Sometimes on deployments, I spent months in the medical tent. Never went into town. Never did anything but put bodies back together."

"Why?"

He drew his brows into a thoughtful expression. "Conditions were very challenging in the Middle East. None of the things we take for granted were available. You had to both boil and filter water and develop an immunity to the bacteria in the food—or live on military MREs. No running water. Sometimes getting any water at all was a challenge."

"So why wouldn't you want a break from that?"

"I was afraid I wouldn't be able to force myself to go back. I didn't want to acknowledge how hideous the conditions were. The men and women I treated had no choice. They'd been deployed—and now they were injured. They deserved a doc who would give them the best he could, not someone wishing he was somewhere else."

Faith's heart twisted in her chest. "I really like you," she blurted. "You're courageous and honorable."

"Don't give me too much credit. My adoptive father always told me the mark of a man was attitude. It's what gets tough jobs done and gives you the fortitude not to quit."

"That was beautiful. I'd like to meet him."

"Wish you could. Cancer got him about a year ago."

Faith looked away, not sure how to respond and hoping she hadn't said something wrong or opened hurt places. "I— I'm sorry."

"Don't be. He had a good life. He was an amazing man who gave me a whole lot."

The streets weren't busy yet, and Reg maneuvered the car into a space. "We're here."

Faith scanned the street. Most of the businesses were still shuttered, but a café midway down the block had a neon sign that proclaimed they were open. Without waiting for Reg, she opened her door and got out, pulling her hood up against a drizzly rain.

He hit the clicker to lock the car before sliding a hand into the curve of her elbow. "This way, but I'm sure you figured that out."

Faith didn't say anything. The way she was feeling, she'd have followed the man by her side anywhere, but it seemed premature to say anything that intimate.

Reg pulled the swinging door outward and gestured her through. A waitress waved cheerily from behind the counter. "Sit anywhere, folks," she called out. "Be right with you. Coffees?"

"Please," Reg replied and guided Faith to a booth near the back.

Lots of firsts, she thought.

First date—sort of.

First meal in a restaurant that's not part of a mission.

First personal conversation with someone other than Glory, Honor, Charity, or Hope.

True to her word, the buxom, gray-haired waitress bustled over with cups, a pot of coffee, and menus. "I'll leave you folks alone for a few. If you want me back sooner than I show up, just holler."

"You got it." Reg smiled at her, and the woman grinned back. He turned to Faith. "Figure out what you want, and we can order. Their crepes are wonderful. So are their omelets."

She met his direct gaze, loving the way his eyes shaded from darker to lighter green from their centers outward. "Do you come here often?"

He shrugged. "Not often. Maybe once a month."

Faith scanned the menu, settling on a fruit-filled crepe. Once the waitress had left with their orders, she tilted her head to one side. "Tell me about yourself."

He laughed. "You stole my line."

Faith turned her hands palms up. "Nothing much to know about me." She lowered her voice. "Born in a test tube. Raised in an incubator and later in a nursery. Never knew anyone but those who lived on my breeding farm, and then in my compound."

"Tell me about the compounds."

"Ach. You don't really want to know."

"Yes, I do." Emotion flickered in his eyes, but she couldn't interpret it, and it felt rude to help herself to the contents of his mind when he couldn't do the same thing.

"Tell you what." She took a sip of coffee and arranged her thoughts. "You tell me about you, and after breakfast, I'll start in on the compounds. If we do it the other way, neither of us will feel much like eating."

He was in the middle of swallowing some coffee when she said that, and half-choked on it. "Aw, Faith. My story isn't any prettier than what I figure went on in those compounds."

"But how can we get closer if we don't share our histories?"

"We can't." He reached across the table and closed a hand over hers. "Milton knows my background. Chalk that up to a weak moment, but I've never told anyone else."

"Why not?"

He shrugged. "I don't know. Ashamed maybe. Here's our breakfast. I'll start once she leaves."

Faith nodded encouragement. She wanted to know everything about the man holding her hand. Everything.

CHAPTER 10

*R*eg took a few bites of omelet as he tried out and discarded ways to paint his family of origin and early years with a more palatable veneer.

"Don't," she said.

"Were you in my head?" he asked softly.

"No, but I recognize stalling tactics. I won't judge. Hell, I don't know enough about normal human ethics to even form an opinion."

He raked a hand through his hair. The more time he spent with Faith, the more attracted he was. What if his background disgusted her? Or worse, made her pity him?

Reg set his fork down. This wouldn't get any easier with procrastinating. "I was born in Chicago in one of the bad parts of town."

"What makes a part of town bad?" Faith leaned toward him, clearly interested in his answer.

"Poverty, but lots more than that. Families can be poor and provide a loving, supportive environment for their children. My father was a habitual drunk, which meant he didn't last long at any job that hired him. Mom tried. She took in laundry and sewing, but often as not we didn't have electricity or gas, so there wasn't hot water to do wash or light for her seamstress work. I watched her withdraw into herself, doing her damnedest to avoid Dad when he was drunk, which was most of the time."

He drank more coffee. Faith was a good listener, and the pity he'd feared wasn't reflected in her expressive eyes. Interest, concern, but not pity.

"Go on," Faith urged. "This isn't any worse than lots of shows I watched on television."

At least on TV, you can shut the damn thing off.

Reg kept that thought to himself, but she might be in his mind. Normally, something like that would've irritated him, felt intrusive, but he wanted the woman sitting across from him to know everything.

No secrets.

Except maybe my role in the breeding farms.

Reg set his cup down and refilled it from the pot on the table before going on. "One of the things I never could figure out was why my folks kept having kids. Hell, they didn't even like each other. There wasn't enough to go around when there were only four of us. By the time we were twelve—"

Faith's eyes widened. "Twelve? Your parents had ten children?"

He nodded. "Yup. I was the oldest. I hated it at home. Cockroaches. Rats. Feeling responsible for my brothers and sisters, who were always crying because they were hungry.

"I stopped going to school regularly around sixth grade and fell in with bad company. Gangs and drugs—except I never cared much for booze or chemicals. Probably a good thing. At least I had pocket money from selling drugs and stealing, which meant I could eat."

Concern flowed from Faith's green eyes. "That's awful, but it made you strong."

Reg screwed his face into a frown. "Not that strong. I got picked up by the juvenile authorities when I was thirteen for selling pot and cocaine. While I was in juvie, one of the—"

"What's juvie?"

"Juvenile Hall. Jail for those who aren't yet eighteen."

"Got it. Go on."

"Anyway, there was an onsite school at juvenile hall. The teacher must've seen something in me because he encouraged me, challenged me, and just kept pushing." Reg looked away from Faith's intense gaze. Now wasn't the time to leave things out, but the next part wasn't easy to own up to.

"I did everything I could to make him leave me alone. Yelled, cursed, told him he was wasting his time, but he never gave up."

"Awww." Faith's expression melted his heart. "He saw the same things that make me care about you."

Faith's words flustered him, but he forged ahead. "Long story short, when my sentence in juvie was up, I went home with Mr. Thomas. He had a wonderful, funny, warm wife who was a nurse. It's because of her that I picked medicine for a career. They'd never had kids of their own, and they welcomed me."

"It's like a storybook tale."

Reg rolled his eyes. "Not exactly. I gave them plenty of grief before I settled down. They never gave up on me, though. Never even got angry." He leveled his gaze at her. "Let me tell you, facing disappointment is way harder than someone being angry. You can fight anger with anger, but disappointment makes you feel like a pile of warmed over shit."

A soft, slow smile lit Faith's face, starting in her eyes and moving to her mouth. "You took his name. That says a whole lot. What was your original family's name?"

"Leary. Irish as they come. It explains all the kids. Irish are good Catholics and don't believe in birth control."

"It's still like a storybook because Mr. and Mrs. Thomas gave you a happy ending."

"What they gave me was my life. They helped me believe in myself and encouraged me to excel in school. Even helped with my medical school tuition—the part the Air Force didn't underwrite—but I paid back every penny."

"I bet they were proud of you."

Unfamiliar emotion thickened the back of Reg's throat. "They were. I'm who I am because of them."

"Is she still alive?"

He shook his head. "No. She never recovered from my adoptive father's death. When people grieve like that, it weakens their immune system. I tried to spend as much time as I could with her, but she'd shoo me away. Tell me to get back to my own patients and clinic."

"What happened?"

"She came down with one of those multi-drug resistant bugs at the hospital. Didn't tell anyone how sick she was until they couldn't save her." Pain beat a slow tattoo against his temples. "By the time they called me, I barely made it to Chicago before she died."

Faith extended a hand, and he clasped it. "I'm sorry."

"Don't be. I'm not religious, but maybe they're together now."

"How about all those brothers and sisters and your original mom and dad?"

Guilt pricked him as it always did when he thought about the family he'd abandoned. Never mind, they'd likely cheered at the specter of one less mouth to feed after he left. "No idea. I never went back. If I had to guess, alcohol killed Dad a long time ago. Malnutrition might've gotten some of my siblings before they even grew up."

He gazed at Faith. "I'm relieved you didn't run out of here. Langley's close enough, you scarcely need the car to get back there."

"Why would I do that? Never mind me. How are you doing?"

"What do you mean?"

"You said you hadn't told anyone about your life—except Milton. Was it hard to tell me?"

Reg smiled. "Not hard at all. You're a wonderful listener."

She tightened her grip on his hand. "Not always, but I care about you."

"I—" Words failed him, so he just said, "Thank you." He glanced at her empty plate. "Did you have enough?"

"Yeah. But part of your omelet is left. Do you want it, or should we take it with us?"

He'd been prepared to walk away from it, but he picked up his fork, chewing and swallowing the last few bites and washing them down with coffee. "There wasn't much left."

"I spent seven years being hungry. I cannot waste food." Faith released his hand and splayed hers flat across the table. "The compounds weren't that much better than the home you grew up in."

"Yeah, they were. At least they were new and well-constructed and probably not riddled with vermin." Words kept flowing, surprising the hell out of him. "And I didn't grow up in a house. More like a tenement, a slum. It was a rundown apartment building where the hallways stank of onions and urine on a good day. Shit and vomit on bad ones."

He grimaced. "Sorry. I don't want to ruin your breakfast, and that was a pretty visceral description."

"Never apologize to me."

"How about only if I've done something wrong?" He smiled. It was easy to smile around Faith. In a distant corner of his mind, he realized he had years of stern expressions to make up for.

"Fair enough. It's my turn to share. The compounds were… sterile. Not in a bacterial sense, but emotionally. I lived in a big room with eleven other women and six bunkbeds. The Nameless Ones rationed everything from food to blankets to toilet paper. We couldn't leave the compound unless they were with us. Ever."

"Go on." He wanted to hear everything about what his creations had become outside their protected breeding farms.

"We continued some protocols from the breeding farms."

"Which ones?"

"Nameless Ones harvested our eggs four times a year.

Conception occurred in test tubes, and some of the women were assigned nursery duty." She hesitated, reluctance clear on her face.

"Whatever it is, I want to know." They'd traded roles, and it was his turn to encourage her.

Faith nodded, but her eyes glazed with pain. "Some of the children weren't right. They were misshapen or had vicious temperaments. The Nameless Ones destroyed them. They were quiet about it. We women found out by accident after Glory hacked into the mainframe hunting for something we could use to escape."

Reg held up a hand. "Wait a minute. What about the women assigned nursery duty? Surely they noticed when some of their charges came up missing."

Faith twisted her mouth into a bitter moue. "Of course they noticed. Nameless Ones told them they'd transferred the kids to another compound, one that specialized in dealing with children who weren't perfect."

"Maybe they did."

Faith shrugged. "Where's that compound then?" Sadness pinched the corners of her eyes. "We barely had enough calories to sustain those of us living in our compound. I have no reason to believe any of the other ones fared better than we did. We never quite figured out how to barter services for money. Consequently, we rarely had cash to take to a local grocery store. Even if we had, it would've been really expensive to feed a hundred plus people. We tried growing what we needed. Some years were better than others."

Reg turned the information around in his mind. It made sense. Faith and those like her had been designed as modern day warriors. No one ever thought they'd have to fend for themselves for mundane things like food or supplies. Consequently, their original configuration lacked blueprints for those things. It appeared V3 had picked up some of that slack, or they'd have died out long since.

"You're quiet," she observed. "Did what I said bother you?"

"No. Not at all. I was just thinking about it." He angled his head to one side. "Don't chalk those lost children up quite yet. They might be alive somewhere."

"Not likely. The odds are something less than forty percent."

A smile tugged the edges of his mouth, and he pulled his wallet from a pocket, laying bills on the table. "Ready to leave?"

"No. I'm enjoying talking with you, and I don't want it to end."

Delight in her total lack of artifice warmed him. "Don't ever change. Promise me."

She smiled broadly. "I'll do my best."

He stood and helped her on with the coat she'd draped over the back of her chair. "What time did Roy say you had to be back?"

"Oh, that's right. We weren't shielding the telepathy, but you can't hear it. Noon. He said I'm off until noon."

"Fantastic news!" His smile mirrored hers. "Focus those kinetics of yours on the weather. If it's stopped raining, we can go for a nice, long run."

"Even if it hasn't, we could spar in the arena."

He stifled a laugh, but it escaped anyway. "Only if you promise not to beat me every single round. Got to leave a man some pride."

She laughed with him, and they were still chortling when he opened her door for her, tucking her inside the SUV. Reg came around and got into the driver's seat. He stuck the keys in the ignition, but didn't start the car.

"What?" she asked. "Why aren't we leaving?"

He leaned across the console and held out his arms. She dove into his embrace. It was awkward with the console between them, but he crushed his mouth on hers, thrilled when she kissed him back. Her woodsy scent surrounded him, making him ache for things he'd denied himself forever.

She threaded her fingers into his hair, and the heat from her hands seeped into his scalp. He'd only meant to kiss her, but lust shot from his head to his toes, sharp and urgent, impossible to deny. What was it about Faith? He'd never had this much trouble controlling his desires before.

Maybe because I kicked open the door to who I am, and she didn't reject me. Being accepted is a hell of an aphrodisiac.

Oblivious to his thoughts, Faith pressed deeper into his embrace, opening her mouth to his questing tongue and sparring with it. He wound his fingers into her thick, curly hair, delighting in how it felt. His cock sprang to a more than full erection and pressed uncomfortably against the front of his pants and the console separating them.

His breathing quickened. So did hers, and the SUV's windows fogged. Reluctantly, he dragged his mouth from hers. "Much more of this," he said, "and we'll end up folding down the backseat."

"Not a bad idea. But maybe here isn't the best place."

He brushed his thumb across her full lower lip. "It's not. When we make love—and we will—I want to take you somewhere very special."

"Why can't we make love now? And then later somewhere special too?"

An unfamiliar feeling coursed through him. He wanted to shield Faith. Protect her from every bad thing in the world. Make up for those seven years she'd suffered in the compound.

"You didn't answer me," she prodded.

"Because I didn't know how." He tightened his arms around her. "I'm far from an expert on falling in love or relationship building— unless you count my relationships with my patients." He blew out a breath. "Collective wisdom says you date and do things together before you make love. So far, we've had a few conversations and breakfast—"

"How many things does this *collective wisdom* demand happen before we can be sexual?" She never took her eyes from his face.

"I have no idea."

"Then how about if we make our own rules?" She grinned impishly. "I did like your idea about a long run, though. We have plenty of time."

Reg took a deep breath. He hoped they'd have years, an entire lifetime together, but it felt premature to say something that far-reaching. He settled for, "Yes, sweetheart, we have lots of time between now and noon. And we've been lucky. My pager hasn't gone off."

"That would mean there's a medical emergency, huh?" At his nod, she went on. "Why are you the only doctor here?"

"Good question. I didn't use to be, and I probably won't be forever. There's a vacant staff position they've been recruiting for these past six months. No one wants to sign on with the government anymore. You can make a whole lot more in the private sector—and every new doc has big med school loans to pay off."

He hated to let go of her, but the sooner they got back to Langley, the sooner they could go for the run he'd proposed. It had stopped raining, and a weak sun was doing battle with patchy cloud cover.

She slid back into her seat. "It's hard to let go of you. You feel right in my arms, like you've always been there except I didn't know it."

His heart hitched in his chest as he started the engine and nosed the car into traffic. "That might be one of the nicest things anyone's ever said to me."

"Feedback is good." She twisted so she faced him.

"Agreed, but you have to say more."

She pursed her mouth into a thoughtful expression. "I don't understand most of how normal humans process the world. I'm never sure if what I say is good, bad, neutral, or indifferent. So when you let me know that I said something right, it helps me."

"Ask for feedback anytime you want, Faith. Keep in mind, my social skills aren't exactly one for the books."

"Well, none of you act anything like the people I watched on TV." She laughed, and it warmed his soul.

"I hope not. They're caricatures. Not meant to represent real life. They're there to entertain." He flashed his creds at the same gate guard, and was waved through the CIA's main gate. "Do you want me to drop you at your apartment so you can get leggings and running shoes?"

"That would be wonderful. What about your things?"

"Good question. How about this? After I drop you off, I'll return to my place, get duded up for a run, and jog over to get you. Shouldn't take more than half an hour."

She fielded a saucy smile. "If you had the injections, you'd be able to run faster. Not as fast as me, but faster."

He pulled the car up in front of her building. "Would you like that?"

"The thing I'd like is being able to share thoughts via telepathy. It's like having a secret language, where it's just you and me."

"And every other freak in a ten mile radius."

Faith shook her head. "More like five miles, and we can shield our communications so only one person can hear."

"Maybe you can do that," he countered. "Milton and Roy and Charlie haven't been able to fine-tune that part quite yet."

"It'll come if they work on it. Especially for Milton and Charlie because of the Cortexiphan."

"Better living through chemistry, eh?"

"Or applied genetics." Faith popped her door open. "You don't have to get out. Hurry. I'll be waiting for you."

He started to say he'd been waiting for her all his life, but it sounded contrived and hokey. "Bye. See you very soon."

Reg backed the car around heading for his lonely apartment. Last time he'd been there was two weeks ago. He had a housekeeper to keep the dust at bay and change the linens, but his home always felt empty. Maybe because most of his things were in storage. Exactly where he'd left them before his last tour in the Middle East.

Would Faith want to live here? Maybe she'd prefer a place in the nearby town of McLean and away from the CIA campus.

Maybe not. She likes being close to Honor, Glory, Hope, and Charity.

He decided the best course would be to ask her what she wanted once they got to that point. He might want to move in tomorrow, but it was a decision for both of them. Not just him.

He reached his underused apartment building and got out of the SUV, intent on a record-breaking wardrobe change when his pager buzzed. Reg dragged it to eye level and groaned.

Milton.

That was never, never good. Nor was it ever something minor.

He switched to his wrist computer in time to see a message flare across it. Also from Milton, this one instructed him to show up at the infirmary, stat.

Cursing all the gods in the universe, Reg slid back into the car. As he drove, he raised Faith on the wrist computer.

"Yes?" She answered immediately, following it with, "Why aren't you back here yet?"

"Because I got paged. I'm on my way to the clinic."

"Do you want me to join you?"

He hesitated. Of course he wanted her next to him every waking minute of every day, but this was her off time, and it wasn't fair of him to intrude.

He probably was silent for too long because she said, "Never mind. Probably one of those questions I shouldn't have asked. The ones you were supposed to tell me about."

He opened his mouth to tell her no questions were off limits, but she'd disconnected. He would've buzzed her back, but he'd reached the infirmary and long years of discipline roared to the forefront. Seconds could make the difference between survival and death.

Not bothering to take the extra moments to lock the car, he hit the ground running hard for the infirmary's open side door. Meant someone was in the ER waiting for him.

His heart cried out for Faith. Just a few more seconds to talk with her, reassure her all was well.

Later. I'll call her just as soon as I see what I'm up against.

CHAPTER 11

Faith stared at her wrist computer. Maybe she'd overreacted, but she'd offered to be there. To help with whatever the emergency was. Instead of jumping on her suggestion, he'd been silent for far too long. Was it because of her lack of medical training? She could fix that in a heartbeat by downloading medical textbooks so she'd have them to refer to.

Maybe she wouldn't be all that fast at first, but soon she'd develop a useful skillset. Besides, she already understood how to heal her own physiology. How much harder could it be to treat non-augmented humans?

Disappointment ran deep. She'd been looking forward to more conversation. And more kisses. Possibly more than kisses. She yearned for the feel of his body against hers. What would he look like naked? Taste like? Hunger to see all of him ran through her like quick fire, igniting her nerve endings.

Maybe I shouldn't go there. I might have scared him off when I jumped on his folding down the backseat idea.

It made sense. That was when he'd launched into excuses about it being too soon.

She glanced down at herself. She was dressed for a run. Just because she was by herself wasn't a reason not to go. Perhaps she'd drop by the infirmary on her way back from a transit of Langley's perimeter. At least that way she'd lay her fears to rest. Or else solidify them so she could move on before she got in any deeper. A dull ache formed beneath her breastbone. She didn't want to move on. She wanted Reg, but he had to want her back.

Faith trotted out of her apartment and down the stairs. Once she was outside, she broke into a lope, covering ground fast. It felt good to move. When she didn't exercise, her body rebelled, growing sluggish and lax. She thought about Reg again, because she couldn't keep her mind off him. Was he sorry he'd told her about himself? Since he'd kept his beginnings hidden, maybe he was having second thoughts about sharing so much with her.

After the intimate conversation and cozy breakfast—and kisses in the car—she'd assumed they were well on their way to becoming a couple. Just like Honor and Milton or Glory and Roy.

Maybe I assumed too much. He said something about collective wisdom and needing more shared activities.

Yeah, but then I suggested we make our own rules, and I thought he agreed.

Faith chewed on her lower lip, thinking. Maybe she should sneak inside his thoughts to reassure herself all was well. Even though they hadn't spent much time together, she longed for him. Ached to feel his arms around her again and inhale his clean scent. Bayberry and forests and something unique to him. It soothed her soul and kindled a bone-deep desire for something she'd never had.

I didn't ask why he'd never married.

Faith ran faster. That was quite an omission. He'd said she could ask anything, so maybe that would be her first question next time they were alone.

"Faith! Hold up." Frank's voice rang from off to her right.

She stifled a groan and cleared her mind of Reg. Just in case Frank decided to go on a fishing expedition. She wanted to tell him to go back to work, but Roy had given everyone the morning off.

Faith slowed fractionally not wanting to give Frank any reason to suspect she didn't want to talk with him. He caught up to her and fell into step, loping by her side.

"Nice morning for a run," he said in a perfectly neutral tone.

Faith glanced sidelong at him. "Not why you flagged me down. What do you want?" She cringed. Not the warmest greeting, but it wasn't out of line with how her kind communicated.

"Just the pleasure of your company."

Faith skidded to a halt and looked square at him. "Bullshit. What's wrong with you?"

Frank stopped running too and faced her. "Why does something have to be wrong with me?"

"Because you're never nice. Competent. To the point, but nice isn't on the radar screen."

He tilted his chin up and looked like he was biting back the orders that used to flow from the Nameless Ones like water. "Did you think about what I said the other day?"

Damn.

She felt his kinetics probe her mind. "Stop that. Yes, I thought about what you said, and I can't."

"Why not? Charity and Tony are happy together." Frank sounded genuinely confused by her rejection.

"Yes, I know Charity is happy. There's a spark between her and Tony. It gave them something to build on."

"We could have the same thing," Frank persisted, "if you'd let it happen. All we'd need is to have sex a few times and—"

"No! I don't feel that way toward you. I never got over how Nameless Ones treated us in the compound."

"That's because you didn't try very hard," he countered.

"Actually, I didn't try at all. I don't ever want to forget. If I do, I might end up in another situation where I'm one step up from a slave."

"Look." He spread his hands in front of him. "I may not have spoken up to alter the status quo, but I never used any women in my lab. Never had them wait on me. I always did all my own laundry and cooking and—"

"Fine. Part of you disagreed with how things were." She inhaled sharply. "This isn't up for discussion. I like you fine as a person to work with. You're steady and reliable and very bright and resourceful."

"See," he broke in. "You could come to like me even better. I ran the odds and they're definitely in our favor."

"They're not. I can't get past you being a Nameless One. And I don't want to get past it. Can't we just be co-workers? Surely there are human women here who'd love to go out with you."

"I don't want them," he said. "I believe we're better off with our own kind. I want someone with my mental acuity, and my—"

"Lots of new women here," she spoke over him. "I'm sure one of them would appreciate you."

"But not you."

Faith shook her head. "No. Not me. I'm flattered by your interest, but I'm not the right one for you."

Something flared in the depths of Frank's amber eyes. A combination of anger and insistence. It frightened her and she drew back, squaring her shoulders. "This is why it would never work between us."

"What?"

"You're trying to come up with a way to coerce me. It scares me, but it disgusts me too. Neither of us knows shit about being human, but that's not how love affairs begin." Faith had had enough. Before Frank could offer dinner, candy, and flowers, she spun on her heel and ran as fast as she could.

She didn't think he'd try to catch up with her—and he didn't.

She sprinted around the perimeter of the CIA installation twice before her emotions stopped roiling like a stormy ocean. Part of her felt bad for Frank. It must have cost him to approach her a second time. That he had meant he'd been expecting her to seek him out.

Nameless Ones had a lot of pride. It was hardwired into their makeup.

She'd just shot him down. Used harsh words like disgust. If they'd still been in a compound, he'd have chased her down and shaken what he viewed as sense into her. He might not have used women as lab workers, but he'd never gotten past seeing them as something to be manipulated.

I'm not being fair. I have no idea how he actually feels. I'm assigning motives to him so I feel less guilty about being honest.

She raised her gaze from the pavement and realized she was close to the infirmary. Should she stop? It had been well over an hour since Reg told her he was tied up in an emergency.

What if he'd changed his mind about her? Had she been premature telling Frank to get lost? Faith shook her head. No matter what happened with Reg, she'd die before she'd link her life to a Nameless One. It might've worked for Charity, but it would never work for her.

She eyed the clinic, debating going inside. She only had about thirty minutes left before she was due to gather her charges for today's lessons. It was long enough. She'd just poke her head into Reg's territory long enough to see what had happened this time—and if it had anything to do with any of the freaks.

Faith offered up a silent prayer. Lots of people worked for the CIA. Just because someone needed a doctor, it didn't have to be because of the group who wanted the planet scrubbed clean of those like her. Decided, she ran to the front door and engaged the palm reader to let her inside.

A quick scan told her Reg was in the emergency room, so she strode briskly in that direction. The double doors stood open, and she walked through, but remained close to the entrance. He was bent over a man she didn't recognize with a mangled leg wound. A nurse stood next to him, handing him things and removing them once he was done. Neither of them noticed her, but Milton must have because his energy closed on her from behind.

He dropped a hand on her shoulder and tugged. Faith understood and followed him out of the ER. "What happened?" she asked.

"Accident in the mechanic's shop." Milton's deep voice rumbled. "I wanted Dr. Thomas to stabilize the man for transport, but he convinced me he could fix the problem here."

Faith looked at Milton. "Why are you standing by?"

"Got to hand it to you. You're sharp. Most people would assume I was keeping an eye on the doc, but my medical skills are so primitive it would be a waste of time. The injured man is my sister's boy. Ace mechanic. Never wanted to be an agent, but I've kept an eye on him since I got him a job here."

"Must be nice to have a family." She shook her head. "Never mind, sir. I was out of line."

"Faith, that you?" Reg's voice carried from the ER.

"Yes, it's me," she called back.

"Were we done, sir?" she asked Milton.

"Yes. Looking forward to your new temporary assignment here, are you?"

"I am. Thanks for approving it, sir."

She hurried back into the ER, but hovered in the doorway. "I took that run for us," she said. "I have to be at the arena very soon, but I wanted to stop by here first."

He raised gloved hands from his patient and spun to face her. "Glad you did. I'll be done here in about half an hour."

"I'll be in the arena by then, working. My afternoons here at your lab don't begin until next week."

He might've smiled. It was impossible to tell through the mask that covered his lower face. "About earlier—" he began.

"It's all right. We can talk later." Faith floated out of the infirmary. Reg wasn't angry, and it didn't look as if he'd changed his mind about liking her.

Milton was waiting for her outside the infirmary. "Mind if I walk you to wherever you're headed next?"

Her stomach twisted into a knot. "Not at all. Did I do something wrong?"

"Relax. Nothing wrong."

Faith nodded, waiting for him to say why he'd waylaid her. She checked her internal clock and broke into a run. Milton was augmented. He wouldn't have any trouble keeping up, and she didn't want to be late. The women were probably feeling nervous about last night.

Milton paced her, running by her side. "Two things, Faith. The first is we scheduled a hearing for next week. You, Honor, and the other women involved will all give statements."

Breath whooshed from her. "Oh my. That's fast. I knew it would happen, but—"

"I requested an expedited hearing. We need to put this behind us, not have it hanging."

She wrestled with an inane desire to bolt, running so far and so fast no one would ever find her, but then she'd never see Reg again. Might be for the best. If the hearing went against them and she ended up in a military prison for years, she didn't want Reg to do something stupid like stand by her and ruin his reputation in the process.

Milton gripped her forearm, forcing her to stop. "Look at me, Faith."

She forced herself to comply.

"Good. Now mind link so you know I'm not selling you a boatload of shit."

She slipped into his mind easily because she'd been invited and didn't need to bother with stealth or subtlety.

His gaze never wavered. "Honor told me what happened. The military court will find all of you not guilty. You acted in self-defense. All the victims had drawn knives clutched in their hands. Don't waste a minute worrying about the outcome. That's an order."

"Got it."

"You still don't believe me. Why?"

She scrunched her eyes shut before opening them. "Because we killed some of you, and people will hate us for it. I can't believe this problem will end here."

"Maybe it won't, but I guarantee you it won't have much of a shelf life. We have bigger problems, and I need everyone focused on them. It's not dissimilar to integrating Asians or Middle-Easterners into our armed forces when we're fighting in those countries."

"You said two things." Faith started moving again. "What's the other?"

"Yes, I did. The second involves you and Dr. Thomas."

Her muscles knotted into blocks. How much could Milton possibly know? Would he forbid her to spend time with Reg? If he did, would that include changing his mind about her working in his lab part-time?

"Why do you always think the worst?"

She flinched. "You were in my mind."

"It's instructive, but you didn't answer my question."

Faith shrugged uncomfortably. "It's not you. It's anyone who has authority over me. I still flinch when Frank or Tony ask me for something, and I've avoided the other freak men who signed on after some of our compound raids."

"Do you feel that way about Charlie?"

"No." Her answer surprised her. "Maybe it's not so much linked to authority, then. I don't know. Just tell me what you have to say about Reg, er, Dr. Thomas."

"You like him. And he likes you. I've worked with that man for years under horrific conditions. He's been alone forever."

"Do you know why he never married?" she broke in and clapped a hand over her mouth.

"How do you know he never married?" The corners of Milton's mouth twisted downward. "More hacking activities?"

Heat moved from her chest upward, flooding her face before she could institute a corrective program.

"I'll take that as a yes on the hacking. No way to keep you folk out of the central databases, but I'd take it as a kindness if you'd requisition information same as everyone else."

"Yes, sir," she mumbled, not daring to ask about her question. Or mention it would have been impossible to requisition information about Dr. Thomas from the personnel department.

"I do know why the good doctor never married, but that's for him to tell you. The only reason I brought him up is I do not want him toyed with. If you're serious about him, I'm happy for both of you. If you're just in it for the short haul, or to experiment with sex for the first time, pick on someone else."

Her face grew even warmer. Were all normal humans this blunt?

"No," he replied to her thoughts, "but I am."

Not sure where her burst of courage came from, she asked, "Did you have this same conversation with Glory or Hope?"

"Not exactly, but I probably should have." He drew his brows into a low, thick line. "It's easy to turn into a confirmed loner in this business. Most of us tried being married, and it went to hell fast. We work hard hours, and even when we are home, we're often preoccupied with work. It's not the kind of job you leave at your desk.

"Takes a special kind of woman to tolerate who we are and not be jealous of our attachment to our work."

Faith shuffled through his words, hunting for what he was telling her. "That's kind of a warning, right? Not to have too many expectations?" At his nod, she went on. "Kind of like today. Reg and I planned to do something after breakfast, but you called him into the clinic."

"Exactly. Until I can rustle up another doc, Reg is on call 24/7 every single day. Sometimes I feel like I'm taking advantage of him, but whenever I bring it up, he reminds me he had it much worse on location in the Middle East."

"He's a good man." The words slipped out. Milton was easy to talk with, and she wasn't censoring what emerged from her mouth.

"Yes, he is. Nothing would make me happier than for him to find someone to share his life, and I'm going to stop there. Eh, maybe I'm not. One more thing."

"Yes?"

"This conversation remains just between us. Do not tell him I butted in."

Confusion reigned. "Not that I would, but you care about him. How could he take exception to that?"

"Men are strange creatures." Milton smiled, a rare enough occurrence it surprised her. "We like to see ourselves as rough, tough, and invincible. Having friends mucking around in our personal business isn't usually appreciated."

"Thanks." They'd reached the building that housed the arena, and she turned toward its door.

"For what?"

Faith glanced at him. "Teaching me more about how normal humans operate."

Milton burst out laughing. Akin to his smile, it was so out of character, she felt taken aback. Before she could ask what was funny, he said, "Never mistake the CIA for normal. Now go reassure your group of women that all will be well with the hearing."

He turned on his heel and ran back the way they'd come. Faith stared after him for long moments before walking beneath the retinal scanner and tilting her head so it would let her into the building. The foyer was deserted, and she took the elevator down to the arena.

The women were gathered in a tight queue waiting for her.

"You're late," one said.

"True enough," Faith agreed. "I'm sorry. It's been a full morning."

"What's going to happen to us?" another asked.

"We've been talking about running away," a third said. "If we all left now, we could cover our tracks so they'd never find us."

"Whoa. Whoa." Faith held up her hands. "You just got here. Why would you want to leave?"

"We're scared," the first woman said.

"Yeah," another chimed in. "Don't want to spend the rest of our lives in jail. It would be even worse than the compounds."

"I was just talking with Milton." Faith opened her mind so the other woman could check the veracity of her words. "He told me there will be a hearing next week—"

A chorus of moans obliterated her next words, and Faith screeched, "Stop it. Listen to me. Use those enhanced genetics to check my words for truth."

When the women quieted, Faith went on. "Milton reassured me we have nothing to worry about. Those men we killed all carried knives in their hands—knives that were out and ready. It supports our assertion that they threatened to carve us into ribbons. We killed in self-defense. Just tell the truth, and we'll be fine."

"Hard to believe that," the woman who'd brought up running away said.

"Yeah. If we'd killed Nameless Ones—no matter what the reason —we'd be screwed," another woman muttered.

"That's because they operated with a hive mind." Faith inserted calming energy into her words. "And they were both judge and jury. An act against one was an act against them all because they were so intent on controlling our every move."

When she heard her own words, they added substance to her earlier interaction with Frank. He might not be as bad as most of the Nameless Ones, but he was still joined with them at the hip.

"Come on," she urged. "Let's hit those practice mats. It's not raining, so if we finish early, we can jog to the gun range for some target practice before the end of today."

"I hate guns," a woman mumbled.

"Yeah, well I'm not fond of them, either," Faith admitted. "But there are times when guns work best and times when kinetics do. Look at it as adding to your arsenal of tricks."

"On a more pleasant note—" the woman smiled shyly "—have you heard from Hope?"

"Yes, have you?" echoed around the group.

Faith nodded.

"Well?" the woman prodded.

"They're having a grand time. They might return early because of last night, but maybe not."

"I can't wait until she's back." Another woman ran her tongue over her lips. "I want all the juicy details."

Faith laughed and herded them to mats covering the floor in one corner of the arena. She remembered pumping first Glory and then Honor for information about their developing love affairs. Of course the women in her practice group would want specifics to feed into their database brains. The more they knew, the greater the odds they'd find men of their own someday.

"There aren't enough to go around," one of the women murmured, and Faith realized her mind was still wide open.

"You'd be surprised," she told the woman. "Lots of men at the CIA, but beyond its borders, there's a whole world out there."

She tackled the woman from behind, driving her to the mat. "Break my hold," she instructed.

All around her, the others paired up and went to work on perfecting their mixed martial arts skills.

Taking care to be understated about it, Faith shuttered her thoughts. She'd calmed the other women's fears about the hearing, but her own hadn't totally settled down. Good no one had done more than scratch the surface of her mind, the part that held Milton's reassurances.

In a surprise flip, the woman beneath her broke free, and Faith focused all her concentration on regaining the upper hand. She'd replay her conversation with Milton to make certain she hadn't missed anything, but that would have to wait for later when she was alone.

CHAPTER 12

*R*eg put in the last of two dozen stitches and angled his head, assessing his work. The jagged wound should heal cleanly. It would leave a hell of a scar, but the man—Milton's nephew—was damned lucky he hadn't taken the full brunt of the explosion farther up his body where it would've done far more damage.

"I can finish up," the dark-haired nurse told him.

"Thanks." Reg checked the IV and fed a dose of antibiotics into it. "I'll come by later to check on him."

"You got it, Doc." She glanced up from sluicing disinfectant over the wound in preparation for dressing it.

Reg discarded his mask and gloves in the biohazard waste container and strode from the room. He glanced at his wrist computer. His half hour estimate had been off by a factor of two. Faith would be busy with the female recruits. At first when he'd heard her voice outside the ER, he'd been convinced he was hallucinating. Hearing her because he wanted to.

He'd been immersed in caring for his patient since laying eyes on him. The man had been bleeding profusely. Getting the mangled vein under control took priority over everything, leaving zero opportunity to raise Faith via computer or phone.

Even though he hadn't reached out to her, she'd stopped by the infirmary anyway. She wasn't angry or disappointed, and her warm acceptance brought out something primitive in him. Remaining with his patient had taken every shred of self-discipline at his disposal. He'd wanted to chase after her, kiss her until they were both breathless, and firm up plans to meet later. He stood over the sink in the small kitchen scrubbing his hands, and then dropped chips, cheese, and an apple into a sack to take to his office. He couldn't leave the clinic yet. He still had to either dictate or type notes on what he'd done today.

Leaving medical notes for later was a mistake, one that became additive and hard to crawl out from under fast. He'd found that out the hard way years ago. He rolled his shoulder blades to release the tension from being hunched over his patient. They cracked and popped, a reminder he was overdue for a workout beyond jogging.

Reg snorted as he made his way to his office. He enjoyed running and biking. He'd always hated weights, but they were a necessary evil.

Yeah. Kind of like medical records.

He pushed open the door to his office. Someone had taped a note to the center of his newly cleaned desk. Milton. His stark script was impossible to attribute to anyone else. Reg could read it upside down from where he stood.

Call me as soon as you're done with Michael.

He grabbed the phone and punched the single number that would patch him through to Milton, who picked up on the first ring.

"Well?"

"Your nephew is fine. He'll make a full recovery."

Breath whistled through the phone lines. "Thank God. I was waiting to call my sister until I had good news. She never liked the idea of her baby working here, but if she'd had her way, she'd have turned him into a total pussy."

Reg rolled his eyes and stripped plastic off a mozzarella stick. "Was there anything else?"

"Yeah. Roy is here, and I've got Charlie patched in via conference call. Any chance you could get your ass over here now?"

"Jesus, Milton. Is that an order or a request? You could use the conference call feature for me too."

"I could, but you're not in Montana."

"Fine. I'll be there in ten minutes. Just need to put on clean scrubs."

True to form, Milton didn't bother with amenities like goodbye.

Reg dropped the phone back into its charging cradle and stuffed the rest of the cheese stick into his mouth. He toed off his shoes, crumpling their paper covers for the waste can. Stripping out of his blood-splattered scrubs, he shoved them into a hamper that lived on the far side of the room and dressed fast. Milton was a good commander, but he could be a total pain in the butt to work for.

He added a note to his virtual "to do" list so he wouldn't forget to update his medical records and bolted out the door. On his way down the stairs, he tapped Faith's ID number into the wrist computer. She might be too busy to answer, but he could always leave a message and maybe set a time for their planned dinner date.

Hopefully, she'd still have dinner with him. She hadn't appeared upset when she showed up for those few moments in the ER, but other people were there. Maybe he'd read her visit all wrong, and the real reason she'd stopped by was to tell him she didn't want to compete with his omnipresent patient responsibilities.

His call dropped into a virtual messenger service, so he tapped *Dinner, 7:30? I'll pick you up* into his display, and got into his car. He pulled up outside Milton's building when the computer vibrated against his wrist.

Expecting a *why the fuck aren't you here yet* message from Milton, he glanced at the display. His heart thumped hard when *7:30 is great* scrolled across it.

He tapped a few buttons, hoping for a brief conversation. Milton could wait.

"Reg?" blared through the wrist computer's tinny speaker.

It was so good to hear her voice, he wanted to drop everything. Walk away from his responsibilities and head for the arena, where he could see her and hold her tight. "Yup. It's me. Shall I pick you up at your apartment?"

"Are we going to the dining hall? I could just meet you there."

He paused. Had she said that because she didn't want to be alone with him? It felt awkward to ask, so he tossed his chips on the table. If she said no, he'd deal with it. "I'd rather take you somewhere more private. Where we can talk like we did over breakfast."

A sharp intake of breath through the speaker made him wince. "We can go wherever you want," he added, talking fast. "I'm about to go into a meeting with Milton. Not sure how long it will run, but I'm sure I'll be done by dinnertime."

"It will be expensive if you keep taking me off campus to eat."

"Is that the only thing you're worried about?" He waited, willing her to answer in the affirmative.

"Of course it is. I'd love to go anywhere with you. I didn't want you to see me as some kind of gold-digger." She paused. "Is that the right term?"

If he hadn't been in the car, he'd have turned cartwheels. "Yes, sweetheart it's the right term, and no I do not see you that way. Seven thirty?"

"I'll look forward to it. Gotta run. We just took a break, but the women need me." The computer's display went dark as she disconnected.

Reg was still staring at in, lost in visions of what tonight would bring when the electronic device blasted his corneas with light. This time it was Milton, the message predictable.

Where the fuck are you?

Right outside, Reg texted back and got out of the SUV. Unfamiliar emotions pummeled him. Faith was concerned about him. She didn't want to be a burden or any kind of drain. Even though she probably had no idea how normal humans managed money, she wasn't taking his generosity for granted. He'd had very little to spend his money on for the fifteen years since he'd completed his residency and begun making a decent salary. Once he'd paid his parents back for floating part of his med school tuition, everything else had gone into savings and investments that had accrued over time.

Money had never been one of his motivators. Frequently, months passed between when he looked at bank or brokerage statements. The CIA provided housing, food, medical equipment, and scrubs. Nothing for him to spend his own resources on.

He hurried inside and made his way to Milton's office. The door stood open, and he walked through.

"Shut it," Milton barked.

Reg caught it with a foot and strode to a chair, nodding greetings at Roy and Milton. "What's up?"

"Hang on," Milton said and clicked keys on a console, presumably to patch Charlie in.

"I'm here, boss." Charlie's voice rang through a speaker system. "What's cooking?"

"Same thing I asked," Reg muttered.

"Who all is there?" Charlie asked.

"Roy and Reg," Milton replied.

"Why not Frank and Tony?" Charlie asked.

"We need to strategize," Milton sounded like his normal, sour self. "There have been some developments."

Reg folded his hands in his lap, waiting and wishing he'd had the foresight to bring snacks. Breakfast had been hours ago. He preferred doing what he did best: assessing and fixing broken bodies. Political maneuverings had never held any appeal.

"Whatever this is," he said, "Frank and Tony will find out

eventually. So will the other genetically modified humans because they'll tell each other."

"I never planned to keep it a secret, but we need to make some decisions. Knowledge about Black Ops operations targeting the genetically modified aren't limited to Black Ops personnel any longer." Milton's nostrils flared, and he looked exasperated. "Bringing the freaks here blew the lid off the seven years Roy and his men spent tracking them. Even though the freaks are more adept at culling secrets from our computers than those without their enhanced ability, hacking is far from new. Nor are they the only ones who engage in it."

Reg made come along motions with one hand. It wasn't like Milton to wander or use extraneous words. "Okay. So everyone at Langley knows what Roy and Charlie and the others were up to for seven years. They also know we've imported freaks and are shaping them into agents. Where are you going with this?"

"Where I'm going—" Milton sent a pointed glance Reg's way "— is full integration. For the genetically modified to be part of our operation, it doesn't make sense to do things any other way."

"It's how we've operated in a *de facto* fashion," Roy spoke up. "Just not on paper. Hell, our IT folk have always known everything about everybody. They're supposed to keep quiet, but people talk, especially when they're upset or worried. It's human nature."

Reg frowned. "Okay, so we're altering our policies and procedures to be congruent with how we do things. Seems reasonable, but scarcely a reason to call a meeting."

"Getting to that part," Milton growled. "Roy located the new freak headquarters and their master computer. We can access it if we get close enough, but we may not want to." He looked at Roy. "Take it from here."

Roy nodded tersely. "It seems our attacks on their compounds have rattled them. The new master computer system includes a Doomsday key—something that will destroy all the compounds and everyone in them. Maybe because I hunted them for so long, my belief is if we take down another compound—or two or three—they'll wipe themselves out."

"That would be a terrible waste," Reg spoke up.

"Agreed," Charlie said. "Should we send out another amnesty offer?"

"Even if we did," Milton cut in, "no guarantees any more of them would see it this time around."

"What we came up with," Roy said, "and the reason neither Frank nor Tony are here, is creating a small group to go to some of the nearby compounds and pitch amnesty. At least that way, we'd be certain they heard us."

"If we could sell the concept to enough of them, they could play it forward," Charlie said. "I like it."

Reg considered the ramifications. "If this goes well, and large numbers accept our offer, we'll need more resources than the CIA can float—"

"Already thought about that," Milton interrupted. "The government would have to develop a program to help them assimilate, probably into various branches of the military since that's where their strengths lie."

"The downside—and it's a big one—" Roy sat straighter in his chair "—is it could backfire. They could activate their Doomsday key the minute they saw a group of us outside a compound."

Reg stood and paced over to the window, thinking. When he turned back, he said, "You don't view Frank or Tony as ambassador material, but I suspect they're far better suited to the task than any of us—or the women. Remember, the women have zero standing in the compounds. That hasn't changed. Means all important decisions are made by Nameless Ones."

"Send fire to fight fire, eh?" Milton laced his fingers together.

"Something like that," Reg replied, amazed that for once Milton had let him finish voicing a complete thought.

Milton tapped a few keys on his computer keyboard. Frank's face flashed on the screen. "Yes?"

"We need you and Tony in my office."

"Who's we?" Frank inquired, clearly not in any hurry.

"Not how it works," Roy moved so he'd be visible at Frank's end. "We have new intel. Your people have a master switch that could annihilate every compound."

"Why didn't you say so in the first place?" The screen flickered and blanked out.

Reg poured himself a cup of coffee before returning to his seat. In less than five minutes, Frank and Tony threw the door open and marched in.

"We were in the middle of something delicate," Tony announced. Kicking the door shut behind them, he nodded at Reg. "Real treasure trove of information in your office. Never got a chance to thank you."

Reg nodded back. "Welcome."

"Treasure trove indeed," Frank cut in. "We know how to stabilize Cortexiphan—and the injections. At least I'm ninety percent sure we do. We'll have to start this particular set of experiments over to rule out a couple of variables." He stopped to take a breath, and then added, "What's this about a mass destruction device?"

"They built it into their new master computer," Roy replied.

"Told you they'd come up with that after our last raid in Maine," Tony broke in. "Hell, the guys who joined us from that compound predicted it."

Reg nodded slowly. "They're tired of hiding. Tired of a marginalized existence. I can see where death would look like a way out. By now, they've run the probabilities and know they can't defeat us."

Frank shot an odd look his way. "You understand because you designed the earlier versions of who we are. We were intended to have a purpose. Not cower in a bunker waiting for the next attack."

"I'm going to cut to the chase," Milton said. "What would be the best way to ensure an amnesty offer makes it to every single freak in every single compound?"

"That's easy," Tony said from where he still stood near the door. "Feed the information into their new master computer. The one with the kill switch for the compounds. Create something like an infinite tape loop so it plays over and over and over."

"Someone will turn it off," Frank protested.

"Not if we do it right," Tony insisted. "They can move away from the broadcast, but they won't be able to eradicate it from the computer's memory."

"How would that ensure the message got to all the compounds?" Milton asked. "My original amnesty offer sure didn't."

"We'd have to encode it." Tony spoke slowly and thoughtfully. "Use a frequency unique to our brainwave patterns. Make certain every single compound knows it's there."

"Far from foolproof," Frank said in his flat, no nonsense voice. "The compound leaders and those like us who had freestanding Internet access would see it. Whether they'd show it to everyone else is anyone's guess."

Tony's comment about brainwave patterns struck a chord, and Reg spoke up. "The women's EEG tracings have some salient differences. What if we made two separate broadcasts, one aimed for women?"

"Might work," Tony said. "They do have Internet access. We'd have to figure out a way to ensure whatever we put together bypassed the filtering mechanisms the men put in place."

"How long would it take to develop something like that?" Milton asked.

"Day or two," Frank said. "It would mean our Cortexiphan project got pushed back, though."

"Do it," Milton said. "The Cortexiphan can wait."

"Do you want to review whatever we come up with before we send it out?" Tony asked, aiming his words at Milton.

"Of course. Now get moving."

Frank rolled his eyes and muttered something that sounded like, "Oh ye of little faith," as he started out the door.

"Watch it," Reg called after him. "You're starting to pick up human jargon. It's the beginning of the end."

Frank stopped and turned around. Tony halted next to him. "Have there been any further attacks like the one on the Los Angeles CIA office?"

Milton shook his head. "Nope. Been damned quiet since then. No more stolen planes or choppers, either. Makes me wonder what they're up to."

Tony drew his brows together. "Crap! Not sounding good. Maybe they plan to activate that mass suicide device, no matter what happens next. If they've stopped fighting back, it's the only explanation that makes sense."

"Let's go," Frank urged, his tone solemn rather than abrasive, for once. "I may not have agreed with the rebellion or how the compounds operated, but it would be an enormous loss for thousands of us to check out."

"Agreed—" Milton began, but the two men were gone.

"Hope and I will be returning tomorrow, probably midday," Charlie said. He'd been silent so long, Reg had almost forgotten he was there.

"You don't have to," Milton said.

"We want to," Hope's voice replaced Charlie's. "I've been listening. I can't stand by and do nothing if my people are on the verge of extinction because they ran out of confidence they had a future."

"Do you need me for anything else right now?" Charlie asked.

"No. Dismissed."

Milton moved his gaze from Roy to Reg. "Thoughts?"

Roy narrowed his eyes. "I hope Frank and Tony can come up with something. The more we kicked this around just now, the more my gut said we're running out of time. Glory will be devastated. Not about the Nameless Ones, but about the women. She's never forgiven herself for the seven in her dorm who didn't believe her and ended up dead."

He pushed to his feet and walked heavily out of the room.

Reg drained cold coffee from his cup and stood too.

"Hold up," Milton said.

"Why? I have patients I need to check on. I'm not totally clear why you even included me in this meeting. I'm not normally part of your inner circle."

Milton's dark gaze softened. "Because of Faith. If you link your life to hers, you get a seat at the table where decisions about her people are concerned."

Reg just stared at the man across the room from him. "That's pretty damned premature, Milton. We're barely getting to know each other."

"Yeah, I told myself that about Honor too, but these women are something else. They get under your skin, and never leave. I wish you all the best. You have no idea how lucky you are. Now go take care of my nephew."

Because he didn't have a reply, Reg turned and left the room. How the hell had Milton guessed anything? Was it because Reg had asked for Faith to be assigned to his lab, and Milton put two and two together? Had Milton talked with Faith?

Doesn't matter. I have nothing to hide.

As he ran down the stairs and outside to his car, his thoughts turned to the freaks and their Doomsday switch. He ran genetic sequences through his mind, searching for reasons the freaks would suddenly give up. Except it wasn't sudden. Roy and his crew had dogged them for seven years. After that, Glory and the other four women had defected, followed by several others in conjunction with multiple raids on their compounds.

Glory had stolen a map highlighting the location of every compound, so the CIA knew where they were. No longer able to conceal their secret locations, the freaks were probably sick to death of posting sentries and watching their backs.

And losing. The CIA had killed hundreds in raids.

Waiting to see where the axe fell next had worn them down.

Despite their hatred for everything human, Reg felt guilty and responsible for the way things had turned out. Compassion smote him. He'd meant for these special creatures, and their supernatural abilities, to be well cared for, not tossed to the wolves to fend for themselves.

He reached his car and drove slowly back to the infirmary. By the time he got there, a plan was forming. One that might salvage the creations he'd held such high hopes for. He'd need Faith's help, which meant he'd have to tell her about his role in the breeding farms, but it was better for her to know.

No secrets was the only way lovers had any hope of staying together.

He'd tell her tonight. Over dinner. Depending on her reaction, he'd ask for her assistance with his plan to save as many of her people as he could. It ran counter to his military training, but he'd do this on his own, which meant not including Milton.

That way, if things blew up in his face, he wouldn't drag the CIA down with him. He would need some of the other scientists, though. There'd been three principal investigators in the V2 fiasco, and he'd maintained contact with the other two. If all of them added their own message to whatever Frank and Tony were cooking up, he was hopeful it would make a difference.

It had to. He'd have one chance to get this right.

Something had to crack through the hatred and vengeance driving the genetically modified. If he turned the right key, maybe they'd let their dreams of retribution fall by the wayside.

Reg pulled a cell phone from a pocket. It was a secret number, not one registered with the CIA. He paid for it through a complex series of fund transfers. Milton hadn't confronted him about it, so it must've escaped detection at least so far.

While he still had the relative privacy of his car, he tapped numbers into the phone's display. He wasn't at all certain the other two scientists would want to be involved since it would rip the covers off their connection to the breeding farms.

The phone at the other end began to ring.

Reg's muscles tensed. He had to make this work. For that he needed cooperation. It didn't require the freaks' augmented genetics to know his odds of success would drop significantly if he took on this project alone.

CHAPTER 13

Faith took a last look in the bathroom mirror. She smoothed her sweater over her breasts and ran her hands nervously down her jean-clad hips. Normally, her clothing was utilitarian and shapeless, but tonight she'd opted for something that hugged her figure, and she was nervous.

Would he like it? See her as slutty?

Not much longer, and she'd find out.

Faith perched on the edge of the sofa and reached for her laptop, scrolling through headlines. Maybe she should get hold of Honor or Glory and ask for pointers, but there wasn't really time for an in-depth conversation.

It will be fine. Just like this morning. He's easy to talk with.

If she could get herself to believe her own words, maybe she wouldn't feel so worried. She still didn't understand why he hadn't accepted her offer to join him at the infirmary when their run was interrupted, but the joy streaming from him when she showed up had been real.

"This is going to take time," she murmured. "We're getting to know each other. He has an edge because he must've had girlfriends before."

She felt his energy approaching and was on her feet before he knocked on the door. Her heart thudded against her ribs when it wasn't doing a delighted two-step.

How can I be eager and anxious at the same time?

She sent kinetics to unlatch the door.

Reg walked through. Rather than scrubs, he wore dark trousers, a cream-colored shirt, and a dark jacket. She'd never seen him in anything other than hospital or CIA attire, and he looked striking. The clothing set off his broad shoulders and slender, but muscular, build.

"You're staring at me." He grinned. "Want me to toss a jacket that says CIA over everything?"

"Might be more familiar." She tried to move her gaze from him, but it was impossible.

"I wanted to bring you flowers," he said, "but I ran out of time."

"You don't have to bring me anything but you." Her throat thickened with unexpected emotion.

He pushed the door shut and walked to her, cradling her against him. The scents of shampoo and a musky aftershave mingled with his usual smell. She inhaled hungrily as she wrapped her arms around him.

Maybe it wasn't the best timing, but she blurted, "Why didn't you want me at the infirmary earlier?"

Reg angled his head so their eyes met. "I was afraid you'd jumped to that conclusion. I'm a thinker. I run things through my mind before I open my mouth. It's a useful skill in medicine. Sometimes if you say what's on the tip of your tongue, particularly if it's not promising news, people panic. My reaction when you offered to come to the clinic was that I was delighted, thrilled, but you get very little time off. Roy had given you a few hours R&R, and I didn't want to interrupt them."

"You were quiet because you were caught between what you wanted and being considerate of me?"

"Exactly."

"I wouldn't have offered if I didn't want to be there."

He cupped the side of her face in one hand. "If I'd been on top of things, I'd have known that. Faith." His green eyes brimmed with something she didn't have a name for. "You're welcome anywhere I am, any time. Like I said earlier, I'm not very practiced at this, but I want you as part of my life."

Her heart did another funny somersault in her chest. "How come you never married?"

He traced her jawline with a thumb. "More hacking?"

Faith looked away. "Maybe. Or it might've been from the other time I went hunting."

"It doesn't matter," his deep voice rumbled. "What does is you cared enough to search in the first place. No wives because I never let myself fall in love. When I was in med school, another student was dating several of us. When all the lies she'd told me unraveled, I swore off women."

Faith waited, sensing there was more.

He drew his brows together, looking both sheepish and determined. "After a while, keeping my emotional life on a shelf got easy. So easy, it was more work to drag my feelings out of the deepfreeze than to leave them be."

"Why me?"

"I've asked myself that."

Faith closed her teeth over her lower lip. "I'm not fishing for compliments, but what did you come up with?"

"You're unique. Maybe it's your spirit or your courage or your determination—or a combination of all three—but something broke through my self-imposed isolation. I tried fighting it, but you've been in my mind and my heart."

His body was warm and solid pressed against her. Desire surged, sharp, urgent, impossible to stuff back under wraps. She tilted her head, hoping he'd kiss her like he had before.

"Do you have any idea how beautiful you are?" The words tore out of him just before he closed his mouth over hers.

Faith threaded her hands through his hair, holding his head while she explored his mouth with hers. She sank her tongue inside his mouth and he sucked on it. The feel of being encased in his mouth made her even hotter, and she traded places, welcoming his tongue inside her.

What would it feel like licking other parts of him? The imagery was enticing, thrilling, and she welcomed the sensual visions tumbling through her mind. He moved his hands down her back, caressing, rubbing, leaving trails of passion beneath his fingertips. His penis swelled against her belly, and she snaked a hand between their bodies to curve her fingers around it.

Even though she'd felt his erection pressing into her before, she hadn't expected it to be so thick and long. It filled her hand, its heat almost singeing her fingers. His cock jerked against her fingers, and he tore his mouth from hers.

"If you want dinner that's not a midnight supper, we have to stop now." His voice held a husky, yearning note.

Faith took a chance. Maybe he'd see her as a slut, but she was so aroused, nothing else mattered. "I want you. If we're hungry afterward, I can pop a frozen pizza into the oven."

"Haute cuisine. A woman after my own heart." Fires blazed in the depths of his eyes, heat spilling from him in waves she didn't need kinetics to feel.

Sudden awkwardness coursed through her. She didn't know the first thing about making love. Warmth moved from her chest to the top of her head. "You'll have to help me. What do we do first?"

He reached between them and uncurled her fingers from his cock. "Let me undress you. I've imagined what your body looks like ever since you visited the infirmary when Charlie was there."

Faith smiled shyly. "Yeah, me too, but about you. I've never seen a naked man except on the Internet."

He slid his jacket off his shoulders, draping it over a chair and laced his fingers with hers. Together, they walked down the short hallway that led to her bedroom and bath. "Sit on the edge of the bed, Faith."

She wanted to ask a million questions. Like what about his clothes? Should she turn the lights out? Would he mind if she linked to his mind so she could feel what he was?

He knelt before her and undid the laces of her boots, tugging them off. Next, he stripped off her stockings and rubbed her feet from toes to instep. It felt heavenly, and she pressed into his touch. He moved his fingers up her jean-clad legs to the button and zipper holding her pants closed, undoing them easily.

"You're pretty good at that." She laid a hand over his, holding it against her naked belly.

"Not for the reasons you might think." He glanced up until his heated gaze augered into hers. "Getting clothes off is essential when I'm assessing injuries. Most of the time I slice through them with a knife, but if I can preserve them, I do. Lift your hips just a little now."

She did, and he shinnied her jeans down her legs, leaving the lace panties she'd donned in a flight of whimsy in place. Reg spanned her hips with both hands, drawing them slowly down her belly and legs until he returned to her feet. Bending his head, he took one of her big toes into his mouth, teasing it with his tongue.

Lust speared her and she writhed beneath his touch. He moved from toe to toe, lazily, taking his time, as sensation cascaded through her. Sex had never been anything she'd waited for. Arousal had been something to deal with just like any other hunger. When she moved a hand between her legs, intent on rubbing herself into the orgasm that hovered, tormenting her, he batted it away and lifted his head from her feet.

"My game," he said, his voice raspy with desire. "My rules. I want to be the one to make you come."

He returned to her legs, this time licking his way up her inner calves and thighs. The combination of tongue, teeth, and lips drove her into an altered state. She'd never been so aroused. Never felt like she'd die if she didn't come.

"Please," she moaned. "Please."

He gripped her inner thighs, moving closer and closer to the dark, secret place between her legs. Her arousal overflowed, slicking her thighs, and he licked and sucked his way through her juices until his mouth hovered over her nub. He didn't touch her, just breathed heat all around her sensitive tissue.

She gripped the sides of his head and bucked her hips, intent on contact. She was so close, anything would send her tumbling over the edge. He twisted out of her grasp and closed his fingers over the edge of her panties, drawing them down her legs.

Reg knelt over her. She felt the heat of his gaze as it zeroed in on the dark curls between her legs, and heard his rapid intake of breath.

"Not fair," she managed through a throat thick with lust. "You still have your clothes on."

His fingers flew down the buttons holding his shirt together, and he shrugged it off his shoulders. Scars crisscrossed his leanly muscled torso, and dark hair tracked across his chest, growing more thickly around coppery nipples puckered just like hers.

Her own arousal receded fractionally, trumped by a need to touch him. She jackknifed out from under him and knelt facing him. Sending kinetic energy through her fingertips, she ran her hands across his shoulders, down his arms and across his chest. The flex of hard sheets of muscle beneath her fingers thrilled her, so she repeated her path from his shoulders downward.

"You feel amazing."

He groaned, leaning into her touch. "You can do that forever," he rasped. "So long as you're up, though." Rather than more words, he latched onto the bottom edge of her sweater and pulled it over her head. Reaching behind her, he unclasped her bra and drew it down her arms.

She hadn't thought the fires in his eyes could burn any hotter, but they turned into an inferno as he surged toward her, filling his hands with her breasts. Tweaking and twirling her nipples between his fingers, he bent his head to suckle her. Added to her already inflamed libido, the heat from his mouth surrounding her nipple seeded a climax. It ripped through her, leaving her wrung out and shaking.

He let go of the nipple he'd been suckling and pulled her hard against him, tumbling them back onto the bed. "Yes, darling," he murmured. "I want to make you come a thousand times. A million."

Faith splayed her hands across his back. Panting and gasping, she ground her body against his. She might have come, but it hadn't taken the slightest edge off her lust. The feel of his bare chest against her breasts defied description. His skin beneath her fingertips was hot, electric, laced with lust.

"Not only will we never get to dinner," she said. "We might not make it to whatever's on the agenda for tomorrow morning."

"Lovely thought, darling, but if my pager goes off, I have to follow it."

She brushed her lips over his. "Then we'd better not waste any more time." Reaching between them, she undid his trousers, but the angle was awkward, so she disentangled herself from his embrace to pull his pants off. Shoes got in her way, but they were loafers and easy to deal with.

When she'd worked her way down to his underwear, she hesitated. The outline of his cock was clear against the distended fabric, and she laid her hand over it, letting its heat and heaviness fill her palm.

"Go ahead." Understated humor ran beneath his words. "Worst thing that might happen is I'll come before I want to, but I'll get hard again."

Slowly, as if she were unwrapping the best present in the world, she slid the elastic waistband of his shorts downward, freeing his cock. It jutted hard and proud from a mat of thick, dark hair. Faith couldn't take her gaze from it, and she moved his underwear the rest of the way down his legs fast.

She curved a hand around his erection, letting its weight rest against her palm. It twitched, surprising her, and she squeezed lightly. A drop of clear liquid formed at the head, and she rubbed it around the velvety top of his penis.

"You don't have to be so gentle. You won't hurt me." He closed a hand around the one gripping him and tightened it before stroking the length of his engorged flesh.

Faith pried his hand off hers, experimenting with light touches alternating with harder ones. His cock grew even more rigid in her hands, and his breathing quickened. His pebbled nipples distended still more, and color splotched across his chest.

Fascinated, Faith bent low intent on taking him into her mouth.

He captured her head between his hands. "That would be wonderful, but let's save it for now. I want to be inside your body, but we're not quite ready for that yet."

Faith felt more than ready, like she'd been waiting for this moment for years, but she let him take the lead. He rolled her onto her back and ran his hands down her body while he knelt between her legs. Closing a hand over each breast, he rolled her nipples between his fingers and ran his mouth down her belly. This time, rather than just breathing over her nub, he fastened his mouth on her engorged flesh. At first he licked, but then he began to suck and heat engulfed her.

She wrapped her legs around his head and ground her nub into his mouth while he worked it with tongue and teeth. Another climax spooled in her belly, waiting. Moving a hand downward, he pushed her legs farther apart and probed fingers inside her body. The combination of stimulation from inside coupled with him sucking on her nub tumbled her into another soul-shearing orgasm.

Instead of backing off, he did something inside her that made another climax seed itself off the heels of the one dying away. Just when she was certain the magic would happen again, he withdrew his hands and mouth, tugging her legs from around his shoulders.

"More," she cried. "I was almost there again."

"I know. This time, you'll come with me inside you." He knelt over her and seated the head of his cock where his fingers had been. "We're going to take this slow." He wrapped a hand around his shaft, stabilizing it, and guiding it inside.

Faith didn't want slow. She wanted to come again, but words were beyond her. Ceding control of her arousal to another was the most sensual experience imaginable. Trusting he'd take care of her, make sure sex fulfilled her, was a potent aphrodisiac.

Her body stretched around his cock as he entered her an inch at a time. She wriggled, anxious for all of him, but he kept to the same, controlled pace. Faith trained eyes that had to be liquid with need on his face.

"I know. I'd love to take you fast and hard until both of us shatter, but not this first time, darling. You'll be sore enough afterward as it is." He let go of himself and thrust forward, burying himself the rest of the way, but not moving after that.

She rotated her hips, experimented with thrusting them. His cock twitched deep inside her body. "You do the same," he suggested, breathing hard. "Snug your muscles around me."

She stopped trying to move and did what he suggested. It intensified the sensations coursing through her, so she did it again.

"That's right. A few more times."

He withdrew slowly, leaving an aching emptiness, before plumbing her once more. She tightened her muscles again, and the climax that had begun with his mouth and fingers developed new life.

Leaning forward, he held his weight on extended arms and quickened his movements. She wrapped her legs around his hips, urging him to go harder, faster, deeper with the movements of her body.

Lust spiraled around them. She latched onto it with her kinetics, and it intensified her arousal tenfold. With the floodgates of her mental control in tatters, she flowed into his mind, reading his desire and how close he was to release.

Faith had no idea if he'd hear her, but she used telepathy. *"Yes. Now. Come with me."*

Her body convulsed around his shaft moments before she felt it shudder inside her. Semen splashed her vault as his cock danced inside her. She tightened around him, wanting to milk every last mote of pleasure from the moment and was shocked and delighted when another peak carried her away.

He let himself down atop her and turned them onto their sides, cradling her in his arms until their breathing slowed.

"Was it— Was I all right?" she asked, needing to know.

"More than all right." He smoothed tangles of hair away from her face. "I didn't hurt you?"

She shook her head, and tensed around his cock, still buried inside her. He twitched back. "It's like our bodies are talking with each other," she murmured.

"They did a whole lot more than talk." He chuckled softly. "Thank you for the most intense experience I've ever had."

"Did you hear me?" she demanded.

"I did. Maybe I should get that injection series on board. There are several and it takes a few weeks before they're fully operational."

"Why is that?"

"They're a type of gene splicing, and it takes time for the body to assimilate the new sequences."

Faith felt light, happy, fulfilled in a way she'd never expected to be. A quick check of her internal clock told her it was late, well past time for dinner. "Would you like me to pop that frozen pizza in the oven?" she asked.

"Are you sure?" He kissed her forehead. "I can still take you out."

"Yeah. I'm sure. If that pager of yours cooperates, maybe we could have sex again."

"Before or after the pizza?" he asked, his expression deadpan.

"How about both?" she suggested brightly and sprang out of bed intent on turning on the oven and getting the pizza ready. The sooner she did, the sooner she could rejoin Reg.

"Have I created a monster?"

She shrugged, feeling suddenly shy. "Guess we'll find out."

He got up too and padded across the hall to the bathroom where he snapped up a towel and wound it around himself. "I'll help you."

She cast a sidelong glance his way. "Seems to me frozen pizza is a task for one."

"Well, I'll follow you into the kitchen. There was something I'd planned to talk with you about over dinner. Since it didn't exactly happen that way, maybe we can cover that ground while the pizza is baking. Do you have any beer here?"

"I do." Faith snagged a robe off a hook near her door and slid it over her shoulders. Something about his words gave her pause, but she was probably imagining the serious undernote that had crept into his voice.

After the intensity of their lovemaking, she and Reg were a couple now. Just like Honor and Milton or Glory and Roy or Hope and Charlie. They'd shared something that would make them indestructible.

If that's true, then why did he sound like that?

Faith buried her concerns and pulled a cheese pizza from her freezer. Reg cared deeply about her. She'd felt it when their bodies were joined. Nothing he could say would change a thing. Breathing easier, she popped the pizza into the oven and got two beers from the fridge.

"Here you go." She twisted off the top and handed him one.

He'd pulled the two kitchen table chairs so they faced each other. "Thanks. Have a seat. There's something I need to tell you."

Fear slammed into her guts. Would she lose what she'd just found? "Is it bad?" she stammered.

He angled his head to one side. "Depends on how you look at it. I would never hurt you, Faith. Not willfully. I'd meant to talk with you before we made love, but sometimes the universe doesn't unfold the way we want it to. Please. Sit."

Clutching her unopened beer bottle, she dropped into the other chair. How bad could it be? He'd said he'd never hurt her.

No. What he said was he wouldn't hurt me willfully.

Watchful, wary, she waited for what he had to say.

CHAPTER 14

Reg drained a quarter of the beer, agonizing over where to begin. He hadn't meant to make love with her, but once that train got moving down the track, he couldn't have stopped it if he'd wanted to, which he hadn't. There wasn't a way to make what he had to say any more palatable. This wasn't unfamiliar ground, though. He'd had years of practice giving people bad news. It was one of the hardest parts of practicing medicine.

Faith's face held a drawn look. "Is it really that bad?" she asked and went to pull the pizza from the oven. She plunked it on the table with plates, forks, and a knife.

That dinner was done told him he'd been quiet for at least a quarter hour. "Yes and no," he replied. "Let me start by telling you about something that happened ten years ago. I'd just gotten back from the Middle East. Granted I was a relatively new doc at that point, but I'd served in war zones since I finished my training. The six months before my tour was up were brutal. Over half the soldiers who ended up in my medical tent died. Maybe a level one trauma center might have saved a few, but not that many."

Faith twisted the top off her beer and drank, swallowing several times. He was grateful she wasn't pushing him.

"Aside from the carnage, one message that came through loud and clear was we were losing to a culture that kept women wrapped in burkas, didn't believe in education except for upper class men, and had enough money from oil to keep the war going forever."

"I appreciate the background." Faith spoke slowly. "But I'm not connecting the dots."

"You will." He drained most of the rest of his beer and set the bottle down. "An idea came to me while I was flying back stateside. I was young and patriotic. This country gave someone like me—a guy who should've ended up doing life in prison—far more than he deserved. I wanted to give something back.

"I connected with some of my professors at Harvard and floated an idea to create genetically modified humans—"

A long, low gasp escaped her. "Aw, Jesus," she moaned. "It was you? You were one of the scientists who…" Her voice trailed off, and a look of horror twisted her face into a disbelieving mask. She wrapped her arms around herself.

He wanted to go to her, gather her against him, but he had to finish what he'd started. "What I discovered was that a project like the one I envisioned was already happening, had been for several years. At that point, there were already several breeding farms, but they'd run into unexpected design snags. The initial version had some significant problems, so I worked on V2 with a handful of other scientists."

"Why'd you all run away?" Her voice was strained.

"You already know the answer to that. Your people were angry—and rightfully so. When V2 ended up having worse problems than V1, they killed every single one of us they could locate during and after the rebellion. I was in the Middle East when all that went down. By the time I heard about it, the rebellion was months-old, and no one knew exactly where all of you were."

"The men did attempt to locate the scientists after the rebellion." Her voice sounded strained. "Revenge was the only thing driving them."

"I know." Reg unclenched his jaw. "Years passed before I returned to the states. I didn't bother altering my identity after I got back. It wasn't as if we were part of mainstream science at the breeding farms. Hell, before Glory and you joined us, Roy had the devil's own time figuring out I'd been involved. And he had full access to U.S. intelligence channels. Milton knew, but he kept my secret."

Reg glanced at the cold pizza, but he wasn't hungry. He leaned back in his chair and leveled his gaze at Faith. "None of this changes how I feel about you, but it may change how you feel about me. That's why I'd planned to have this conversation before sex rather than after."

"Do Frank and Tony know?"

"Yes. Roy let it slip the other night when we were dealing with John and the cyanide." He shook his head. "None of that matters. I've put plans in place, started wheels turning. Soon my identity won't be secret any longer."

"Plans?" her voice shrilled. "What plans?"

"Faith." He reached across the table intent on covering her hand with his, but she jerked hers away. "Talk with me."

She moved her troubled green gaze to her lap. "Not much to talk about. That's a major omission. And it feels like I just had sex with my father."

His eyes widened. Out of all her possible reactions to his disclosure, he hadn't anticipated incest. Launching arguments to counter her feelings was a shitty idea since it was impossible to argue anyone out of how they felt. Even knowing it was the wrong approach, words slid out anyway. "You were alive long before I even knew the breeding farms existed."

"Not my point. You mucked around in how I'm made." Pain sluiced from her, pinching the corners of her eyes into spirals. "V2 was a disaster. Some of us exploded. Burned to death. No one could put out the fire in time to save them."

Guilt, a constant companion since he'd heard about what

happened to the version he'd helped create, rolled over him in choking waves. He wanted to make excuses, but there weren't any.

"I know. And I'm sorry."

"Sorry, is it?" She jumped to her feet. "Sorry doesn't come close to making up for the suffering you caused. If it weren't for V2, we'd never have left the breeding farms. Never have gone on the run. Never have—" Her face twisted into a rictus, and she started to sob. Turning away, she bolted from the room and he heard a door slam.

Reg pushed heavily to his feet and walked down the short hallway. The bathroom door was shut, and the sound of her crying tore at his heart. He rattled the knob, but it was locked.

"Faith, please."

"Go away. Get your clothes and go. This was a mistake."

The finality in her words hit him like a lead weight right in his guts. He dropped the towel over a chair and dressed fast. The bedroom still smelled of sex—and her. His soul ached. Would things have turned out like this if he'd told her over dinner, or would she have bolted from the restaurant just like she had from her kitchen?

She was still crying. If he hadn't lived with iron discipline for so long, he'd have broken down too. He hesitated outside the closed bathroom door, not sure how to articulate what was in his heart.

"I know you're standing there," she said between sobs. "What I don't understand is why. I can't do this. Not anymore than I could've hooked up with Frank like he wanted me to. You're not a Nameless One, but you're not any better than them." A thin, mewling howl obliterated her next words.

Reg swallowed around a thick place in his throat. "I'm standing here because I love you. I didn't handle this well, but I never, never intended to hurt you. Jesus, Faith. You're the first woman I've ever wanted in my life. You might think I've had lots of female company, but you're wrong. The sad truth is I've always been afraid to let anyone close enough to hurt me."

Her crying escalated. He considered kicking down the door. It was thin enough, he wouldn't have any trouble defeating its flimsy lock, but that would probably upset her further. If he was trying to get away and someone came after him, he'd react like a cornered animal.

"I will leave because it's what you want. What I can't do is stop loving you." His heart flooded with all the things he wanted to say. That he hoped she'd change her mind. That he'd do anything to have her back in his life. Instead, he trudged down the hall and let himself out her door.

Luck was with him because he didn't see another soul between her apartment and his car. His chest felt like a fifty-pound gorilla was sitting on it, and his eyes stung. He'd figured she'd be angry, but he'd never believed she'd slam the door on him. Something she'd said rattled around his brain.

Frank.

Apparently Frank had hit on her, and she'd turned him down. Her antipathy for Nameless Ones ran deeper than her desire for a relationship. Or maybe she didn't have feelings for Frank. She'd made it clear that even if she did, she'd never accept a Nameless One. Charity had, but the women were all unique, despite their genetic similarities.

He drove back to the infirmary, parked the car, and got out. The night was cold and clear, so he shoved his hands into his pockets and set off at a brisk pace. He had to find the cold, detached place that allowed him to patch up broken bodies with landmines exploding all around him. The place where emotions didn't touch him.

The next twenty-four hours would be critical to put his plan to help salvage the genetically modified into play—before they could activate their Doomsday switch. He had to be on top of his game, not crying in his beer over Faith rejecting him. He'd reached both the men he'd worked on V2 with. Neither had any interest in his plan. Both were ensconced in cushy academic positions. One at Harvard, the other at Princeton. As far as they were concerned, what had been well concealed should remain that way.

Because their work at the breeding farms had rolled out beneath the radar, it hadn't been sanctioned by any scientific institution. They hadn't had any choice. Not really. The ethics of gene manipulation, particularly to create human beings, was questionable. They'd have had religious groups breathing down their throats. Plus, the original plan was to use the clones as soldiers. The less their enemy knew about that, the better. Reg had no doubt Middle Eastern governments would have hustled to create their own genetic copies, if they'd known. Under far less humane conditions.

The veil of secrecy had turned out to be both a blessing and a curse. As one of his fellow scientists pointed out a few hours earlier, anonymity lent them more good than bad. When Reg dissected that statement, he realized it was true for those like him—the researchers—but the clandestine nature of the labs had been the freaks' undoing.

If we'd been honest with them, we'd have had a whole different outcome.

He didn't blame the other researchers for not wanting to risk their careers and carefully constructed lives on his plan. It had holes in it and might not work beyond painting a target on his back for the freaks to come after him—just before they pulled the Doomsday switch.

Nothing like a little witch burning to make up for a whole lot of grief.

Not quite the right analogy. Should be something more like death being more palatable if your enemy dies right along with you.

His thoughts were sobering. The freaks viewed all humans as enemies, but those like him were archenemies. He'd fucked up in a major way with V2, and then hadn't been there to pick up the pieces. What was it Tony had asked? *Why'd you do such a shit job?*

It was a fair question, and one that didn't come with any easy answers. So why was he even trying to right an old wrong now? One of the men he'd spoken with, Christophe Drakis, a Greek biochemist who'd survived an autocratic regime before emigrating, said something about dragging buried bones out to chew on. And that it was never a good idea.

Reg retraced his steps, moving toward the infirmary. He had no idea how long he'd been walking. If he turned his back on the freaks and their Doomsday button, and they blew themselves to Hell, he'd never be able to forgive himself. Divine intercession wouldn't clear his conscience, either. He remembered times he'd entered the confessional as a child—where he'd admitted to petty theft or impure thoughts—and laughed grimly.

His remorse and responsibility over his role at the breeding farms inhabited a whole other universe. There weren't enough Hail Marys and Pater Nosters in the world to save him from himself. If the freaks were truly intent on mass destruction, he'd do everything in his power to alter their path.

He'd planned on help from Faith's kinetics, but it appeared she'd written him out of her life. Thinking about her made the place beneath his breastbone throb dully. No wonder the term broken heart had come into fashion and never left. It was where you hurt when dreams splintered into shards of agony.

He clamped his jaw into a hard line. His thoughts were edging into melodrama. This wasn't the time. He'd hoped to keep his plan out of Milton's gunsights, but for it to have any chance of coming together, he'd have to throw himself on Frank and Tony's mercy. They might not be any more inclined to help him than Faith was to love him because of what he'd done, but he was out of options.

If they shot him down, maybe he could convince them not to tell Milton.

Reg let himself into the darkened infirmary. Interesting he'd chosen to come here, rather than go home. No one had paged him, and he didn't have any patients who needed him to check on them.

"Who am I bullshitting," he muttered as he ran up the stairs. "This is my home. I only keep the other one so people won't give me grief, or know how truly cut off I am from any semblance of life outside of being a doctor."

The words were harsh, but it was good to get them out. He hadn't spent fifteen years doctoring, immersing himself in the fragile balance point between life and death, to lie to himself about why he did things.

Lights were on in his office, and the hum of Frank and Tony's voices reached him before he got to the door. Good. Saved him the trouble of tracking them down.

Frank looked up, surprise etched into his expressive features. "You're about the last one I figured we'd see tonight." He and Tony sat on the floor, surrounded by stacks of papers. Laptops whirred as banks of flickering computer simulations scuttled across half a dozen screens.

Reg rolled his mental eyes. His office looked a whole lot like it had the day Milton showed up and chided him for being a slob.

Tony peered intently at him. "You look like hell. Did something happen?"

Reg smothered an inane desire to spill his roiling emotions. Problem was, he'd always viewed psychiatry as a wasted residency. No way talking about his hurt places would make them heal faster. Picking scabs off his fresh wounds would draw his longing for Faith even closer to the surface than it already was.

A prick of kinetic energy tickled the side of his head. "No," he snarled, lips drawn back from his teeth. "You will not probe my mind."

"Fine." Tony held both hands up in front of him, palms outward. "Would you like us to leave?"

"No. It's convenient you're here. I need to talk with you." Reg caught the door with a foot and shoved it closed.

Frank exchanged a pointed look with Tony. "Before you get rolling with whatever you need us for, our last experiment went well—thanks to a few tidbits we picked up in your files."

"Indeed it did." Tony sounded excited, which was out of character for him. "We believe we can mimic the results Roy and Charlie and the rest of the men achieved with just two injections spaced a week apart. Not much in the way of side effects, either. We removed the hydroxyl ions from the original configuration of Cortexiphan, added an isomer of it, and—"

"I thought you were supposed to be working on hacking into the freaks' mainframe with a tape loop message." Worry filled Reg, but he rode herd on it. Frank and Tony would be able to read strong emotion without any kind of kinetic incursion into his mind.

Was he the only one worried about the freaks' future?

Frank waved a dismissive hand. "Already done. That was far easier than we anticipated. Dropped it off with Milton a couple hours ago."

"Soon as he approves it," Tony cut in, "that project will be done, and we can line up volunteers to test our chemical cocktail."

"I will," Reg said.

Frank's amber eyes widened. "You? Don't you want to slice and dice it nine ways from Tuesday?"

"Sure, but I want the augmentation more." He hunkered near where the men sat. "How hard would it be to add something from me into whatever you prepped for the freaks' mainframe?"

"What do you want to add?" Tony asked.

"And why?" Frank angled his head to one side, assessing Reg.

Reg sucked in a ragged breath and blew it out. Here it was. He had to tell the truth because they'd know if he left anything out.

"V2 is my fault to a large degree. I've searched for an opportunity to fix it—"

"It's fixed." Frank spoke over him.

Tony made a chopping motion with one hand. "Let's hear him out. We're not exactly guiltless. When V2 didn't pan out, we piggybacked onto its failure and told everyone scientists were killing the V1s and 2s to make room for V3."

"Not exactly a lie." Frank shrugged. "The killing may have been indirect, but we needed an excuse to get people fired up to exact revenge on the scientists before they all vanished into thin air."

Reg shunted his surprise to a back burner and kept talking.

Seven-year-old history wasn't important. The ball was in play. No going back now.

He addressed his first words to Frank. "Working together, we can come up with a better, more permanent fix than V3, but that's beside the point. You two came to terms with my scientific role at the breeding farms. It's not that different from me coming to terms with appreciating you for your skills and abilities. Much of your enhanced ability may have originated from my test tubes and agar plates, but the totality of who you are is ever so much more than the way those experiments began."

Frank opened his mouth, but Reg waved him to silence. "Wait. Let me finish what I have to say. Then you can comment or ask questions or say I'm full of shit." At Frank's nod, he went on. "I want to tell as many of your kinfolk as I can that I'm sorry about V1 and V2, but we can't go back. I want to offer my reassurance that I will work tirelessly to see they're integrated as full members of human society, not anomalies stashed away in hidden enclaves."

Frank and Tony were watching him, unreadable expressions on their faces.

"It seemed to me—" Reg met their unwavering gazes "—the best way to accomplish that would be for me to record something you tack onto your tape loop."

"It's a nice thought," Tony said, "but why would they believe you?"

"Because I plan to tell them who I am. I'm done hiding. They can come after me if they want."

Frank whistled long and low. "I like it. It's simple, elegant, and it just might work."

"Agreed," Tony said. "We were worried they'd know our voice tracings belonged to us. We're not exactly heroes in freak circles these days. They view us as the worst kind of traitors. We took skills they needed and are using them to help you."

"We kicked around not saying it was us," Frank went on. "But we decided that would make it worse." He drew his brows low across his forehead. "Does Milton know what you want to do?"

Reg shook his head. "Nope. I'd like to keep it that way."

The subtle buzz of kinetics pricked his skin, and he gritted out, "If you're going to discuss it, include me."

"All right," Tony said. "We were just running the odds of Milton finding out and reading us the riot act."

Reg grinned crookedly. "I'd say around ninety percent. What'd you come up with?"

Frank grinned back. "Ninety-two point four."

"Will you do it?" Reg asked.

Tony nodded slowly. "I'm game."

"Me too," Frank said. He cast an appraising glance Reg's way. "What does the rest of your night look like, Doc?"

Reg shrugged. "Not much. Writing out what I want to record. What'd you have in mind?"

"If you came back to our lab, you could be our first guinea pig. We'd set you up with infusion number one." Frank furled his brows in invitation.

"We could make that recording to add onto ours while you're there," Tony said.

"Yeah." Frank got to his feet, dragging piles of papers beneath one arm. "Probably better that way. We can help shape your message and maybe lessen the odds of some disgruntled freak showing up here with blood in his eyes."

"I'm in," Reg said and pushed upright.

Tony selected a few more file folders and stood. "You don't mind if we borrow more of your experimental data?"

"Not at all. How long will this infusion take?"

"Maybe an hour." Frank shrugged and looked Reg up and down but didn't comment on how he was dressed. "You might want to change into scrubs. In case you bleed on anything."

"Will do. I'll meet you over there."

The men left his office with the hum of kinetics bouncing around them. Soon, very soon, Reg would be able to hear them—unless they shielded their speech. He strode to the closet and swapped out his dress clothes for scrubs and a CIA sweatshirt. His discarded shirt still smelled like Faith, and her loss twisted his stomach into a hard knot.

Can't think about her. Not until after this next part is done.

His yet-to-be recorded message would throw down the gauntlet. It would also set his life's path for the next several years. Assuming no one killed him. Maybe the infusions to augment his ability were more timely than he imagined. They'd boost his sensitivity and make him a more deadly opponent if someone did come after him.

He clipped his pager to his waistband, killed the lights, and left his office.

If the freaks believed him and accepted his help, his assistance would be a two way street involving normal humans as well. They'd have to get up to speed on everything from the inception of the breeding farms to the present day.

Some would be distrustful of the genetically modified. Others would welcome them with open arms. After a while, they'd assimilate, and no one would think much about them being different. America was nothing if not a melting pot, but integration took time.

If he were fortunate, Milton would keep his word and rattle some cages. Someone would form a government agency to address getting all the genetically modified settled. Reg got into his car, tapped the ignition, and headed for the far side of the CIA's campus. Rain splattered his windshield, but it wasn't heavy enough to bother with the wipers.

If he were less fortunate, Milton would kick him out of the CIA. Not the end of the world, and maybe for the best. Not running into Faith by accident might be a plus at this point.

A deeply submerged part of him mourned, urged him not to give up, but Reg tuned it out. He'd tried. She'd told him to get lost. End of story. He'd be a bigger fool than he'd already made of himself to show up on her doorstep begging.

A thought slammed into him. If he could still smell her on his discarded clothing, Frank and Tony must have been able to as well. Right along with the scents of sex. That they'd had the decency not to pepper him with questions surprised him.

Maybe they used one of their stealth tactics and plucked the information out of my mind without me knowing.

The buzz of their telepathic conversation as they'd left his office took on whole new ramifications, but Reg pushed everything aside. Parking the car outside the building that housed Frank and Tony's lab, he hustled inside. If Frank and Tony knew, they'd had the good grace not to mention it in his office, which probably meant they wouldn't bring it up at all.

Faith cried until her eyes hurt, but the tears kept coming. Time got away from her, maybe as much as a couple of hours, but it might have been three or four. She felt betrayed, even though Reg hadn't deceived her. Not really. Still, she had the same sick feeling she'd had when Frank hit her up to go out with him. She hated the scientists who'd botched making them as much as she hated Nameless Ones.

"Why can't anything ever be easy?" she moaned and stared at her blotchy face in the mirror. The scent from lovemaking clung to her. She looked at the shower, thinking she should scrub the residue away, but she couldn't stand to eradicate the last traces she'd ever have of Reg.

I'm being stupid. I have to take a shower sometime.

Yeah, but not right now.

Reg was long since gone. She'd heard him leave. Heard the door close with the finality of a coffin lid slamming shut after she ordered him out of her apartment. She'd had to take a hard line, so she didn't yank the door open and fall into his arms. His words from the other side of the closed bathroom door ran through her mind over and over like a radio broadcast she couldn't shut off.

"I'm standing here because I love you. I didn't handle this well, but I never, never intended to hurt you. Jesus, Faith. You're the first woman I've ever wanted in my life. You might think I've had lots of female company, but you're wrong. The sad truth is I've always been afraid to let anyone close enough to hurt me."

She bent over the sink and sluiced cold water on her face, feeling like absolute crap. There wasn't any reason to remain in the enclosed space, so she padded into the hallway that smelled like him, woodsy and enticing. The bedroom was worse. Before a fresh spate of tears crushed her resolve not to go after him, she went into the kitchen and threw the pizza in the trash.

She pulled another bottle of beer out of the fridge, but then put it back and dragged an unopened fifth of bourbon from a cupboard. She'd never been a drinker, but maybe it would dull the edges of her misery. Faith sat heavily in a chair, staring at the liquor.

Why hadn't he told her before?

"Oh for Christ fucking sake." She answered her mental query out loud. "He never said anything because none of the ones who ran the breeding farms wanted to be found. They became targets after the rebellion, and the ones we didn't kill scattered."

Her eyes widened, and she bit down hard on her lower lip. Reg had said something else. She extracted his exact words from her database brain.

"None of that matters. I've put plans in place, started wheels turning. Soon my identity won't be secret any longer."

She fisted one hand and sent it crashing into a nearby wall, leaving a hole in the sheetrock. What the hell was Reg up to that would reveal his role at the breeding farms? Didn't he understand Nameless Ones would come after him until he was dead? Seven years might have passed, but the hatred fueling their rebellion had only grown stronger.

She dropped her head into her hands. "Aw shit," she groaned. "What should I do?" Warning him was logical, except surely he understood the consequences of outing himself.

The safest path was to do nothing. The same survival mechanism that had chased Reg out of her home earlier resurrected itself, but she pushed it aside. She had to talk with someone, figure out what to do. Her normal ability to examine every angle and plot a course of action wasn't working as it should. The only question was who to raise via telepathy.

Faith wanted Honor or Glory or Hope, but Hope was still in Montana. This might be her last night alone with Charlie before they returned to the craziness at the CIA. Faith couldn't bring herself to disturb her. That left Honor or Glory, but Honor would almost certainly talk with Milton and Glory with Roy. If Reg were up to something, maybe it was secret and...

Faith dug her nails into her palm. Her mind was starting to resemble a hamster running on a wheel that wouldn't stop. Or even slow down.

Charity was the only one left. Faith bit her lip so hard it bled, and she licked the salty liquid away. She felt guilty as sin. She'd avoided Charity, first because her genome had been unstable and later because she'd settled in with a Nameless One.

Faith hadn't been a very good friend. She knew it, and it felt wrong to raise Charity to help solve her problems. Any of the new women would sit with her, listen to her, but she didn't know them like she knew the other four. Plus, they'd just arrived in the normal human world, so their observations wouldn't be worth as much.

She was still staring at the unopened bourbon and feeling wretched when a brisk knock on her door sent her flying to her feet. She'd have dropped the booze, but her reflexes were quick enough to catch it before the bottle shattered on the tile floor.

Who the hell was out there?

Had Reg come back after all? Part of her wished it was him, but another part wanted to disappear out a window if he'd returned. She wasn't ready to see him again. Hell, she might never be, but tonight she felt raw and bruised and vulnerable.

The knock sounded again, followed by Charity's mind voice. *"Faith. I know you're in there. If you don't let me in, I'll use kinetics."*

Faith sent her own jot of kinetics to spring the lock and plodded into the living room.

Charity walked in. Pushing the door shut behind her, she scanned Faith from head to toe and then sniffed, nostrils flaring. "What's with the booze?" she asked.

"I was considering having a drink." Faith's voice sounded as dull and dead as she felt inside. "Why are you here?"

"Tony sent me," she said blandly. "There are things you need to know."

"Huh?" Confusion swept through Faith. What did Tony have to do with anything?

Charity moved around Faith, sat on the sofa, and patted the place next to her. "Sit. We need to talk."

Faith rocked back on her heels. "Can't whatever this is wait until tomorrow morning? It's getting late."

"Do you really want it to wait?" Charity's harsh green gaze softened. "Jesus, Faith. Look at yourself. You've been crying, and pretty damned hard from the looks of things. This place reeks of sex, and you're clutching that booze bottle like a life preserver. None of us drink, so the fact that you're even considering it tells me something's gone bad wrong. I'm bearing good news. Seems like you could use some."

Kindness from Charity was so unexpected, Faith felt the quick, hot bite of tears again. She swiped the back of one hand across her eyes. "I do not want to cry anymore. It's counterproductive."

Charity shrugged. "Yeah, but sometimes counterproductive helps. Sit. Open that bottle, and we'll pass it back and forth."

"You don't have to be nice to me," Faith muttered. "I haven't been very nice."

"Sure you have. I get it that Tony makes you cringe. It's because you don't know him very well. He's nothing like the men in our compound. Neither is Frank, but that's not why I'm here.

Things are afoot, and you're the only one who doesn't know about them. Tony sent me over here to make sure you're in the loop."

Panic closed a fist around her heart. She perched on the edge of the couch next to Charity, who pried the bottle out of her hands and opened it. "Things?" Faith inquired around a tongue that felt thick and uncooperative. "What things?"

Charity tilted back the bourbon and took a tentative swallow, making a face. "Shit! How the fuck does anyone ever get drunk on this stuff? It burns like a bitch."

"What things?" Faith's voice shrilled.

"The men found the master compound—and its computer. Seems our erstwhile kin are tired of playing cat and mouse. They built an override switch into the new mainframe that will blow up every compound at the same time." Charity paused for effect. "Killing all of them."

Faith doubled over as if someone had punched her in the gut. Breath exploded from her lungs. "How'd you find that out? Are you sure?"

"It was Roy who discovered it, and then the others corroborated his intel. I'd peg it at around eighty-five percent for accuracy. The only thing we're not sure of is if they have some plan to go out in a blaze of glory and take as many normal humans with them as they can."

Charity took another swallow of liquor and made a face. "Before you ask how it works, they piggybacked onto cloud technology to make certain the destruction code hits every compound at exactly the same moment."

Faith straightened and reached for the bourbon. It really did burn going down, but she swallowed two more times before handing it back to Charity. "That's terrible. We have to do something."

"We are. Frank and Tony made a recording that they're seeding into the master computer. It's probably done by now. Reg added his own plea to theirs. He told them he was one of the scientists responsible for V2, and a whole bunch of other stuff too."

Charity's usual taciturn expression crumpled. "I listened to it, and it damn near made me cry. He's one hell of a man. Not many can admit they were wrong. Even fewer are willing to ask for forgiveness or put their own lives on the line to make something right. His message isn't long, maybe only ten minutes, but he clarified his hopes and dreams for our kind. He still believes in that dream, and he invited everyone listening to step forward and make it a reality. Said he'd stand with them every step of the way."

Faith swallowed hard around a growing lump in her throat. "So Reg is with Frank and Tony?"

Charity nodded. "Yeah. In the conference room across from their lab. Everyone is there—except you. Roy was afraid things were escalating fast, so we had to get this master computer project in place pronto."

"I get that part." Faith held out her hand for the bottle. "Where I'm having trouble is exactly why you're here."

"Focus, goddammit," Charity snapped, sounding like her temperamental self. "I've already told you that."

"Fine," Faith snapped back. "Tell me again."

"To make sure you knew about the Doomsday switch and our attempts to reach everyone before it's truly too late." Charity's tone dripped reproach at having to repeat herself. "You were the only one who didn't know. Except for the new recruits, of course. The other part is that Milton's ordered full integration. No more Black Ops, at least not where freaks are concerned."

Faith's mind was reeling. It wasn't relevant to Charity's disclosure, but she muttered, "We really need to come up with another name for ourselves."

"Yeah. It might happen but probably not tonight." Charity eyed Faith. "Feel like a run? I'm headed back to the conference room."

Faith replied with a question of her own. "How come you're not asking why I was crying? Or trying to dig the info out of my head?"

Charity shrugged. "If you wanted me to know, you'd pony up the info. It's none of my business unless you want it to be."

Faith set the bottle on the coffee table. Her eyes still felt hot, gritty, and swollen. She shook her head. "If I look as crappy as I feel, I shouldn't go anywhere."

Charity got to her feet. "Think about it, Faith. We're all there. You should be too. We're waiting on reactions from the compounds, so we might be there all night." Before Faith could demur again, Charity trotted to the door and let herself out.

She turned back before latching it. "One more thing."

"Really?" Faith stood. "How much more could there possibly be?"

"This one's at least potentially good," Charity countered. "Frank and Tony came up with a major improvement in the injection series Roy and his men took. They added a stripped down version of Cortexiphan, and—"

"I don't need the long version. Why is that important? We're already augmented."

"Because Reg volunteered as a test subject. He already got the first of two infusions and is doing really well." Charity's green eyes danced with enthusiasm. "It's awesome he trusted us enough to step forward. Frank and Tony might've twisted his arm a little, but he wouldn't have agreed if he didn't believe in their ability."

Faith's mouth gaped open, but Charity pulled the door closed. The sound of her footsteps pelting down the hall faded as she hit the stairwell. Faith stalked to the door and pulled it open, looking out on the empty hallway. She could call Charity back, pump her for more information, but no amount of secondhand info would take the place of seeing for herself.

She pushed the door shut and ran through her living room, down the hall, and into the bathroom, intent on a fast shower while she instructed her body to repair the reddened places around her eyes. Fear for Reg dogged her, clawing at her guts.

Milton had taken those injections, and they'd damn near been the death of him because of his age. Granted Reg was maybe ten years younger than Milton, but still.

She shuffled through physiological and biochemical information in her overstuffed brain. By the time she was done showering and mopping most of the moisture from her long hair with a towel, she'd come to the conclusion that human reactions to both the injection series and Cortexiphan revolved around a combination of the chemicals and each person's unique physiology. Biological markers could predict some of the reactions, but not all of them.

Had Frank and Tony been thorough?

After what happened with Milton, she sure as hell hoped so. When you cut to the bone, they were still Nameless Ones, and arrogance was where they lived.

I'm not being fair. They saved Milton's life. Charlie's too.

And Charity's.

Faith dragged on dark sweats with the CIA logo blazoned across her back. She pushed her kinetics outside to check both conditions and temperature. It wasn't raining, so she laced into running shoes, and secured her hood over her head. On the move, she zipped into a jacket and donned gloves before running out her door.

Maybe Reg wouldn't be happy to see her. He'd had time to think about her rejection, process it, and react. That part wasn't important. She had to assess him for herself and make sure Frank and Tony hadn't started wheels in motion that would harm him.

Faith threw her kinetics wide open and ran hard for Frank and Tony's lab building. It was on the far side of Langley, quite a way from her apartment building. While she ran, she thought about the compounds. She'd been consumed with hating the men, but they'd had their own share of problems. Their original design lacked many basic skills they needed to live independently.

Coming up with V3, the third iteration of their genome, had exhausted most of their resources for the first year after the rebellion. But that first year also laid the groundwork for a society lacking in damn near everything. It had been easy to hate the humans who'd created them. Once the men heavied up, establishing themselves as masters in the compounds, it was easy to hate them too.

Maybe if we hadn't been so immersed in animosity, we'd have accomplished a whole lot more.

The insight rattled her. If they hadn't been so set on revenge, they wouldn't have needed to hide in their compounds. Normal humans wouldn't have been afraid of them. The CIA wouldn't have established a Black Ops taskforce to take them down.

They'd been masters of their own doom. Why the hell hadn't any of them realized that and changed something? Sadness for her kind filled her, and she silently thanked every single normal human who believed in them, saw the value in augmented genetics, and were willing to overlook the places they fell short of being entirely human.

She reached the building where the men's lab was and stopped at the door. The entire second and third floors were lit up, shedding light around the building. A gaggle of cars parked along the street suggested that Charity's depiction of "everyone" being there might not be far off the mark.

Faith took a few deep breaths. Lots of people wasn't a bad thing. It meant she and Reg wouldn't have to do more than nod at each other. She could hang with Honor and Glory and Charity while they waited to see if the compounds reacted to the message seeded into their master supercomputer.

She stood near the door, collecting her thoughts and gathering her scattered emotions. Could she take down the barrier she'd thrown into place after Reg revealed who he was, what he'd done?

I already knew who he was. Her precise, data-driven brain stepped in, correcting her. *The only new part was his role in the breeding farms.*

Yes. Fine. But can I lay it aside? Not hold it against him?

Faith pushed her hood back and raked a hand through her still-damp hair. She needed an answer because it wasn't fair to either of them if she indicated she could get past her antipathy for the scientists—but fell short. Her heart ached from earlier. Pushing him away had been hard. She'd done it because she didn't see any other path.

Had anything changed?

Yes. Two things. She answered her own question.

He signed up to make himself more like me.

He offered himself up in an attempt to get freaks in the compounds to rethink...everything. Who they are. How they came to be. What kind of future they wanted. And he promised to stand by everyone who stakes a claim to the future he's offering.

Faith felt small, petty. She'd held onto the same negativity that had all but destroyed her people. Every time she'd considered rethinking how she felt about Nameless Ones, a host of reasons cropped up that mired her in old, nonproductive thought patterns.

Maybe I blew it with Reg, but my bigotry stops here. I'm not going to perpetuate my own narrow-mindedness any longer.

Change starts right now. With me.

She'd apologize to Reg. And Frank and Tony. Maybe not tonight when everyone was on tenterhooks waiting to see if the freaks would listen to reason—or if it was truly too late for them. But she'd say she was sorry very soon. And mean it. Prejudice was like a cancer. Once it got a toehold, it set down a network of roots that were hard to eradicate. Realizing they were there was a first step. It might take her months to claw her way down to bedrock, but she'd do it.

Tilting her head, she activated the retinal scanner, and the deadbolt clicked open. Faith hadn't been here before, but familiar energy drew her upstairs. Everyone was congregated in a good-sized room at the end of the second floor hallway watching a screen that took up an entire wall. A cheer erupted as she entered the room, accompanied by Tony pointing at a new light flashing on the display.

Faith glanced at it and realized it was the map of all the

compounds in the country. Maybe half the locations sported flashing white lights.

"We got another one," Milton exclaimed, looking stoked. He punched Frank's upper arm. "Damn if this isn't going to work."

"I am so relieved," Roy said from his place next to Milton in the front of the room. "I was afraid we'd waited too long."

"It was Reg's message that did it." Frank sounded somber. "Hey! Look! Two more lights."

Reg detached himself from where he'd been lounging against a wall. "Nah. You're giving me way too much credit. Besides—" he smiled and it broke Faith's heart "—credit isn't important. Results are the only thing that counts." He focused on Milton. "We're going to need government resources and support to take care of the GAs. You'll note I came up with new moniker. It's more respectful than freaks."

"Already in process with HHS," Milton said gruffly. "Not that tonight was a foregone conclusion, but I like to be proactive. Sometimes it skews the energy in the universe in our favor."

"See?" Reg grinned broadly. "Success has a thousand parents."

"GA is genetically altered, right?" Roy quirked a brow.

"Exactly," Reg replied. "It was either GAs or GMs, and I preferred the former."

Faith clung to the shadows. Reg hadn't seen her yet. Maybe she should leave. Tonight had turned into a triumph for him. She was happy for his success. Touched beyond words he'd cared enough to risk himself reaching out to her people. She wanted to hear his recorded message—the one that had finally battered through the freaks' intransigence—but it could wait. Everything could. She'd be damned if she'd dilute his achievement with anything negative. After her reaction earlier where she'd thrown him out, she felt ashamed.

Cursing herself for cowardice, she faded back through the open door as three more lights flashed white on the screen. Everyone fist pumped the air and cheered louder. Amid their joy, she turned to retrace her steps.

"Faith!" Reg's voice sounded behind her, and she stopped dead.

She tried to talk, but her tongue was glued to the roof of her mouth. She didn't dare turn around or look up. What would she see in his eyes? Anger? Pity? His energy drew closer as he covered the distance between them. If she could've leveraged kinetics to beam herself out of there, she would have, but those things only happened on television.

CHAPTER 16

*R*eg felt Faith's presence the minute she stepped into the room. He was shocked by how quickly the infusion was working. His senses were already much, much sharper. Perhaps the addition of an isomer of Cortexiphan to the mixture was responsible. Frank and Tony had been ecstatic, and Reg was wondering if he'd even need the second treatment.

None of that was important, though. Faith's presence won out over everything. She was here. She'd come after all. Charity had reassured everyone that Faith would show up, but Reg had been far from certain.

Why wasn't she moving deeper into the room? He expected her to make her way to where Honor, Glory, and Charity sat, chatting up a storm in telepathy. Soon he'd be able to make out the words. So far, the buzz of the energy was much louder.

Amazement and relief had coursed through him when the screen began lighting up half an hour before. White lights meant someone in the compound was keying their agreement with full amnesty. Tonight was long overdue. If he hadn't been overseas, he'd have found a way to intervene on the heels of the rebellion. And he should have been more proactive once he was home.

Would haves and should haves don't buy much.

He'd kept a close eye on Faith's energy, still expecting her to join her friends, the women who were like sisters to her. When she began edging out of the room, he sprinted after her. No way was she leaving before they had a chance to talk.

"Faith!" he cried once he was outside the room.

For a long, gut-wrenching moment, he was afraid she was going to bolt. If she did, he'd go after her, but the odds of him catching her weren't good. Not yet. The infusion needed more time to alter his physiology.

She ground to a halt but didn't turn. Hell, she didn't even look up. Confusion—and shame—streamed from her in multihued waves of light.

"Is it so bad you can't even look at me?" The words tore out of him. "Sorry. I'm sorry. I don't want to make you any more uncomfortable than I already have."

She did look up then and turned to face him, her green eyes liquid with pain. "You don't owe me any apologies. That should go the other way around. I've been a worse hypocrite than the Nameless Ones I professed to be so much better than. At least they were honest about feeling superior to everyone else. I hid behind every slight, every wrong word. Hell, I made myself quite the martyr."

"It's all right. I should've told you about myself well before we ended up in bed together." He angled his head to one side and held out his arms, yearning to feel her against him.

She shook her head. "I'm not done. What I did earlier was more about me than about you. I needed to pull my head out of my ass long enough to see that." She tilted her chin. "The hard truth is I might not have if Charity didn't stop by. I haven't treated her fairly, either. At first, I distanced myself because of her unstable genome— almost as if it was contagious."

Reg dropped his arms to his sides. "You're being too hard on yourself."

"No. I'm being honest—for the first time maybe ever. After Charity got better, I kind of avoided her because of Tony being a Nameless One. She never held it against me, but she's a better person than I am. And then when Frank made it clear he was interested in me, I could have been nicer saying no. Instead I was abrupt. Made it clear he was subhuman because of being a Nameless One."

"Jesus!" She shook her head. "I was awful."

Reg fought with himself, told himself to hold his tongue, but he had to know, so he asked, "Do you like Frank?"

Faith's eyes widened. "Oh hell, no. Not that way. But that's not a reason for me to treat him like yesterday's garbage. He took a chance accepting Milton's amnesty offer, and he's turned himself inside out working hard for the CIA. I should respect him for that. And I do."

"But you don't love him?" Reg persisted.

"No. And you shouldn't love me. Not after how I behaved."

Reg closed the distance between them. She might not accept his embrace, but he needed to touch her, so he dropped his hands onto her shoulders, reveling in the feel of her beneath his fingertips.

"Those things I said while I stood outside your bathroom door feeling like the worst kind of fool are all true. Nothing's changed."

Her gaze skittered away from his. "I don't deserve you—or anyone, really. Not until I get my act together."

He tightened his hold on her. "I was kicking myself hard when I left your place. Blaming myself. Rehashing all the mistakes I'd made." He shrugged. "No one is perfect. Not me. Not you. I still want you. I haven't given up hope that you'll be my woman, my wife. I was afraid you'd never talk with me again, but I was going to show up on your doorstep and not leave until you let me inside."

"Really?" She did look up at him then, her eyes shiny with tears.

"Really." When he moved his hands from her shoulders and circled her body with his arms, she didn't draw away.

Faith leaned into him. "What you did for my people, for the freaks—"

"Uh-uh," he broke in. "GAs. Short for genetically altered. I want that one modification well underway before everyone from the compounds converges on Washington D.C. They're full partners in this. Not some genetic aberration."

"What you did for the GAs," she went on, her voice partially muffled in his shoulder, "was unprecedented. Thank you."

He cradled the back of her head in one hand. She was going to give them another chance. He felt it in the press of her body against him. A tense place deep in his gut that had been knotted ever since he'd left her apartment began to relax.

"There you are," Milton's voice boomed. "Get back in here, both of you. We're only two lights shy of every single compound."

Reg met Milton's dark eyes over the top of Faith's head. "We'll be there presently."

"Five minutes, no more," Milton admonished and trotted back into the room.

"We can go inside now," Faith said. "From what I understand, tonight belongs to you. You should be where everyone can applaud you."

"Not before I've kissed you. Just for the record, the only one whose acclaim I ever wanted was yours." Reg tilted her head and closed his mouth over hers. He kept the kiss brief, just enough to reinforce their earlier passion. He felt his body come to life when she opened her mouth to his probing tongue. Faith wrapped her arms around him, holding him close, and his heart took flight. She might have felt betrayed, but she still cared about him.

She moved her mouth away from his. "I'm glad you didn't run away forever when I told you to go."

He kissed the tip of her nose and let her go. "It's one of the curses of being a scientist. I draw my own conclusions—even if they fly in the face of evidence to the contrary."

"So you didn't give up on me? On us?"

"Oh hell, no. You'd have had to do a whole lot more to chase me off than you did. Come on. Milton may have made going back inside the room sound like a suggestion, but it was actually an order. He gets far less jovial when people don't follow his instructions."

Faith rolled her eyes. "Yeah. I've seen him in a temper. Lots of times." She wriggled out of his embrace, but laced her fingers in with his, and they headed back into the conference room.

"Come up to the front with me," Reg murmured low next to her ear.

Faith shook her head. "I'm going to sit next to the women."

"So long as I can find you once we're done here, that's—"

"Oh no, you don't, you cocksuckers," Frank roared.

Reg jolted to attention. What the hell had happened?

"Go on." Faith let go of his hand and hustled toward where the women were.

Everyone in the room had bolted to their feet and were moving toward the screen. Reg stared at it as the flashing white lights flickered and died, one by one. Had the GAs changed their minds?

"I've got this," Frank shouted, typing with frantic speed into a keyboard Reg assumed was linked with the CIA mainframe.

"I'm helping," Tony said. "Won't hurt if they hear it from both of us."

"Hear what?" Milton bellowed. "Will one of you fill me in on what the fuck just happened?"

"My best guess," Roy said, "is one of those two compounds who refused our offer engaged the sequence to start the Doomsday key counting down."

"That's exactly right." Frank never looked up from his keyboard.

"Can't you hack into the damned thing and abort it?" Milton demanded.

"No," Tony said. "What we can do is give each compound the code that will terminate the operation at their end."

"All they have to do is feed it into their individual mainframes,"

Tony said. "It will recognize the self-destruct instructions and defeat them."

"Jesus!" Milton clamped his jaw into a tight line. "Did any of you memorize the pattern on that board? So I can determine which compounds to blow out of the water."

"We probably all did," Honor spoke up.

"Yeah," Charity broke in. "One was that place in Maine where we chased everyone out of the bunker. The other was where I assume they moved their headquarters. It would have to be for them to have access to the master computer to start the countdown."

"Where exactly is that?" Reg asked.

"West Texas, a few miles north of Ft. Stockton," Roy replied.

Reg walked to where Frank and Tony sat, still typing like madmen. Lines of code rolled across their screens. The longer he stared at it, the closer it came to forming a pattern that made sense until something shifted, and he could read it just like any language.

He squeezed his eyes shut, opened them, and looked again. The code was still legible. Would this be another benefit from the infusion?

Frank blew out a frazzled breath and leaned back. "Now we wait. Again."

"Are you sure there's nothing more you can do?" Milton stalked over. "How long is the latency between when they activate Doomsday and everything blows up?"

"Don't know," Tony answered. "Probably not long, though. The whole point is genocide. If they gave people even half an hour, some would probably decide they had zero interest in being part of someone's poison Kool Aid pact."

"If you think of anything," Reg said to Frank and Tony. "Anything at all, sing out."

"Nothing more we can do." Frank's usual smartass demeanor had fled, leaving naked anguish stenciled into his features. "I was so sure we had this."

"I was too," Tony said. "We thought we knew our people, but we're more than machines and capable of acting out of character."

"No shit," Frank muttered. "I didn't exactly factor that into any of the probability models."

Reg opened his mouth to say something about them trying their best, but it might not go over well, so he settled for, "Thanks. Sometimes no matter how hard I tried to save someone, they died anyway. It's not a good feeling. I've wasted a whole lot of time running scenarios detailing how I could have done things differently. But my patient was just as dead."

Frank quirked a brow. "That's a decent analogy."

Reg made his way toward where Milton and Roy stood dead center watching the blank display. The women formed a group off to one side. Everyone wore grim expressions, and the women were conversing telepathically. The air around them held a luminous aspect, and electricity crackled. Faith and Charity had their heads together. So did Honor and Glory.

Reg's hands were balled into fists so hard his hands ached. He knew he was wound tight, but the fists surprised him. He flexed his fingers and skirted the back of the group, heading for Faith.

She nodded solemnly at him. "Won't be much longer," she said. "Either the board will light up again. Or not."

Glory turned to him, her pain palpable. "Almost all the compounds have nurseries and incubators where they're growing babies."

"Makes sense," he replied. "It also means there are older children."

"Yes," Honor concurred. "The normal kids—not the ones who got culled—are all sent to a handful of compounds when they're around five. The original idea was to keep them in specialized children's units until they were maybe thirteen or fourteen."

"At which point, they'd be returned to their home compound," Charity said.

"We never actually got to that point because the oldest kids in those units are around twelve now," Faith added.

Reg had been watching the board intently. "Look!" he pointed at a flashing white light somewhere in central Oregon. "Frank and Tony saved at least one compound."

Before his words were out, lights flared all over the board. Whoops and cheers filled the room. Except from Milton. He could have been carved from stone, with his gaze trained on the display.

"Did we get everyone who was here before?" he growled.

Frank pushed in next to him, scanning the flashing lights. "Almost," he said. "We're missing one here." He tapped a spot in eastern Tennessee. "And here." He pointed at northern Oklahoma. Almost as if his finger urged it to life, the Oklahoma light began flashing bright white.

"Not good enough," Milton growled. "I do not want anyone snared in a mass suicide pact who didn't sign up for it. Raise that Tennessee compound on the phone."

Frank pulled a cell phone from his back pocket and tapped on its display.

"That's not a CIA issue phone," Milton snarled.

"Really?" Frank angled an incredulous look his way. "You're going to give me grief over that?" Without waiting for an answer, he began talking to whomever had picked up on the other end, rattling off the code sequence.

After a long, gut-wrenching moment, the Tennessee light popped to life, and Milton exhaled briskly. "I'd deploy fighter jets to annihilate the GAs who activated the Doomsday sequence, but—"

"No need." Frank glanced up from his call. "We saved Tennessee with like thirty seconds to spare. The other two compounds just exploded, including headquarters, which isn't a bad thing. I do have a question, though. The man I'm talking with wants to know what happens next."

"How many are you, total?" Milton asked.

Frank fed the question into his phone. A moment later, he replied three thousand eight hundred sixty-seven."

"Have him tell you how many are children," Glory called from across the room.

"He already did," Frank replied. "Six hundred eleven."

Milton squared his spine. "What happens next depends on what they want. I'd like everyone to show up in DC, but that might not be practical."

"It would work if we did it in groups," Tony said.

Milton held out his hand for the phone. Frank handed it to him, saying, "Watch it. It's not CIA issue."

"Shut up," Milton growled before angling his mouth over the speaker and activating it to make the conversation public. "Milton Reins here," he said. "I run the Central Intelligence Agency. Please give every single genetically altered human my personal guarantee regarding their safety. You do not have to run or hide any longer. We'll find homes and jobs for you. See that your children attend school and are raised in families."

"What if some of us wish to remain in our compounds?" the man on the other end of the line asked.

"Fine by me," Milton said. "We'll see that you have vehicles and driver's licenses, and jobs so you can buy the things you need." He paused a beat. "If any of you would like to work for us, we always have spots for scientists, doctors, computer gurus. We're also always recruiting for every branch of our military. The gates are wide open. Speaking on behalf of the U.S. government, we did you a great disservice. Allow us to rectify it."

"That goes double from me." Reg cupped a hand near his mouth to project his voice across the room.

"Who was that?" the man on the phone asked.

"Dr. Thomas, the V2 scientist in the podcast we sent to all your computers," Milton replied.

"We all want to meet him. I'll spread the word, sir," the man said. "How can we reach you with our decisions?"

Milton glanced at Frank and Tony, who nodded in unison. "I'm going to hand the phone back to Frank, one of your geneticists who works for us. He'll figure out the fine points of how this will roll out."

"Got it, sir. Thank you."

"Drop the sir," Milton said. "Unless you come to work for the CIA." He handed the phone to Frank, who huddled over its speaker with Tony.

Honor linked a hand under Milton's arm. "Looks like an unmitigated success." She beamed. "The war is finally over."

"Moving in that direction," Milton said in his usual gruff tones. "Moving in that direction at least for this war. There's always another. We've done all we can for tonight. Time to turn in."

Faith edged closer to Reg. "Maybe," she murmured near his ear, "if there are a whole lot of us, normal humans won't be scared anymore."

"It runs deeper than that," he told her, enjoying the trust spilling from her eyes. Something he never thought he'd see again.

"What do you mean?" She drew him away from where they'd been standing. The tight knot of women had dissipated. Glory and Roy were heading out of the room. Honor kept a hand firmly on Milton, and Charity hovered near Tony.

"When Charity came to find you, did she tell you I had an infusion to make me more like you?" At Faith's nod, he went on. "This is a new mixture. At least so far, it seems powerful and easy to tolerate. My best guess is every single person who serves in any military or law enforcement capacity is going to want the augmentation."

"I get it." Faith's expressive features gleamed with understanding. "There will be so many who can do exactly what we can, no one will think twice about it anymore."

"Exactly." He threaded an arm around her waist. "Ready to come home?"

"With you?"

He nodded. "With me. I apologize in advance for my living quarters. I've never spent much time there. Mostly I'm at the infirmary."

"We could come back to my apartment—at least for tonight." She offered a shy smile.

"You're inviting me back? After kicking me out."

Faith elbowed him. "I am, but you'd better decide quickly. The offer just might self-destruct in—"

He laughed. "You, my love, have watched one too many episodes of *Mission Impossible.*"

"You've got my number. This is going to be fun."

He herded her from the room. Frank and Tony were still deep in conversation with the man from Tennessee. "What will be?"

"Getting to know each other."

"Fun and exciting and scary sometimes. I never wanted anyone in my life as much as I want you. When you ran me out a few hours ago, I was devastated." He held the stairwell door and they walked down the stairs, hips bumping companionably.

Faith eyed him as they walked outside. "You made a pretty good recovery."

"On the surface. I'm used to running a steamroller over my emotions so they can't get in the way. It's one of the things you'll need to help me with."

"Deal." Faith stuck out her hand.

He grasped it. "What'd I just agree to?"

She grinned, her face illuminated by a nearby streetlight. "Oh yeah. The quid pro quo part. I have a temper. And up until Charity showed up in my apartment, I needed a fairly harsh reality check."

Reg drew her into his arms. "We'll figure it out as we go." He kissed the tip of her nose. "I have a car here, or we could walk."

"Let's take the car. The faster we get to my apartment, the quicker we'll be back in bed."

He splayed his hands across her back. "You liked that, did you?"

She nodded. "A whole lot. That's why we need to do it again. To make certain what happened earlier wasn't a fluke."

"It wasn't." He spun her in his embrace and pushed her gently toward where he'd left the car. "Come on, my little vixen. I may have created a monster."

"Would you still like me if I demanded sex every day?"

"Oh yeah. Not much you could do that would make me not care about you. Faith, darling." He opened the passenger door and tucked her inside.

When he came around and got in, she said, "I like it when you call me that."

"Good. Because you are my darling."

Her smile crumpled.

Alarmed, he asked, "What's wrong?"

"The hearing. For those men we killed. I'd forgotten about it. What if it goes sideways? Maybe we shouldn't spend any more time together until after—"

"Ssht. It will be fine. Trust me on that." He started the car and drove across the darkened campus.

"Do you really think so?"

"I know so, and I'll never lie to you. If I thought you had reason to worry, I wouldn't hide it." He pulled into a parking place and killed the engine, but didn't open the car door. "Tonight is for us. What happened back there when almost all the compounds chose life over destruction was a victory."

"I thought so too," she said, a catch in her voice. "I didn't truly believe they would."

"It's because you misjudged the men."

"I know. That was one of my less attractive insights. I came to terms with it on my way across campus."

"Can we leave all that here in the car?" Reg cupped her face in one hand. "When we go inside, I want it to be just you and me."

"I can do that. Will you stay all night?"

"What's left of it."

She pushed her door open. "Guess that means we need to hurry."

"This won't be our only night together, Cinderella. Just the first of millions." Reg got out and came around to her side of the car, closing her door once she was in his arms.

"Millions," she echoed. "I like the sound of that."

"Good. Get moving, darling. A man could freeze out here."

"Not with me in your arms you won't."

He linked an arm through hers and guided her to her door, following her through. Visions of a naked Faith cascaded through his mind, and he loped up the stairs after her. The way he was feeling, they'd end up fucking like bunnies on the living room floor.

"Great imagery." She tugged him through her open door.

He realized she'd been in his mind. "Pretty soon," he said and kicked the door shut, "I'll be able to do that too."

"I can't wait. Now about that living room floor idea…"

Reg pulled her hard against him and crushed his mouth over hers.

CHAPTER 17

Three weeks later

Faith emerged from the hearing chamber flanked by Honor, Charity, and the other women who'd been involved in the attack that night. The flood of GAs had taxed CIA resources, and the hearing had been postponed until today. Milton, Tony, and Reg hadn't been with them because of how the military justice system operated. No one who wasn't directly related to an incident was allowed in the hearing room.

"Well?" Milton shot out of a chair and grabbed Honor's hand.

"It was fine," Honor said.

Tony didn't say a word, but he scooped Charity into a tight embrace, and she hugged him back.

"We told the truth," Faith added, "and the officer who heard our case said we'd been cleared of wrongdoing."

Reg burst through an outside door wearing blood-splattered scrubs. "It's over, right? I tried to get here earlier, but I was in surgery."

"Yeah, it's done," Milton said. "Justice was served."

"Good thing this is behind us," Tony murmured.

Reg hovered near Faith, but didn't touch her because of the gore on his clothing. "Bet you're happy this is over," he said low into her ear.

Faith nodded. She figured he'd stripped off his gloves and come on a dead run from the infirmary. A peek at his feet, with his shoes still encased in paper covers, confirmed it. She glanced at the women milling around the foyer. It was closing on dinnertime, but Milton might want them to do some time in the arena since they'd blown the entire afternoon with the hearing officer.

She opened her mouth to ask about her assignments for the remainder of the day when Charlie ran into the lobby with Hope next to him. Roy and Glory were right behind them. Their worried expressions shaded to joy as they sensed the jubilation streaming from everyone.

Milton clapped his hands sharply together. "I propose a celebration in the dining hall. See everyone there at nineteen thirty sharp. It will give the kitchen time to make something special."

"Can we invite some of the new GAs?" one of the women asked, avoiding direct eye contact.

Faith bit back a smile. Looking right at Milton took some getting used to, even for them. His intensity never wavered.

"So long as I have a headcount within the next thirty minutes." He angled his dark gaze her way.

"Yes, sir. On it, sir." The woman turned and fled, flanked by half a dozen others.

Milton rolled his eyes. "I am not that big of a badass."

"Yes, dear." Honor tugged on Milton's hand. "Let's get out of here. I can fill you in on the proceedings later."

Faith smiled at Reg. "Want me to walk back toward the infirmary with you?"

He grinned back. "That would be great. I need to do a little bit of finish work, but then I can clean up for dinner."

She longed to touch him, but understood he'd broken protocol by leaving the clinic coated with potentially contagious bodily fluids.

There wasn't much danger, so long as the stains weren't exposed to anything. Like her bare fingertips. She'd enjoyed her brief time working in his lab. Part of her indoctrination had been learning about infection control practices. The CIA had standardized policies, and she'd downloaded them, absorbing the information.

Once they were outside, Reg set a quick pace across campus. Over the last few weeks, he'd become almost as fast as she was. He hadn't opted for a second injection because the initial one worked so well.

"Are you going to tell me what happened?" he asked.

"Not very much, really. The hearing officer had already studied our statements. He had a bunch of questions. Some he asked us privately in a little room off to one side, which was kind of a joke since all of us could hear everything."

Reg cast a sidelong glance her way. "Did you tell him?"

"Oh hell, no. No percentage in it. He'd just have dragged us farther away, which would've meant we'd still be there."

"True enough. Did he ask all of you the same things in that private room?"

Faith thought about it. "Yes, for the most part. The ones of us who actually cast the kinetics that killed the men got one set of questions. The other women didn't have to answer as much."

"What was in the extra questions?" Reg persisted.

"If we felt threatened. How we'd been threatened. What we tried before we resorted to lethal force. How worried were we about the other women. Stuff like that."

"Did he ask about anything else?"

"No, but Honor read a statement at the end when he asked if we had anything further we wanted to add."

"Really?" Reg narrowed his eyes to thoughtful slits.

"What?" Faith stopped shy of the clinic. There'd be no privacy once they crossed through its doorway.

"Means Milton was worried enough to make certain every single point about the incident being self-defense, pure and simple, got hammered home. I bet you anything he wrote it."

"Now that you mention it, Honor's statement did read like a checklist, but once she was done, the officer nodded and told us we'd been cleared and were free to go. I got the impression he'd come to that conclusion before he grilled us today, and the question and answer session was just a formality."

"That's possible. How are you feeling?" He reached for her, but then dropped his hands to his sides. "Damn it. I want to hold you, but I can't."

She chewed on her lower lip. "In terms of how I'm feeling, relieved kind of trumps everything. I'm glad it's over, plus it would have been a bitch explaining a different outcome—one where we ended up in the brig—to all the GAs here."

"I'm guessing most of them know about the incident."

Faith nodded. "We can be thicker than a pack of thieves since we don't just use words to communicate." She checked her internal clock. "I was going to stop in at the clinic, but how about if I meet you at home?" She paused. "I like the sound of that."

"Sound of what? Home?"

"Yes. Our home. It seemed like maybe we were moving too fast when I agreed to share your apartment, but it hasn't hurt us."

"Quite the opposite. Home is perfect. I'll be there by eighteen thirty."

"Oh good." She clasped her hands together and switched to telepathy. *"Means we might have time for a quickie before dinner."*

"You do know how to motivate me." His telepathy was still fairly primitive, but easy enough for her to understand. He blew her a kiss and ran lightly up the steps into the infirmary.

Faith switched directions, heading for the building where Reg lived. Charlie and Hope were on the top floor in an obscenely large apartment that had once been Milton's. Hope had always been a special friend, so proximity to her turned out to be an unexpected plus.

The genetically altered had poured into Langley after the night Frank and Tony told the compounds how to escape the Doomsday sequence. Some GAs only remained long enough to confirm someone knew who they were, and to reassure themselves no one would hunt for them any further. Everyone wanted to meet Reg, shake his hand, and thank him for his candor.

As time passed and no one showed up with a chip on their shoulder and blood in their eyes, she'd relaxed. So had Reg. He'd believed enough in what he was doing to reveal his identity, and her kin respected him for that. She saw it in their minds and in their eyes when they stopped by the infirmary or Frank and Tony's lab to meet the man who'd had the guts to apologize.

Frank had surprised her by wishing her and Reg well. There hadn't been a hint of jealousy or discontent as he told them he was happy for them. When she'd murmured that maybe one of the newly arrived GA women would love and appreciate him, he'd winked and told her he was already working on it.

She let herself into the building where she lived now and made her way to the third floor. Reg's apartment had been devoid of much of anything personal. Not anymore. She'd added her things, and they'd made several shopping trips into nearby communities, selecting furnishings that appealed to them both. He'd told her he had a boatload of stuff in a storage unit, but that it could stay there until they bought a house someday.

Faith walked into her new home, inhaling deeply as the door shut behind her. The place smelled like them. Him and her, and she loved everything about sharing her life with Reg. It was just past eighteen hundred. Plenty of time for her to get out of the formal black suit she'd donned for the hearing.

She kicked off leather pumps and slid her pantyhose down her legs, snagging them on a fingernail. Faith held the flimsy heap of nylon at eye level. Yup. Definitely a hole.

Who the hell designed a piece of clothing that wouldn't even last through a single wearing? Disgusted, she tossed them in a wastebasket. She might never have to wear nylon stockings again for the rest of her life, and it would be fine by her. She slid out of her jacket and blouse on her way into the bedroom and stopped at the closet long enough to hang her suit back on its padded hanger. Her skirt joined the other items, clipped to another hanger.

Shucking her bra and panties, she headed for the bathroom and flipped the taps, standing under the shower once the water was hot. It felt heavenly pummeling her. They'd gotten three-minute showers once a week in the compound, and sometimes the water had been cold.

That life is truly over. Even in the compounds.

Some GAs had opted to remain in their compounds, but compound life had joined the modern world. Someone, maybe Frank, maybe Tony, maybe Milton, made it clear to the Nameless Ones that women were to be handed full rights. No one had objected, so maybe it was a relief. As she thought about it, the Nameless Ones couldn't have been comfortable hiding truth from the women. Living in fear of the fallout once the women discovered they'd been powerful enough to tell the men to go to hell all along.

Hell hath no fury...

Faith laughed. Her sensitive hearing picked up the sound of the front door opening. Meant Reg was home. She hurried to sluice water over her soapy hair and body so he could have the shower. Before she was done, the glass door opened, and he stepped into the steamy enclosure, his arms surrounding her from behind.

He nuzzled her neck and cupped her breasts in both hands. "I was hoping I'd catch you in here," he said.

"Oh really? Why's that?" she teased, knowing full well what he meant. The press of his erection into her backside provided ample proof of his intentions.

Reg turned her in his arms and crushed his mouth down atop hers. Faith threaded her arms around him, feeling her nipples pebble where they pressed against his chest. Sex had been magical between them, and it just kept getting better. He was an endlessly inventive lover, and they'd gotten into the habit of linking their kinetics to drive each other higher still.

He moved his arms until his hands cradled her butt and then lifted her effortlessly. She wrapped her legs around his waist, opening her body to his probing cockhead. Faith wriggled until he slipped inside her.

Reg tore his mouth from hers. "Damn, you feel amazing. It's scary how hard I want you."

"Not any harder than I want you," she countered, breathing fast. Faith pressed her distended nipples against his chest rubbing them from side to side as sensation ratcheted through her.

He drove into her, holding her in place. She watched his face, loving the lust spiraling through him. His arousal fueled her desire, and she tightened her muscles around him as he plumbed her. His cock swelled even more, but he'd wait for her. He always did.

Her belly clenched with heat and need as she welcomed the hunger engulfing her. This might be a quickie, but the higher she rose before tumbling over the edge into pure, unbridled sensation, the hotter those feelings were.

He angled his head and ran a string of biting kisses up her neck. His fingers dug into the backs of her legs. She moved her focus from her nipples to her neck to her thighs to her vault in a round robin of heat and desire. Faith clung tighter with her legs and wrapped her arms around his upper body, raking her nails up his back.

It elicited a long, low groan from him, and he closed his teeth over her shoulder, biting and sucking. His thrusts grew faster, more frantic, and her commitment to hold her orgasm off as long as possible crumpled. Spasms shot through her, and she felt him release in blasts of juddering heat.

They clung to each other with the shower's spray pummeling them.

"You're wonderful, amazing," he managed, still breathing hard.

"You're pretty incredible yourself," she countered. "Good thing you had your nurse put that IUD in for me, or I'd be pregnant by now."

"That wouldn't be the end of the world." He pulled out of her body and disentangled from her. "But I'm selfish enough to want some time alone with you before we add to our family."

"It's not selfish. It's practical." She leaned back, letting the luxury of endless hot water lave her.

Reg pumped liquid soap into one hand, washing himself. "That's a good lead in."

"To what?"

"I have a totally impractical suggestion, but I cleared it with Milton."

"What might that be?"

"How would you like a week away from the CIA?"

Her eyes widened. "I'd love one, but I haven't been here long enough to qualify for a vacation. The P&P manual is quite clear about that. Section IV, Subsection C states—"

"Milton overrode it. What sounds better to you? Hawaii? Florida? Cabo San Lucas? Whatever you'd like, I'll make it happen." He turned off the water and pushed the glass door open. Grabbing towels off hooks, he handed her one.

"What about the infirmary?"

"I'll get a locum doc to cover for me." Reg snorted laughter. "That, if nothing else, will ensure Milton treats me like royalty after we get back. No one else will work the hours I do—or provide quite the level of patient oversight." He wrapped another towel around her streaming hair, tucking the ends in. "Those are housekeeping issues, Faith. Do you want to get away for a while with just the two of us?"

Her heart cracked open and spilled over. She nodded because she didn't trust herself to speak.

"Then it's settled. It won't happen right away—because of those housekeeping issues—but I'll start the ball rolling. All you have to do is tell me where you want to go."

"I—I don't know," she stammered. "I've never been anywhere. It might be better for you to choose for us."

Reg chuckled. "Yeah, I've been to some of the world's garden spots. If it ain't choked with rubble from bombed out buildings, I probably haven't been there. How about this? After dinner tonight, we can haul up possible destinations on the Internet and get a feel for where we'd like to go."

"It's a good plan. There's always Milton's ranch or that place in the San Juans where Roy took Glory."

"Yes," he agreed, "those are possibilities, except I want to take you somewhere special. A place that's just yours and mine. If it works out, maybe we can go back to wherever it is every single year to celebrate being together."

"And if it doesn't?" She quirked a brow.

"Then we go somewhere else until we find a spot we both agree is perfect."

Faith draped her towels over hooks and threw her arms around Reg. "I love you. I still feel like I don't quite deserve you, though."

He wound his arms around her. "Sweetheart. I'm the one who doesn't deserve you. I'll always be grateful you—"

"Hush. No apologies. From either of us."

He licked his way up her neck and settled his lips over hers for a brief, sweet kiss. When he moved his mouth from hers, he said, "We need to get moving if we're going to make nineteen thirty. As it is, we'll need to drive."

Faith checked her internal clock. How the hell had they burned up forty-five minutes in the shower? She dove for the hair dryer and used the high setting to get some of the water out of her hair. "Guess our quickie wasn't all that quick," she called over the noise of the dryer.

"Did I hear a complaint?" He headed for his side of the closet and started dragging clothes out.

"Nope. Never from my lips." She padded into the bedroom and

looked at Reg who'd put on dark slacks and a pale green shirt, topped by a dark sports coat. "What should I wear?"

"How about that long, teal skirt and black tunic we picked up the other day?"

"Really?"

He nodded. "Really. You'll look like a goddess in them."

Heat swooshed from her chest over her head, and she knew she was blushing, but she didn't waste kinetics redirecting the blood. She pulled on underthings and then the soft, woolen skirt and beaded tunic that she'd thought were a ridiculous splurge at the time. A quick glance in the mirror stopped her dead.

"I don't know about the goddess part," she said, "but these are attractive. Much more than I thought they'd be when I saw them in the store."

"That's because you refused to try them on. Grab some shoes. We need to be gone."

Faith ran into the living room and shoved her feet back into her discarded black pumps. Her hair hung in curls to her waist, but she didn't have time to tame it.

Reg draped a black shawl over her shoulders. "I'm a lucky man, Faith. You've made me very, very happy." Winding an arm around her shoulders, he guided her out the door.

Faith leaned into him. "I'm happy too. So much so, it's unnerving."

He didn't answer. Just kissed the tip of her nose and helped her into the car. Before they got to the dining hall, he said, "We'll have lots of happy times, lots of tomorrows. We'll have times that aren't so perfect, either."

"But we'll get through them because we have each other."

"Exactly." He brought the car to a halt in a parking place.

Milton and Honor stood next to the door, clearly waiting for them, along with Roy and Glory, Hope and Charlie, and Charity and Tony. Frank was part of the group as well. Faith got out of the car and waved to the other women.

Reg joined her, and together they hurried toward the others.

"Good thing you got here," Honor said. "You had thirty seconds to spare."

"Or what?" Reg countered. "We turn into pumpkins?"

Faith laughed, recognizing the Cinderella fairytale analogy. They all talked at once as they moved into the dining hall, and joy filled her. Not only was this a new beginning for her people, but a new life for her and her four sisters too. They'd all found special men and a life that had meaning and purpose.

It was impossible to ask for more, and Faith didn't intend to tempt fate by doing anything other than offering up her undying gratitude for the future unfolding before her.

You've reached the end of *Keeping Faith*, and the end of the *GenTech Rebellion* books. Will there ever be another one? I'm not sure, but if you enjoy science fiction mixed with your romance, you might like *Icy Passage*, a novel that came out of my love affair with Antarctica and the Southern Ocean. A sample follows.

ABOUT THE AUTHOR

Ann Gimpel is a USA Today bestselling author. A lifelong aficionado of the unusual, she began writing speculative fiction a few years ago. Since then her short fiction has appeared in a number of webzines, magazines, and anthologies. Her longer books run the gamut from urban fantasy to paranormal romance to science fiction. Once upon a time, she nurtured clients. Now she nurtures dark, gritty fantasy stories that push hard against reality. When she's not writing, she's in the backcountry getting down and dirty with her camera. She's published over 50 books to date, with several more planned for 2018 and beyond. A husband, grown children, grandchildren, and wolf hybrids round out her family.

Keep up with her at www.anngimpel.com or http://anngimpel.blogspot.com

If you enjoyed what you read, get in line for special offers and pre-release special reads. Sign up for Ann's newsletter on her website or her blog.

ICY PASSAGE, CHAPTER ONE

Micah Greenwich sucked air as he pushed up from his squat, a weight bar balanced across his shoulders. He did one more squat before a wave of dizziness threatened to bring him to his knees. Gasping, he shucked the bar onto pins protruding from the back of the squat rack and grabbed one of the metal stanchions for support. A headache pounded behind one eye, and he felt nauseous.

"What the fuck is wrong with me?" he muttered, still clinging to the metal cage shoved in a back corner of the gym at McMurdo Station, Antarctica. No one was in the gym. Not at this hour. Granted, the perpetual night for part of the year, followed by perpetual day, yielded some odd circadian rhythms, but Micah rarely had competition for any of the gym machines or weight equipment late at night.

He glanced at the weight plates balanced on the ends of the forty-five pound bar, thinking perhaps he'd misjudged and put too much weight on it, but that wasn't the issue. He shrugged. Maybe he was getting sick. Something was going around. So far, he'd been lucky during his brief stint at the southern end of the Earth and had avoided the colds and flus McMurdo residents passed among themselves like candy.

He wiped sweat from his face with a ratty towel and decided to call it a night—at least for working out. He still needed to stop by his lab. Because he was the newest and greenest microbiologist, he'd been assigned archaea, the most ancient single-celled life form on the planet. His cultures had taken a decidedly odd turn, though, a couple of weeks back—growing like mad and not looking like any prokaryote he'd ever seen. While he might have started with archaea, what was in his bins didn't look much like them anymore.

Another wave of nausea battered him, and he folded his arms around his midsection, wondering if he was going to vomit. Saliva flooded his mouth, but he choked it back. Even though he didn't feel like doing anything beyond finding his bed, he left the gym and made his way three buildings over to his lab. McMurdo was a series of prefab buildings with interconnecting doors and insulated tunnel-walkways, so you didn't have to go outside into the weather. Antarctica never got particularly warm, and nights were always bitter.

He glanced out a window at an inky sky shot with stars, and a reluctant smile split his face. It might be minus something outside, but it was beautiful too. He'd always loved wild, remote places, and Antarctica was about as wild and remote as it got—shy of signing up to be an astronaut, which was a long-standing dream of his.

Micah frowned, wondering if the astronaut gig was even possible. The United States had cut their funding for the space program rather dramatically. Besides, he needed more in the way of credentials to even be considered for something like that. With another swipe at his still sweaty face—the more he thought about it, the surer he was he was coming down with the flu—he pushed open the door to his lab and froze, not believing his eyes.

"Britta?" he called. "Marguerite!"

The women didn't answer. They sprawled face down on the floor in front of his main workbench, clearly passed out. Wondering if they'd gotten into the high-grade, ethyl alcohol he used to preserve things, he called their names again, louder this time. The longer he looked at them, the weirder he felt. They were too still. Sudden fear gripped him, making the nausea worse.

"Jesus fucking Christ. Why me?" he muttered, and raced to the women. He bent, grabbed Britta's shoulder, and shook her. When she didn't respond, he flipped her over and stared at her cherry-red face.

Fighting a deeply sinking feeling, he turned Marguerite over. She looked just like her friend and roommate. Micah squatted next to them and laid his fingers across their necks, searching for a pulse.

Nothing.

He placed his ear over their hearts, willing there to be something, anything, before he started CPR. Still nothing. He ground his teeth together, unnerved. How could there possibly be two dead women in his lab?

Even though he was pretty sure it wouldn't do any good, he tilted Marguerite's head back and breathed into her mouth before doing chest compressions. When he looked over at Britta, he understood he had to have help and lurched to his feet. Snapping up the wall phone, he punched in the afterhours code for the clinic. As soon as one of the nurses answered, he screeched, "Send help now. Third micro lab."

His headache worsened. So did his twisting, roiling guts, but he went back to the women. He didn't need to be a doctor to recognize death. Despite the futility, he alternated CPR from one to the next. Five long minutes passed—but they felt like five years—before the door burst open.

"Christ!" One of the docs—Stewart maybe, Micah was too rattled to take a good look—pulled him off Marguerite. A tall, broad-shouldered woman Micah didn't recognize examined Britta.

"Looks like carbon monoxide poisoning to me," the female medic said flatly. "This one's well past CPR."

Dr. Stewart rocked back on his heels. "Yeah, her too." He trained his blue eyes on Micah. "What happened?"

Micah shook his head. "Damned if I know. I just got here. I had dinner in the mess hall, worked out in the gym, and then I swung by here to check on my cultures."

The woman narrowed her eyes and half-crawled to where Micah sat on the floor. She folded her fingers over his wrist and took him in with practiced hazel eyes. Her reddish hair was short, almost in a butch cut. She pressed her lips into a harsh line, frowning.

"I'm Ariana," she said, letting go of his wrist. "One of the nurse practitioners. How have you been feeling?"

"Bad," he admitted. "Think I finally succumbed to the community disease everyone else has."

Dr. Stewart joined them and squatted next to Micah. He ran a hand down the side of Micah's neck and listened to his chest with a stethoscope before exchanging a pointed glance with Ariana. "Where's the CO meter in here?" he asked.

Micah gestured behind him. "On that wall." He twisted to look at it, but the indicator light was green—safe. Maybe it was defective. His scientifically trained mind arranged informational bits into an unpleasant pattern. "The women," he said. "If I'd been firing on all cylinders, I'd have figured it out as soon as I looked at the color of their faces. They died from carbon monoxide poisoning, didn't they?"

"Probably," Dr. Stewart said cautiously. "But it's conjecture at this point."

"That cherry-red color is a dead giveaway," Ariana said with conviction. "Nothing else will do that."

"We'll wait for an autopsy before we make statements like that." The doctor eyed his colleague coolly.

"Yes, Doctor. Sir. King of all things medical." She set her lips in a thin line, clearly biting back further sarcasm. "Meantime," she ground out, "I'm pretty sure he—" she jabbed a finger at Micah "—

has whatever killed these two." She stood and punched numbers into the wall phone. "I'm calling security."

Dr. Stewart sifted his hands through his untidy, blond hair. "Tell them to alert maintenance. Until we figure out what killed these two, we've got to get out of here. Now."

Micah straightened. "Wait a minute," he sputtered. "The meter says it's safe. For all we know, Britta and Marguerite got poisoned elsewhere and just happened to be in here cleaning when they collapsed."

Dr. Stewart got to his feet and hauled Micah upright. "For tonight, we'll put you in the infirmary and run tests to check if your hemoglobin's been compromised. I've got to alert the boss and talk with base security. We'll to get to the bottom of this."

"But my lab—"

Dr. Stewart made a chopping motion with one hand, and the rest of Micah's protest died unspoken.

Ariana hung up the phone and nodded at Dr. Stewart. "You take care of the boss. I'll deal with security and maintenance. Need to get the gas sniffer in here to make sure there's not a leak."

Micah tried to focus, but the room spun crazily. He really was wiped out. Much more tired than a thirty-year-old man had a right to feel.

"Can you walk?" Dr. Stewart nudged him.

Micah focused bleary eyes on the physician. "Yeah. I think so."

"How are you feeling?" Ariana asked the doctor.

He shrugged. "Normal. But it takes time for exposure to take a toll. Micah probably lives in this lab, except when he's asleep."

"Yeah, but," Micah pointed out, "those women didn't. They clean all the science labs. Maybe one of the other ones is the problem."

The doctor folded an arm around Micah's waist supporting him, and led him out of the lab. "I'm on it. By the time you wake up, we'll know more."

Micah staggered through the door, flanked by Dr. Stewart and Ariana. "What are you going to do about the women?" he asked.

"You were there when I alerted base security. They'll take care of them," Ariana assured him. "For tonight, focus on getting well."

~

IT HADN'T BEEN JUST that night, though. Micah spent the next three days in the infirmary sucking bottled oxygen. When that didn't clear his red blood cells fast enough, the doctors ordered chelation treatments. In the meantime, he had a chance to think, and he didn't care for what he came up with. Besides, it was so fantastic, no one would believe him.

Maintenance had given his lab, and the other three microbiology studios, a clean bill of health, which meant he could go back to work tomorrow. Even more disturbing, the entirety of the science wing where the dead women cleaned showed zip in the way of evidence of a gas leak. In the interest of thoroughness, maintenance had checked the female dorms too, and found exactly nothing. Autopsy was conclusive regarding cause of death, but no one could figure out how the women had been exposed to a big enough dose of carbon monoxide to kill them.

The same was true for him—major exposure to something pigging up his hemoglobin, but without an identifiable source. Another few hours without medical intervention and he'd have been just as dead as Britta and Marguerite.

Armed with that knowledge—and a phalanx of unanswered questions—Micah spent his downtime in the infirmary mapping out a series of tests to run on his strange archaea colonies. He had suspicions, but needed facts before he presented them to Jack DeVoe, the man in charge of McMurdo operations. If he went to him now, Jack, who had a Ph.D. in biochemistry, would laugh him right out of his office. And there would go Micah's hopes of earning his chops, so he could go on to something more prestigious than working at McMurdo Station.

ICY PASSAGE, CHAPTER TWO

Jack DeVoe sat behind his desk staring at his computer monitor. He snagged a bottle of whiskey from a drawer and belted back a slug, but it didn't make the news any more palatable. Russia and the U.S. were at it again, arguing over Ukraine like a pack of feral dogs battling each other for a juicy bone. The U.S. threatened to send troops, and the Russian president was screaming threats over network news. Unfortunately, Jack was fluent in Russian, and the barrage of words sounded like much more than posturing.

He'd been in Antarctica for years. Maybe now was a good time to go for early retirement—before World War III stranded him at this remote outpost. The more he thought about it, the better he liked the idea, especially in light of the two dead women who'd shown up in the micro lab the other night. Despite him harassing maintenance until they ran the other way every time they saw him, they hadn't come up with a goddamned thing.

He straightened in his chair and rolled his shoulder blades to loosen the tension making his neck hurt. How in the fucking hell could two women die from carbon monoxide poisoning with no leaks? Not just two women, either. The young microbiologist would've been just as dead—but he got lucky. Jack ground his jaws until his teeth ached. He'd figure out what was killing his people. No matter what it took.

Then he'd leave Antarctica.

His phone buzzed and he picked it up, growling, "What?"

"Hey, boss. Micah here." He hesitated. "Is this an okay time? You seem miffed about something."

Nothing much. The world's imploding and a mystery gas leak is on the loose.

"Nah, I'm fine, Greenwich. You still feeling all right? What do you need? It's ten at night."

Micah cleared his throat. "Thanks for asking, but I made a good recovery." He paused a beat. "I suppose in a backhanded way, I owe my life to Britta and Marguerite. If it weren't for them, I'd be dead too."

"Get on with it." Jack rolled his eyes. "You didn't call to swap philosophies."

"Right, sir. Sorry. I know it's been a while since you did much with your biochem background, but I'd appreciate it if you could stop by the lab."

"Now?" Jack straightened in his chair and screwed the top back on the liquor bottle. "Is the lab on fire or something?" He shoved too-long blond hair out of his face and listened intently.

Micah laughed, but it sounded strained. "I've been running tests on my single-celled samples, but I keep coming up with odd results." He hesitated. "The other problem is a critical mass issue. Something bizarre happens when the colonies reach a certain size."

Jack squeezed his eyes shut. "Bizarre, how? Did you run it past the other microbiologists?" When Micah didn't answer, Jack prodded, "Well, did you?"

"Yeah. They're so freaked out by this, they don't want anything to do with it. They'd rather chalk it up to me being nuts."

Jack clicked away from Yahoo! News. He couldn't do a damned thing about bad decisions on either side of the political fence. Or dead staff, apparently. Focusing on the phone in his hand, he said, "I still don't understand exactly why you need me," and followed up with, "Can it wait until morning?"

"I really think you should come see this, sir. If you tell me I've spent too much time at this Godforsaken outpost, I'll pick up my marbles, and no one will ever hear another word about my concerns."

Breath hissed from between Jack's teeth. "Fine. Be there in ten."

He dropped the phone into its cradle before the other man said goodbye and pushed heavily to his feet. The cold and isolation of Antarctica did things to people's minds. Maybe Micah had fallen prey to what Jack labeled the, "Aw shit, I'm stuck at the ass end of the world," syndrome.

He flexed his fingers, stretching them after long hours at the keyboard. Maybe a side trip to the lab wasn't a bad idea. He'd worked as a senior researcher in biochemistry at the National Institutes of Health before accepting the job running McMurdo, and he missed being in a lab teasing out thorny problems.

Besides, if he retreated to his quarters, he'd polish off the whiskey. A wry grin split his face. Compared with a lot of McMurdo residents, he was practically a teetotaler. The base went through buckets of booze, but it kept other problems at bay. He booted down his terminal, told the base operator he'd be on the sat phone if anyone needed him, and left his office.

The halls bustled with activity. Between the times when they had twenty-four hours of daylight, and the months of twenty-four hour darkness, no one kept much of a regular schedule. He nodded to a few folk as he passed them, clapping a shoulder here and punching an arm there as he made his way to the microbiology laboratories.

Located near the end of one of McMurdo's many wings, the labs housed state of the art equipment for studying the rich array of unicellular life forms that inhabited the Antarctic. He pushed the door open and strode inside. Not seeing Micah in the outer room, he yelled, "Greenwich!"

"In here, boss."

Following Micah's voice, Jack walked into one of four smaller rooms that shot off from the main one like wagon spokes.

The other man straightened from where he'd been bent over a binocular microscope. Tall and lanky, he wore hazmat gloves. Blond hair stuck out at crazy angles around the mask perched over a full beard. Bright blue eyes regarded Jack. "Thanks for coming."

Jack grunted and grabbed a mask and gloves of his own. "What's got you so fired up, son? And why the major hand coverings?"

Micah shook his head and twisted his stool to face Jack. "Should I start at the beginning?"

"Just hit the high points and let me ask questions." Jack hooked his foot around a stool and dropped into it.

Micah pulled his mask aside. "Okay. I've been here four months. Because I was youngest and new kid on the block, the others stuck me with archaea, you know the prokaryote colonies."

Jack snorted. "Yeah, no one's ever very interested in proks, probably because their structure's so simple." He narrowed his eyes. "You never answered me about the fancy hand coverings. Did the little bastards get away from you?"

Color stained Micah's face above his beard. "Now that you mention it, yes. Things were fine until the colonies developed a certain mass, but then things shifted."

"Are you talking about quorum sensing?" Jack asked, referring to a bacterial mechanism of population control based on density and several other factors.

"That's exactly what I'm talking about." Micah exhaled softly, fogging the lab glasses perched atop his nose. "Before we go further, come look at this." He got to his feet and pulled a sample bin across the table. Beige plastic, it was about eighteen inches long and a foot wide.

Jack got to his feet, frowning. The bin was large for bacterial colonies, which grew just fine on agar plates. Micah removed the lid, and Jack's mouth fell open when he stared at towers of cell colonies growing up the sides and along the bottom of the bin. Instead of the gray-green he'd expected, the colonies were violet, blue, red, and bright green.

"Holy crap!" He grabbed a sterile instrument off Micah's tray, pulled the plastic protector off, and gently prodded the mass in the bin. The tower nearest the tip of his instrument recoiled and flowed into a nearby glob of cells.

"I wouldn't get my hands too close," Micah cautioned.

Jack dropped the spatula back on the tray and motioned for Micah to put the lid back on the colony bin. "So instead of limiting their growth in response to quorum sensing, they're going nuts?" he asked.

"That's what it seems like to me," Micah replied. "But it gets worse. You asked about my gloves. I started feeling bad last week—a few days before I came in here and found Britta and Marguerite. Because of them, Dr. Stewart and Ariana caught my downhill slide in time to save me." He shrugged sheepishly. "The symptoms of carbon monoxide poisoning are subtle, and I'm a guy. I probably wouldn't have ever thought to turn myself in to the medics."

He shook his head. "During my stint in the infirmary, I had a lot of time to think, and I figured out what might've happened. It was pretty off-the-wall, though, and I needed to run some tests, first—"

"Cut to the chase. I'm all ears." Jack sat back on his stool. His stomach tightened, and he wished he'd either laid off the booze—or finished it.

"This will sound farfetched—"

"You already said that. Skip the fucking caveats. Just spit whatever it is out."

Micah inhaled sharply, exhaling in a rush before words tumbled past his lips. "You know how some proks have an affinity for iron?" At Jack's nod, he continued, "My best guess is I got sloppy with my gloves, and the proks worked their way through my skin, latched onto my red blood cells, and displaced their ability to bond to oxygen. It's the same mechanism carbon monoxide—and any other toxic gas—uses to kill you. Basically, you suffocate."

Jack felt like someone had sucker punched him. Before he could stop himself, a long, low whistle escaped. "I can see why the other researchers would want to discredit your theory. Distance themselves."

Micah colored again and studied his hands. "Sorry to bother you, sir. Like I said, you'll never hear another word—"

"Shut up," Jack snapped. "I didn't say I didn't believe you. Did you experiment with mice?"

The color mottling Micah's face deepened. "Er, yes. I know I'm supposed to requisition—"

"I don't give a flying fuck about that. What'd you find?"

Micah straightened his shoulders. "I introduced normal proks into a bin with two mice and these proks into a bin with two others. The mice with the normal proks are fine. The others are dead. When I examined their tissues, they died from oxygen starvation. Just like Britta and Marguerite." He stared hard at Jack. "Since maintenance couldn't find any gas leaks, my best guess is the women looked in the sample bins, were fascinated, and touched the colonies."

Jack felt old when he got to his feet and went to look into the bin with the crazily growing bacterial colonies. Micah's theory made a whole lot of sense. Plus it explained why maintenance had come up dry. After he replaced the lid, he gestured to the microscope. "What's under there is stained samples from this bin?"

"Yes."

"What's unique about them?"

"It's why I called you, sir. We finally made it to where I need your biochem background. These don't exactly look like proks anymore."

Jack strode to the microscope, adjusted it, and peered through the eyepieces. What he saw gave him pause. The prok structure was there, but these had more to them—lots more. He straightened slowly. "What happens if you separate the colonies?"

"Funny you should ask, since I already did. After a day or two, they revert to regular proks. My assumption is they'll stay that way until they divide enough to reach whatever critical mass spurs them to shift into that." He pointed at the sample bin.

"Mmph. Let's limit access to this lab to just you and me. For now, keep the colonies small, even if you have to jettison some material."

Micah shook his head. "I don't think tossing anything is smart. These guys thrive in almost any environment including extreme cold and salt water, but I'll do my best to keep the colonies under critical mass."

"Douse the ones you want to get rid of with ethyl alcohol and see how they like it." Jack stripped off his mask and gloves. "I'm going to call a friend of mine, Brynn McMichaels. He's a microbiologist I worked with at NIH. Just so happens he's stationed at South Georgia Island. Proks were a big interest of his."

"What's he doing with them?" Micah perked up, the flat, worried expression leaving his face.

"Building boutique antibiotics or some such thing. It's been a while since we've talked, so I'm not totally certain. Anyway, his contract must be close to up. If he hasn't signed on for another stint on South Georgia, maybe I can talk him into coming here. We might be onto something fascinating with these mutant proks."

Micah smiled for the first time since Jack had entered the lab. "Thanks, sir. I appreciate it."

"Hang onto your gratitude. Let's see if we can get Brynn to come here, first. At the very least, I'm sure he'd be willing to bat ideas around on the phone or via email."

Jack headed out the door before Micah could thank him again. He remembered what it was like to have ideas no one else endorsed. The scientific community could be pretty shitty to researchers they viewed as renegades.

As he walked McMurdo's corridors, he rolled Micah's idea around in his head. Whiskey sloshed in his belly, and for the first time in years, he wished he had a pack of cigarettes. To quell his craving for tobacco, he scrolled through the contacts list on his sat phone on the way to his quarters. He had no idea if Brynn would be up yet, but it was morning on South Georgia, so he punched the buttons to put the call through.

After three rings, a sleepy-sounding Brynn said, "Hello?"

"Hey, old buddy. Jack here."

Sputtering blasted through the phone. "What the blazes are you doing calling at this hour? Must be the middle of the night there. Did McMurdo implode?"

"No, but the world might. Are you following the news?"

"Yeah, sure, but that's not what you woke me up for. Or is it? Hang on." Something clinked against the phone—probably a glass. "Damn. It's past eight. Time for me to get up anyway. Back to why you called. You speak Russian. Do I need to beat a path home?"

Jack grunted. "I was actually considering that earlier tonight, but no one's declared war—not yet, anyway. The reason I'm calling is we've got an unusual situation in the lab here with proks that've gone wild—"

"Aw, shit!" Brynn cut in. "You're kidding, right?"

"Wish I were." Jack pushed open the door to his small suite of rooms and kicked it shut behind him. Instincts working overtime, he asked, "You having the same problem?"

"Not exactly, but my colonies are acting oddly. Growing like mad. For some reason quorum sensing isn't slowing them down one whit, and once the colonies get to be a certain size, they almost demonstrate a group intelligence."

Air left Jack's lungs in a whoosh. Brynn had always been the most level-headed of researchers. "Are you certain?"

"Of course I'm certain," Brynn snapped. "What I haven't figured out is what to do about it."

"Be very careful while you're figuring it out. It's likely the proks here killed two women."

"What?" Brynn screeched. "They're single-celled life forms. How could they possibly harm a human?"

"This batch has an affinity for iron. Once they drill through the skin and get into the bloodstream, they have a heyday." Jack paused. "I've read about that phenomenon, but never come across it before."

Time dripped by before Brynn spoke again, still sounding agitated. "Maybe mine have a different problem. If they were going to get me, they've had lots of opportunity, and I feel fine."

"When's your contract with that Brit bio firm up?"

Brynn snorted. "Very soon. I already gave notice. I've had it with the southern ocean. Two years was plenty."

"Would you consider coming here and bringing your colonies with you?" Jack forged on before Brynn could protest. "It's good science to look at both mutating colonies side by side. Maybe we'll learn something critical."

A low rumble—maybe compressed frustration—preceded Brynn's next words. "I don't know, Jack. If I don't charter a flight back to Argentina, I might be stuck here if the political mess heats further."

"You could catch a plane from here to Christchurch," Jack pointed out, not bothering to mention he'd be on it right along with Brynn.

"How would I get there? We're heading into winter, and the weather's unpredictable."

"Does that mean you'll come if I can figure out the logistics?" Jack pressed.

After a lengthy pause, Brynn said, "Yeah, I guess that's what it means, but I'll be damned if I know why I just said yes."

"Because we go back a long way, buddy."

"Yeah, we do. Keep me posted. If I don't hear from you in a few days, I'll make arrangements to get to Ushuaia or Buenos Aires."

"Fair enough. One more small favor."

"Hard to imagine it could be any bigger than what you just asked. What?"

"Can I give one of the microbiology staff your number? He'd love to have a blood brother to talk with, and the other three here have pretty much blown him off."

"Sure, Jack. No problem. As long as he waits until a little later this morning to call."

"I won't even tell him how to reach you before tomorrow morning here—and I'll remind him about the fifteen hour time difference. My admin staff will figure out how to transport you and your cultures to McMurdo. Stay tuned."

"Gosh, guess I'll make myself some breakfast now that you've given me something to look forward to. A reason to get out of bed and all that."

"Spare the sarcasm. Talk to you soon." Jack disconnected and booted up the computer in his quarters to check the weather window.

As his fingers flashed over the keys, he kept seeing the bacterial colony with its multi-hued towers of one-celled organisms. It seemed absurd, beyond the pale, that they'd attacked Micah and the two women. Regardless, Jack felt certain that if the young researcher hadn't stumbled over the lab cleaning staff, he'd be just as dead as them—and the mice in his experiment.

An uncomfortable sensation tracked down Jack's spine. It took a moment before he recognized it as fear. Thank Christ he'd warned Brynn.

www.ingramcontent.com/pod-product-compliance
Lightning Source LLC
Chambersburg PA
CBHW071251190726
48292CB00007B/2490